One Night in Boukos

A.J. Demas

CHAPTER I

IT WAS A spring evening in the city of Boukos. The air in the courtyard had a wet tang, like a suggestion of rain, nothing as definite as a promise. Above the brick wall, against the dark blue sky, the pale blossoms of fruit trees showed like tiny clouds. The trees themselves were planted in a row of pots along one side of the courtyard. Along the opposite wall, echoing the trees, stood a row of painted statues. A pale-haired goddess with bare breasts and a mantle draped in chiselled folds over one arm held out a golden apple. A young soldier, naked but for a pair of tooled greaves, leaned in a muscular pose on his tall spear. A man with horns and a tail propped himself against a tree stump and raised a cup to his lips. A princely figure in a short, belted tunic and sandals held the hand of a naked child with wings. They were eerily lifelike in the fading light, and Marzana could easily imagine that one of them might move at any moment.

Perhaps, Marzana thought, to an inattentive observer, he would look like another statue himself, standing still in the torchlit colonnade of the house, feet firmly planted, hands clasped behind his back. A statue very different from the row along the wall: a tall, dark-eyed man with an aquiline profile never seen in Pseuchaian art. Against the chill of the evening he wore a long coat, with woven bands of leaves and birds decorating the wide sleeves and the hem. Beneath it, his linen shirt and loose blue trousers also bore subtle coloured patterns. A red sword-belt lay across his chest, and a curved blade hung sheathed at his side. His pointed beard was lightly hennaed; beneath his tall felt hat, his dark hair fell to his shoulders, and small gold rings winked in his ears.

He destroyed his resemblance to a statue by unclasping his hands and looking guiltily down at the string of prayer beads he held. He moved his thumb slowly over the polished surface of the one where he had left off, and looked back out at the statues that had distracted him. He found them, like all Pseuchaian art, both admirable and unnerving in their striking approximation of life. Zashian artists, he supposed, being of course second to none, could have created sculptures of equal naturalism if they had wanted to. It was simply not the way things were done in Zash. He was very far from home, and there was no forgetting it.

He thumbed the remaining beads in the string with a renewed, though still half-hearted attention, silently finishing his evening devotion. He was on the point of turning back into the house when the gate at the far end of the courtyard opened. He saw the sentry, silhouetted in the light of his lantern, nodding curtly to someone, but not bowing. Not His Excellency returning home, then. Marzana stayed to see who it was. A familiar figure in a red coat came sauntering down between the statues and the fruit trees.

"Bedar?"

The owner of the red coat extracted a hand that had been tucked into his sash and waved in greeting. He arrived in the torchlight spilling out from the colonnade, and he yawned elegantly.

"Hello, Marzana. You are not waiting up for His Excellency, I hope."

The red coat was expensively embroidered with winged lions in gold thread. Its owner was younger than Marzana—how much younger Marzana had never been able to discover—and smaller, his figure soft with feminine curves under his expensive clothes. He had a child's clear olive complexion, delicate hands like a woman, and the shrewd, hard, calculating eyes of a bandit king.

"Not waiting up, no," said Marzana. "I was not expecting him so soon. Is he on his way?"

Bedar shook his head, the gold pendants of his earrings swinging against the backdrop of his long, silkily black hair. "The party continues unabated. His Excellency remains." He leaned against a column, arranging himself decoratively. The shrewd eyes were beautifully almandine and finely outlined in kohl, his sleekly folded eyelids just touched with aquamarine. "Much good may it do him."

Marzana frowned. "He sent you home?"

"No, I left. When he inquires about it tomorrow, I will have been taken ill—I very probably *would* have been taken ill, should I have remained much longer. You laugh."

"I do."

Bedar produced his own string of prayer beads from his sash and flipped them irreverently around two fingers. "This is why I like you, Marzana. You laugh at me."

Marzana hadn't been sure that Bedar *did* like him, and found he was pleased by the revelation, flippant as it might have been.

"You astonish me! You simply left? Are you not the perfect servant that you are rumoured? Do you do this sort of thing often?"

"Of course not. I should never have got where I am if I did." He poured the string of beads from one hand to the other. They flashed red and gold in the torchlight, inappropriately well-matched to the colours of his coat. Prayer beads were not supposed to be items of jewellery; the thrice-holy Vaksha had made this very clear. "His Excellency was enjoying himself, as far as I could tell, and scarcely noticed either my presence, when I was there, or, I daresay, my departure, when I ceased to be. Certainly I was not greatly needed."

"No doubt. But you were the only one he took with him— now he is there without any attendance."

"The Pseuchaians will think nothing of that—it's quite usual for them, and they don't have a proper sense of His Excellency's rank. *He* won't mind, either. Believe me. He will do very well on his own. The Boukossian ministers are fawning over him, even as we speak. This is the faction that is very eager for the alliance—they wish to make up for that unpleasantness in the Basileon two days ago." Bedar balled the prayer beads up and tucked them back into his sash without attempting to tell them properly. "You are still vexed, I take it, that he refused an escort from your men?"

"Vexed? No. Soldiers are not vexed—that's a word from the women's quarters."

"Oh, well—pardon me. Darkly brooding? Bitterly vengeful?" He put a little growl into the words that was amusingly unsoldierly.

Marzana laughed. "Let me put it this way. Had he hired me himself to oversee his guard, and then refused like this to let me do my job, I should resign the commission. But my orders come from my commanding officer—and beyond him, from my king. I know where my duty lies, and I shall go on trying to do it, whether His Excellency likes it or not." He shrugged irritably. "He should have taken an escort—it was pure folly not to. But I wash my hands of it. If he will not listen to me, then I have tried to do my duty, and no better may be. Why did you leave the party? What was it like?"

"An ordeal, in a close little dining room with hard couches and a roaring fire—the Boukossians were all half-naked, of course, so they weren't bothered by the heat." Bedar affected a careless tone, but Marzana was not convinced.

"Were they offensive?" he asked.

"Oh, well—" Bedar studied the meticulously filed nails of one hand for a moment. They were stained slightly around the edges with ink—the only thing about his appearance that gave any hint that he did something to earn his keep besides being decorative. "Offence is in how one takes it, I suppose. I was the subject of much speculation. I was twice taken for His Excellency's wife—once for his son, and His Excellency nearly choked on his wine at that point. Those who did not ask stupid questions contented themselves with staring. They drink from cups the size of washtubs, you know, and there is *all manner* of merriment if you suggest watering their ghastly strong wine like a civilized person. There was some threat of dancing—that was when I made up my mind to leave."

Marzana winced. "That was probably wise. I am half inclined to send a couple of my men to the minister's house to wait for His Excellency. But I think I will not."

"They would only have to stand around in the cold—possibly in the rain, if this silly foreign weather ever makes up its mind—to be snapped at when His Excellency decides to come home."

"Precisely. No one would get any thanks for it. Tomorrow is this festival of the Boukossians', is it?"

Bedar nodded. "They have already begun preparing—I saw them in the streets, on my way back here. I anticipate horrors."

"I daresay. But look here—will you tell Smar and the others that they need not be afraid to go out in the streets, that there are no crowds of jeering youths with cudgels? I have tried to tell them that this place is not like that—but they won't take my word for it."

"I shall tell them," said Bedar with a smile. "I shall tell them that I walked all the way home from Sosikles's house tonight *by myself*, though I did see some hard-looking men in the street—they will think me a very reckless fellow, I am sure."

"I don't need them to be reckless—to tell the truth, I'm not sure what I think about you walking around alone after dark, but I'll let that go. It's just that I'm tired of Smar sending my men out to run errands for him—they have their own duties, and Smar and the rest have theirs, which they can't do if they are afraid to leave the house."

"My dear Marzana, I shall tell them. Don't worry."

"Thank you." He half-stifled a yawn. "I must go check on the sentries before I fall asleep on my feet. I beg your pardon."

"Of course. God guard your sleeping and your waking." He gave a beautiful, unstudied version of the pious gesture that went with the words.

"And yours."

As he crossed to the door of the house, Marzana felt a sharp twinge in his bad hip, which had been aching on and off all evening. It would certainly rain tonight, he thought, or tomorrow. If tomorrow, that would be a pity for the Boukossians and their festival. As for him, he had no plans to go anywhere.

He was right about the rain. The sky was pale and clear when he rose the following morning, but there were puddles on the windowsill. It had grown colder, too, and he buttoned his coat as he went on his rounds to inspect the sentries. He arrived in the queer little Pseuchaian kitchen at the back of the house in time to be of assistance in interpreting between the Zashian cook and a shop-boy who had come to deliver some peculiar local produce. A Pseuchaian cook had been provided with the house when the ambassador's party was installed a week ago, but he had been hastily dismissed. Apparently the Boukossians had not imagined that the ambassador would have brought his own cook with him. Indeed, they had seemed astonished by the sheer size of His Excellency's entourage; the house they had provided, which they had probably thought flatteringly grand, was actually barely large enough to accommodate everyone.

The cook gave Marzana an almond pastry, apologizing for the quality of the local ingredients that he had been obliged to use in its creation.

"Is there any cheese?" Marzana asked wistfully. He had been craving some good cheese almost ever since they left Suna a month before.

"Not in my kitchen," said the cook primly. "Haven't you heard? The only milk you can get in this country comes from the Horned Beast."

"Really?" said Marzana, trying uneasily to remember whether he had drunk milk or eaten yogurt during the last week. Surely, he thought, if one ingested something from an unclean animal, one would in some way be aware of it? He considered that for a moment and concluded that it might only apply in the case of the extremely pious. He doubted that he would qualify.

He walked back through the colonnade of the house's inner courtyard, thinking to sit on one of the benches by the door and finish his breakfast. His right hip was aching again, and he looked at the sky, wondering whether there would be more rain. There were a few dark streaks of cloud. From inside the open door he heard voices: Bedar's, calm as usual, and Smar's, clearly agitated. Marzana stepped through the door to see if there were anything he could do.

Smar stood in the middle of the atrium, in coat and hat and boots, as if he had just come in from the street. Bedar, listening to him with arms folded and a look of rather elaborate sympathy in his long, dark eyes, was still in his dressing gown. He could, as Marzana had observed, be up and busy before dawn, if the service of his master required it; when it did not, he apparently liked to sleep late.

"I don't blame you, Bedar," Smar was saying, with pompous insincerity. "I'm sure you weren't to know—but I tell you about it for your own good, because you were quite wrong, it is *not* safe to go out there. People who carry on in that way might be capable of anything. Anything!"

"God guard your going and coming, Smar," said Marzana. "Is something the matter?"

Smar turned on him with pursed lips. He was rather white in the face, Marzana observed; something had obviously given him a scare. But whatever it was, he seemed to think it was none of the captain of the guard's business.

"No, indeed," he said thinly. "We are surrounded by ghastly barbarians—nothing whatever is the matter." Turning back to Bedar, he added, "Not that I blame you, I'm sure—you weren't to know, were you?"

He turned on his heel and stalked away into the house, leaving Marzana to look questioningly at Bedar.

"What doesn't he blame you for, exactly?"

"Oh—he ran into a procession outside. Something to do with the festival—apparently it got started at dawn. They were carrying … well, I don't know what they were carrying, really, but he seems to think they were puppets, with gigantic … " Bedar made a fastidious gesture, and finished the sentence apologetically: "gigantic … *parts*. He is convinced that they were worshipping them."

Marzana pressed his knuckles to his lips. "I'm sorry," he

said, when he had regained control of himself. "This after I told you to assure him that it was safe to go out of doors."

Bedar smiled slightly. "He says they tried to make him join in some sort of dance."

"How distressing for him. Is there something else amiss? You look … worried." It was not precisely true, but he looked as close to worried as Marzana had yet seen him.

Bedar looked up, now visibly startled. "Worried? Oh." He brushed back his hair with one hand, tucking it behind his ear. "It is early—I suppose I am not dissembling up to my usual standard yet."

"So you are worried."

"I don't think His Excellency came home last night." He spoke quietly.

Marzana was a moment taking this in. "He is not in his suite?"

Bedar shook his head. "I woke up feeling guilty about having left the party—you were right, it is not the sort of thing that I do, as a rule, and His Excellency is by no means the worst master I have served. I got up, thinking that I would go and make my apologies, and I met one of the boys in the hall, coming with His Excellency's breakfast tray, so I took it from him and went in myself. His bed has not been slept in. I don't know who else knows—your sentries may not have noticed, since they have their separate watches, and no one knew when to expect him. Some of the slaves must have been up, waiting to put him to bed—but I don't think anyone has told Smar yet. He didn't say anything about it. He was on his way to the market, he told me, when he ran into the procession."

"The Boukossians must have invited His Excellency to stay the night. It is probably their custom when they have been drinking hard—as you told me they were."

"Yes—doubtless you are right. Still, I feel horribly at fault. I ought to have remained—his Pseuchaian is not so good as mine, and had he needed anything, and not been able to tell them—had he been taken ill, perhaps … I am greatly to blame for not having been there. I must make what amends I can. I intend to go to Sosikles's house directly—I was on my way back to my room to dress when Smar came in."

"You should have an escort. I will have one of my men accompany you."

Bedar smiled. "I am not afraid of Pseuchaians inviting me to dance, if that is what you mean. But if you think I should have an escort, by all means, I shall take one."

"Thank you. I wish your master would be so reasonable. I will send Aza with you—he is a trustworthy fellow."

"Thank you. And, Marzana—should anyone begin to worry that His Excellency is not at home … "

"I will tell them that he spent the night at his host's house, which is a Boukossian custom, and that you have gone to fetch him—as arranged beforehand. Will that do?"

"You are a mighty cedar tree of compassion, and I kiss the hem of your coat."

Marzana laughed.

Bedar retired to his room to dress, and Marzana finished his breakfast and went to find Aza. He sent him to wait in the courtyard, then returned to the atrium. Bedar emerged from his room, putting in his earrings, but otherwise looking like he had been dressed for hours: immaculate in white trousers and a black, embroidered shirt, his eyes discreetly painted, his hair smelling of lilies.

The front door was opened, just then, by a sentry. A handsome, blond Pseuchaian youth in a blue cloak was ushered in, followed by a curly-haired boy carrying a painted jug.

"Good morning," said the youth jauntily, addressing Marzana across the atrium. "I have come to see the ambassador."

"You honour my master's house with your presence," said Bedar in lightly accented Pseuchaian, bowing to the youth. "I regret to tell you that His Excellency cannot see you at present. May his humble servant be of use to you in any way?"

"Oh, hello," said the youth breezily. "You were at our party last night, too—I remember you." Turning his attention back to Marzana, he said, "I am Leusiklos, son of Sosikles. My father has sent me with a gift for the ambassador, to thank him for coming to our party last night. Phormion, come here," he said to the boy with the jug. "We have an expression, you know: the weapon that made the wound will heal the wound. This is the best vintage from my father's own estate—he trusts the ambassador will enjoy it as well as the wine at dinner last night. Oh, and the boy is part of the gift, of course." He grinned pleasantly. "We hope that he'll prove as pleasing as the wine."

"Your father is the soul of generosity," said Bedar. "His Excellency will be desolate to have missed your visit."

"Quite all right—I understand how it is, the morning after. Still asleep, I suppose. Everyone at our house had to get up early today for the festival—we hadn't the luxury of lying in. Well, I must be off. No, Phormion," as the boy made a move to follow him out, "you heard me—you're to stay here."

When the youth was gone, the boy stood clutching his jug, looking at the two Zashians in front of him, his eyes darting from their trousered legs to Marzana's beard and back again with undisguised terror. As for the two Zashians, they looked at one another.

"Sosikles is the man whose house you were at last night," said Marzana.

"Yes," said Bedar.

"And he has just sent his son here with a—" glancing at the boy with distaste "—with a gift for His Excellency."

"Yes."

"Which means that Sosikles thinks His Excellency is here—which means that His Excellency is not at Sosikles's house."

"Yes."

"Then where is he?"

"I have no idea."

CHAPTER II

THE ATRIUM OF Sosikles's house was a chaos of scurrying slaves carrying dishes and garlands and leafy boughs with ribbons tied to them. A young man wearing nothing but a loincloth came through from the garden, leading a couple of white animals with chains of flowers around their necks. Bedar backed hastily against a wall to get out of their way, making, in spite of himself, the sign against bad luck. On the whole, he agreed with the opinion of the Vanian theologians, that avoiding a particular type of beast was mere superstition. But he had been born in a tiny mountain village in a remote province of Zash, and a very few aspects of his early childhood had died hard.

Sosikles, a lean, eager man with greying hair, appeared on the stairs, trailing a purple mantle that a slave who followed him was trying to pin in place as he descended.

"You've caught me just in time, Bedar," he said cheerfully. "I'm on my way out to our local shrine, to officiate in the Psobion—our annual festival, you know, in honour of our city's patron god."

"Yes," said Bedar, with a smile that was all one motion, not remaining fixed for more than an instant. "I am indeed fortunate to have intercepted you, sir." He caught himself trying to deepen his voice as he spoke, and was vexed by it. That, in this case, was the right word.

"What can I do for you, my lad?" Sosikles inquired, hitching up the purple mantle, which his slave had finally succeeded in pinning. "Did your ... did the ambassador receive my present this morning?"

"He did," said Bedar, "and charged me to convey his very great gratitude. I am almost reluctant, in light of your generosity, but ... "

"No, no! Is there something else? Something I can do?"

"Well, sir, His Excellency regrets to trouble you on this festival day, but he wished me to inquire whether any of your staff has found a blue silk purse, which he fears he may have left behind him last night. It contains a few trifles which he would be sorry to lose."

Sosikles creased his brow for a moment. "None of my slaves brought anything like that to me last night—or this morning, though we're all so busy here, with the festival, that I wouldn't be surprised if it had been overlooked."

"It is perhaps more likely that His Excellency lost the purse on his way home. Unfortunately, I was not with him. May I inquire if he was conveyed home in a chair, or escorted by some members of your household?"

"Oh dear no—didn't he tell you? He didn't go straight home from here. The party broke up around the fourth hour—no later than that. I was for bed myself, thinking of how busy I'd be today—but most of the rest went on somewhere else, to lengthen the night, as we say in Boukos." He smiled pleasantly. "I believe the ambassador went with them. Yes, I'm quite sure he did. At any rate, when they left here, he was certainly one of the party. It's a shame you left when you did, Bedar—it was quite a good night."

"Indeed, sir, I regret it. His Excellency did not mention

to me where he had gone after leaving your house. Is it possible that you might tell me, and so spare me a journey back home to inquire?"

Sosikles laughed. "You have quite a way about you, Bedar—you know that?"

"Sir." Since he had no idea what this meant, Bedar thought it best not to commit himself to any particular response.

"Well, they went to Gorgion's, as far as I know. Astragalos had the idea—I believe Lekythos decided to go home, but the rest of them went on. Gorgion's is in Fish Street, on the corner. But you won't want to be rushing off there now, will you? I don't expect your ambassador would miss you if you didn't come straight back. I tell you what—come and see a bit of the festival with me, and I'll order you a chair to take you to Gorgion's and back. Are we agreed?"

It was the way that Sosikles's gaze had fastened on him, rather than the words he used, that suggested to Bedar what this offer really was. A Zashian man would have put it differently—supposing he had seen fit to speak of it at all—but if he had been very bold, he might have indulged in just such a hungry look. This time Bedar's smile was even more perfunctory.

"I am terribly sorry, sir," he said.

The street outside the minister's house was as busy as the interior of the house had been. Owing to a strange Pseuchaian custom of mixing shops and dwellings together, the door of the house, though decorated by marble columns and set back a little from the street, opened right between a spice merchant and a perfume shop. Both were closed for the holiday, but the street was busy with foot-traffic.

Marzana stood outside the perfume shop, where Bedar had left him, arms folded, ignoring the staring and pointing of the clean-shaven, bare-legged men and unescorted women who passed by. He looked, Bedar thought, like one of the Lords of the Dawn, as they were carved in black basalt on the face of the great temple in Suna: stern, broad-shouldered, unshakeable, armed for all eventualities.

He was rather Bedar's type, actually, but Bedar knew the feeling was not mutual, and didn't mind. He fancied Marzana had more value as a friend, anyway.

"Well?" Marzana said, when he saw Bedar. "Do we know anything more?"

"Yes. Apparently His Excellency and the other Boukossian ministers left the party to go to a fish market in the middle of the night."

"A *fish* market?"

Bedar shrugged. "That was the best sense I could make of it. At the fourth hour—what is that? I've never quite understood their way of telling time."

"The fourth hour at night? That's two hours before midnight. We would say the tenth hour. That was when the party broke up? That doesn't seem very late—I thought these Boukossians were great revellers."

"Yes, well—apparently they need fish at that time of night, to keep the revelry going. Shall we walk, Marzana? We are in some danger of becoming a tourist attraction here."

Marzana nodded. They set off towards the end of the street which opened out into one of the small public squares that were patchworked across the city of Boukos.

Bedar went on, thinking out loud, "Possibly the place where they went did not sell fish—Sosikles said that it was in the street with the fish markets, but I suppose it might be something else. A wine shop, do you think?"

Marzana looked doubtful. "I don't see why His Excellency would have gone out to such a place."

"He may have thought it would be rude to refuse. For

that matter, perhaps it would have been. I should have been there." Bedar ran a hand through his hair and looked up at the sky, which had grown overcast. "But no amount of saying that now will change the fact that I wasn't. The question is, what do I do now?"

"What do *we* do now, you mean," said Marzana.

Bedar looked at him, smiling in spite of himself. Bless his heart, Marzana wasn't trying to say, "You have created a problem for all of us," but rather, "We're in this together." Yet Bedar knew he had only himself to blame.

"That is very kind of you, my dear Marzana. But I am the one who neglected his duty."

The truth was, quite apart from worrying about what might have become of His Excellency, he felt personally ashamed at having let him disappear. For most of his life, his masters had entrusted him with things—secrets, money, members of their households—and he had guarded them, one way or another. This was the first time he had lost anything, and it was not one of his master's treasured possessions but the master himself.

Marzana made a dismissive gesture. "You were provoked, from what you told me. Well—we were both provoked. But you are certainly not the only one who was negligent. Indeed, the worse fault was mine. You merely neglected His Excellency's convenience—I neglected his safety. I feel as guilty over this as you do, I daresay. We are in it together, and that's that. The question is," he added reluctantly, "do we need to involve anyone else?"

Bedar considered this, for about as long as he thought it deserved to be considered. So far, they had not mentioned to anyone that the ambassador was missing. To Smar they had told the planned story about His Excellency spending the night at his host's house, trusting that the rest of the household—the ambassador's half-dozen aides and all his lesser servants—would hear the news eventually from Smar. They had left the curly-haired boy and the wine in his charge as well, not having known what else to do with them. For a moment Bedar pictured how Smar would react if they told him the truth, the panic among the ambassador's aides that would result, the shouting and hand-wringing and loud declarations about the folly of trusting barbarians not to murder honest, civilized Zashians …

"No," said Bedar, "I do not think we need trouble anyone else with this just yet."

"Good," said Marzana briskly. "Nor do I. This may yet turn out to be a trivial matter, easily solved. It would be foolish to sound the alarm unnecessarily."

"And diplomatically unfortunate if the Boukossians should hear it," Bedar added dryly.

They had reached the square by this time, and found it dominated by a cluster of carts with tent-like awnings, from which people were selling food. Men and women in flower-decked festival clothes were clustering around and walking away eating off of skewers and out of folded vine-leaves.

"How can there be so many of them?" Marzana wondered. "The whole population cannot be in the streets—some of them must be minding the stalls—and some of the shops are open."

"I think they come in from the country. Look at those two, for instance." Bedar nodded towards a pair of men in broad-brimmed straw hats, with leather satchels. "Do they look to you as though they just came down from one of these apartment blocks?"

"No. I see what you mean."

They walked around the outside of the square, keeping clear of the crowds, and discussed what they should do. Marzana had some idea where the street of fish markets was, having passed it a few days before in the course of an errand. He thought it might be worthwhile to seek out Gorgion's, whatever it was, and see if anyone there had useful information. Bedar, thinking he could guess what dreadful ideas Marzana cloaked in those dispassionate, professional words, "useful information," did not ask for more explanation than that. He said that he thought it might be a good idea for him to call on Kottabos, another of the ministers who had been at the party, to see if he could tell a better story than Sosikles about the previous night's events.

Marzana nodded. "An excellent plan. Shall we agree to meet back at the house at noon? If one of us has found His Excellency by then, or if he has come home on his own, well and good—if not, we can discuss further strategy at that point."

"Further strategy … now those are *not* words from the women's quarters."

"No?" Marzana smiled. "And what would you say instead?"

"'What in the name of the angels of the Almighty we are going to do,' perhaps."

"I suppose that would also be apt. Until noon, then?"

"Until noon. God guard you."

"And you."

They clasped hands, in the fashion of their country, and parted.

Bedar set off into what he hoped was the street that would lead him to Kottabos's house. If he had to, he would ask directions—but not until he was satisfied that he could not find the place on his own. In Suna, where he had lived for three years but still found it easy to get lost, he was never hesitant to ask directions. Here things were different. In Suna he knew his place, and would not have presumed to look men of a certain rank in the eye; but at least people did not stare in surprise every time he opened his mouth.

He found the house, which he remembered from the day after their arrival in Boukos, when the ambassador and all his staff had been invited to dine with Kottabos. There had been a feverish debate between His Excellency and his aides over whether or not Kottabos expected him to bring Bedar, who had been present when the general invitation was issued, but who would never have been thought to be included in such an invitation in Zash. In the end they had brought him, and it seemed to have been the right choice; the Boukossians had been fascinated with him, if only because they seemed not to have any clear idea what he was.

Kottabos's house was large, and stood in a quiet neigh-bourhood where the buildings were set a little apart from one another, as in certain parts of Zash. It was quiet inside, too, with none of the festival chaos that had prevailed at Sosikles's. Bedar inquired for the master, and a well-trained, soft-spo-ken young slave asked him to wait, and then showed him through to a chilly colonnade facing a large, wet Pseuchaian courtyard-garden, centred on a fountain dominated by a marble group of a naked boy and girl. The master of the house reclined on a couch in the colonnade, sipping at a cup of steaming wine and looking, from the greyish cast to his heavy face, as if he was probably testing out the Boukossian adage about the weapon that made the wound.

"*Bee*-dar, isn't it?" he grunted, eyeing his visitor.

"Sir." He had always thought his name was a simple one to pronounce—Beh-*dar*, nothing to it—but he had been surprised how many ways there were to get it wrong.

"Message from your ambassador?"

Bedar supposed it was a good sign that Kottabos thought

His Excellency might be sending a message this morning; that must mean, at least, that he did not know of any fatal mishap befalling him the night before. He repeated his story about the blue silk purse, embellishing it with further details. He had gone, he claimed, to Gorgion's in the street of the fish markets, but being unable to find his master's property there, he begged Kottabos's pardon for disturbing him this morning, but wondered if Kottabos could tell him how His Excellency had gone home from Gorgion's.

Kottabos gazed at him uncommunicatively for a moment out of dull, hooded eyes. "I don't think he did go home," he said finally. "We had a few games at Gorgion's, then we left. Nobody could agree about where to go, so we split up. Some of them went on to Temple Walk, I think. The rest of us went to Old Pottery Street." He sipped his wine slowly. "I don't remember where the ambassador went." He did not appear to be thinking about it, to try to recall; evidently there was little hope of his remembering anything much from that period of the night. After a moment he added, "Aristygion might know. He seemed pretty sober."

"Indeed, sir? If you will forgive me one further question, would it be possible for you to tell me where Aristygion lives?"

Armed with an explanation of where the sober Aristygion might be found, Bedar left Kottabos's house, and stood for a moment in the street outside. He had seen people being carried in sedan chairs through the streets of Boukos, and Sosikles had offered to hire one for him, so it must be possible, might even be permitted. In Zash he would have known how to go about it, but here he did not know where one found chairs for hire, let alone how to determine which ones were for the use of foreigners, which only for women, and so on. At any rate, he doubted it would have been easy to find a free one during the festival. Small matter—it was early yet, and he did not mind walking. And certainly his task was enviable compared to what he suspected Marzana would have to face. Kottabos had spoken of "a few games" at this Gorgion's, the place where Marzana was headed. It must not be a fish market after all.

CHAPTER III

FISH STREET ON the morning of the Psobion was a narrow prospect of shuttered storefronts, with a stale, aquatic smell in the air. Marzana walked the length of it, unhopeful. He stopped in front of a whitewashed building on the corner, shuttered like the rest, but with the look of being something other than a shop. What, exactly, Marzana could not guess. There was some tidy red lettering over the door, but this was no help. Though among his fellow soldiers Marzana had always been considered rather a bookish fellow, that was only in his own language; he could not read a word of Pseuchaian.

At any rate, the whitewashed building seemed as closed as the fish markets. The small intersection of streets on which it stood was empty except for a couple of old men seated on a bench at the opposite corner, wrapped in their cloaks, with walking-sticks propped beside them. They were eyeing Marzana with frank disapproval. One of them scratched his stubbly chin and muttered something to the other. Marzana supposed he ought to ask them about the whitewashed building, since they obviously belonged to the neighbourhood. He tried to recollect what was the polite address in Pseuchaian for an elderly man. He had heard that these people set almost as much store by respecting their elders as Zashians.

The door to the whitewashed building opened before

he had remembered the proper address, and a thin-legged, brown-haired man with a broom appeared, sweeping the dust from inside out into the street. Marzana turned back.

"Good morning," he said. It felt bald and impious as a greeting, but he did not know which of their many gods the Boukossians invoked for such a purpose, and wasn't sure it would be quite right of him to mention them anyway, since he did not believe in them.

The man with the broom looked up, and his eyes widened a little.

"Hello, foreigner! Are you looking for something?"

"Yes, I am. Is this the place that is called Gorgion's?" He tried to pronounce the name as he had heard it, but his accent when speaking Pseuchaian was far thicker than Bedar's.

"It is," said the man, evidently understanding him nonetheless. "We don't open up until evening, though, on account of the festival. You looking for a game?"

"I … " He had not quite understood what the man meant by this, and wondered if it was his grasp of the language that was at fault, or something else. "I am looking for a man. Another Zash—ah, Sasian—like me. I think he was here last night."

The man leaned his broom against the doorframe and folded his arms. "He owe you money or something?"

Marzana took an instant to consider. This man seemed the sort who might give him information about the ambassador, for a price, even if he thought Marzana was hunting him down for something unpleasant. On the other hand, he could think of another story which would be more likely to produce results, and had the additional advantage of being the truth.

Making a show of digging his purse out of his sash, Marzana said, "No—I work for him. He is missing." He extracted the purse. "If you have information to help me find him, I can pay you for your trouble."

The man's eyebrows went up. "Generous of you. Well, there was a Sasian here last night. I don't know if he was your man—there's a few of them in town, for this trade alliance business. But I suppose if you thought he was here, it might have been him. I just noticed him because of the beard—but I suppose you'll want to know when he left, and who he was with, and so on. Stamnos might know—he's inside cleaning up. Come on in."

He held the door open, and Marzana ducked to pass through the low doorway into the building's dim interior. For a moment, he took the place to be some kind of cook-shop or tavern, because it was filled with small tables and clusters of wooden stools. And there did seem to be empty wine cups on some of the tables; a round-faced youth in a dirty tunic was walking among the tables with a tray, gathering them up. But though they might have sold wine on the side, the real purpose of the place, Marzana realized, was something else. Each table was furnished with a small stone cup which was not for drink, and number of knobby pieces of bone with different figures incised on their faces. At one side of the dim room was a wooden counter with a rack of coloured tokens and a large strongbox. Everything seemed clean, in spite of the clutter from the night's custom, and in good repair, as if the place did a brisk business and served a respectable clientele. Yet Marzana almost shuddered as he realized what this was. Such places were of course illegal in Zash; but to a gentlemen they seemed one of those things, like brothels, that scarcely needed to be prohibited by law. After all, no respectable man would have so sullied his reputation as to enter one, even if the law had permitted it.

There was no help for it now, Marzana thought. But surely

the ambassador had not stayed long in this place himself, once he had realized what it was.

"Stamnos," the man with the broom was saying, "this man's looking for the Sasian who was here last night."

"What for?" said the youth with the tray of cups. "Does he owe you money?"

"No, you daft lump," said the man with the broom. "He's gone missing! The other Sasian's gone missing. So you just think whether you saw anything helpful, and can remember it."

"Sure." Stamnos set down his tray and gave Marzana a friendly grin. "I was just thinking, if he *did* owe you money, you'd be in luck—because *he* was, last night. I was working counter when he and his party left, and I cashed him out—he made a bundle. His friends were all congratulating him and saying it was beginner's luck, that sort of thing. He came with a bunch of purple cloaks—and left with them too … yeah, I think they all left at the same time. It was late, but … I didn't think they were going home to bed—I think they were headed off somewhere else. Actually, I remember when it was, because I saw they almost bumped into the watchmen when they went out—some of them had got a good look at the pictures in the bottom of their cups—and I remember he was calling seventh hour when they almost knocked him down."

"There, you see," said the man with the broom. "I said he would know something."

"Thank you," said Marzana to the youth. "That is very helpful. May I ask—when you said 'purple cloaks,' what do you mean by this?"

"Oh, that's just what the young people call the ministers of the Basileon—the civic assembly, you know," said the man with the broom. "On account of the purple cloaks they wear when assembly's in session."

"I think they were six or seven of them, besides your man," said the helpful Stamnos. "They took up two tables, and they had a horde of slaves with them that hung about outside. Oh—and I've remembered something else, but I don't know if it's any use to you."

"Yes?" said Marzana.

"It's just that your man was playing with another group, for a while. I didn't see how he got to join them, but I did notice he had a game or two with them, and then went back to his own party—and I didn't think they'd even really noticed he was gone, because they were losing to the house pretty badly just then, and some of them were so drunk anyway. Only … these other men, the ones he had a few games with, I noticed they weren't drinking much. There were four of them, I *think*, though I'm not sure. Oh, and when they cashed out, I heard them talking, and a couple of them had Ariatan accents. They cashed out right after the purple cloaks did, I remember that."

"They were Ariatans, for sure," said the man with the broom. "They were dressed like Ariatans."

"Yeah, *and they had Ariatan accents*—I said. I thought it was funny, because the Ariatans are the ones who were at war with Sasia last, right—only seven years ago?"

"Yes," said Marzana. "Seven years ago. But we have had a new king since then. Many things have changed."

"Oh, right, yes—I suppose so."

"How do Ariatans dress?" Marzana asked. Seven years ago he had been on campaign in Smerdin, and he had never, to his knowledge, seen an Ariatan.

"Like peasants, the lot of them," said the man with the broom. "Undyed wool, and boots like soldiers on the march."

"They wear their hair short, too," said Stamnos.

"Ah," said Marzana, looking at the sandy hanks of hair that barely concealed the youth's ears, and wondering what he considered *short* hair. Stubble?

"Anyway, that's all I remember—I hope it's some help."

"Thank you. It is indeed a great help." He untied the mouth of the purse that he had taken out and tipped a few coins onto the table beside the youth's tray, shaking the purse carefully so that he would not have to touch the coins with his fingers. "Please take this for your pains."

He offered the man with the broom a somewhat smaller reward, and left the building. The door closed behind him, and he stood in the chilly street, wondering what to make of all this. One thing seemed quite clear: the ambassador had spent close to three hours in a gaming house. What was more, he had not sat by and looked on with distaste; he had taken part in the games himself, and actually stooped to collecting his winnings. If Marzana did manage to track him down alive, it was clear that he would have to pass over in silence the details of where he had been to search for him. It would never do to let him know that he had heard about this.

Across the narrow street, the old men were still sitting on their bench. Marzana saw them staring at him again, and approached, bowing respectfully. One of the old men stood up, grasping his stick and drawing himself up as tall as possible. He still had to look up to meet Marzana's eye.

"Go home, Sasian!" he said loudly.

The other old man looked terrified by his companion's boldness; his eyes had fastened on the sword at Marzana's side, as if he feared that this barbarian might not scruple to strike them both down in the street. Marzana found himself more offended by this than by the other's open defiance.

Caught in a posture of greeting cut off by their rudeness, he could at first think of no appropriate response.

"We don't want your kind here!" the bolder man declared. "We remember Minarta!"

"And I do not," said Marzana, "because it was a battle fought a month before I was born. But my mother remembers it. My father was killed at Minarta. And yet, as you see, I am here, in a time of peace. Truly, forgiveness is a blessed thing."

He left them staring after him with much the same expression as before.

CHAPTER IV

ARISTYGION WAS NOT at home. As a slave was explaining this to Bedar in the minister's lavishly tiled and painted atrium, a young woman in a clinging blue gown, with a beautiful aureole of pale, trailing curls, came through from the back of the house, followed by a small slave girl carrying a folded cloak.

"Good morning," said the woman, smiling at Bedar as she made some minute adjustments to her bracelets. "Psobos bless your bed!"

This struck Bedar as a shocking thing for a woman to say to a stranger, even in her own house, and he was not at all sure that it would do for him to reply, "And yours."

"May the heavens smile upon you, my lady," he said instead.

"Goodness! What a pretty thing to say. Are you looking for Aristygion? I'm Tysistrate Phoreia—his wife."

For an instant Bedar was on the verge of saying, as he might have done in Zash, that Aristygion could surely have none finer. He caught himself in time. Of course he couldn't. This was Pseuchaia. He only had one wife.

"Ari is out already, I'm afraid," the singular wife was saying. She turned to the slave girl to take the cloak she was carrying and shake it out of its folds. "I'm on my way out too, to watch the processions from my sister-in-law's. They have a lovely roof garden. You must be one of the Sasians from the trade thingy. Ari talks about it over dinner—I believe he thinks it's an excellent idea, whatever it is."

Bedar smiled at her cheerful indifference to her husband's politics. "Indeed, my lady, I am a member of His Excellency the ambassador's entourage. My name is Bedar. You may rest assured I did not come here to trouble your husband with business on a festival day." He gave a slight, regretful shrug. "His Excellency has sent me on a … rather tedious errand."

"Oh, do tell!" said Tysistrate sympathetically, tucking her cloak around her. "I don't suppose there is any way I can help?"

Bedar sighed, as if to say that he wished there were (which he did), and he told her the story of the blue silk purse. He found by this time that he was beginning almost to believe in the thing himself. He was trying to retrace His Excellency's steps, he said, and could not find out whether he had gone to Temple Walk or Old Pottery Street.

Tysistrate stared at him open-mouthed. "Doesn't he *remember*?"

Bedar looked up at her through his lashes, and shook his head slightly. He did not like to be spreading slander about his master, but he had already realized, at Kottabos's, that he was going to have to depend on the assumption that the ambassador had been too drunk to recall where he had been the night before. Short of revealing the truth, he could see no way around it.

"Oh! That's *shocking*!" She seemed to relish it as an excellent piece of gossip, and evidently felt she should offer something in return. "Well—I can tell you … though some would say I shouldn't—Ari went to Temple Walk. He always does.

He has some little tart there—I know the perfume she uses by now. Dreadful cheap stuff." She gave a little, unhappy laugh.

"My lady, I am desolate to hear of this."

Evidently there was a brothel in Temple Walk, then. He had known such things were common in Boukos, so he was not particularly surprised. He *was* fairly desolate, however, at the thought that he was going to have to ask after his master in such a place. How far, he wondered, had His Excellency's politeness extended? Had he actually accompanied the ministers to their assignations with tarts? Or had he chosen instead to join the other party, for whatever diversion was to be had in Old Pottery Street? Bedar supposed it all depended on what that other diversion was.

"Well, I'm sorry Aristygion isn't here," said the wife. "He might have been able to tell you where your ambassador went—he came home quite sober himself, when he *did* come home. But I couldn't tell you where you'd find him now. I'm awfully sorry."

"I beg you do not trouble yourself on my account, my lady."

A slave had come out from the inside of the house and was hovering nervously. Tysistrate turned to give him a questioning look.

"Mistress, I can't find either of them, *or* the chair."

"Oh, I expect they didn't come back. Ari took the sedan chair with him last night," she explained to Bedar. "Not for himself, but for your ambassador, in case he should want it to take him home. I suppose that's what happened—and it doesn't surprise me that those two lazy fellows didn't bring it back afterwards."

Bedar could not feel quite so sanguine about this, but he kept his doubts to himself.

"My lady," he said, "I hope this will not mean that you are unable to travel to your sister's house as you had intended."

"Dear me, no! It isn't far—I am quite able to walk the distance."

Of course. Barefaced, apparently, in a dress that left little to the imagination, and with only one female attendant. This was Boukos, after all. Still, out of a sense of Zashian propriety, Bedar offered to escort her there. She accepted, probably out of a sense of Boukossian frivolity.

The walk to the sister-in-law's house was not long, but the streets were crowded, which slowed their progress. On the way they chatted amicably. Bedar had always found it easy to talk to women, and the minister's wife, who was of a similar rank to many he had known in Zash, was to him both readily comprehensible and at the same time fascinatingly foreign. They had a pleasant discussion about the climates of their respective countries. She had never seen snow, and was intrigued by the idea of the king migrating from one palace to the next according to the seasons. He found it hard to credit what she said about the heat of the Boukossian summer, and his disbelief amused her.

"Where did you get your earrings?" she asked.

He touched one, to recall which they were: a pair with slender ivory pendants inlaid with gold. He remembered he had bought them for his own birthday, since his master, unimaginatively, had given him a present of cash.

"In Rataxa, my lady—Ratases, as you call it—at the bazaar. His Radiancy the king winters in that city on occasion, and my master went there to join him last year, for the hunting."

"They are lovely earrings. Such a becoming style. I suppose if this trade alliance gets passed, we may be able to get such things in our markets here. Do you know, when I think about that, I feel I could get almost as interested in the whole business as Ari does?"

"Could you indeed, my lady? I feel it would be quite a feat—as I recall from the first meeting of the Basileon, your husband's enthusiasm for this alliance knows virtually no bounds."

Tysistrate laughed. "You remember Ari, then?"

"I do, my lady. He is an impressive figure in the assembly."

This was true; but it was not all that he remembered. He also recalled that Aristygion was much older than his wife. He had always thought Pseuchaian wives fortunate, each having a man all to herself; now he found himself feeling sorry for this one.

"Thank you for saying so," she said, smiling prettily. "I am sure of it myself. When we were first married, he used to repeat his best speeches for me, sometimes. However, I believe he thought that I was bored—and so, eventually, he stopped."

They had arrived at the great central marketplace of Boukos, the agora, the heart of the city. Bedar had been here before, when the ambassador's household was shown around after their arrival; but he found the place almost unrecognizable now, it was so transformed for the festival. Banners and garlands had been hung on the fronts of all the stately marble and pink brick government buildings, and the clutter of market stalls had been swept aside, leaving the open space bare for the processions which would gather here throughout the day. On a pale green hill which rose just beyond the edge of the agora, a painted Pseuchaian temple seemed the scene of much activity. A row of what looked like brass pots on stands, set up on the steps in front of the temple, jumped with flame, ethereal in daylight, and beyond them the columned porch was thronged with people.

"That's the main temple to Kerialos, our wine god," Tysistrate informed him. "He is particularly honoured in the Psobion, because of course Psobos is a member of his train. Psobos himself doesn't actually have a temple, you know—but all those little posts with heads on them, that you see around the city, those are sacred to Psobos."

"Indeed, are they, my lady?" He had wondered about those posts. They had other things on them, besides heads.

"Yes. They're called the Psobioles. And now, you see, for the Psobion, each district of the city, and each village on the rest of the island, sends a procession around by the local shrines, to greet the other gods, and to bless all the Psobioles, and then they all wind up here, in the agora, with dancing and music and the images of Psobos and so on. It's quite delightful, if you've never seen it before—well, it's a lot of fun, even if you *have*. Then in the afternoon there will be the contests, which are here as well, and in the evening the Kerialos Play. You see, my sister-in-law is quite fortunate to live so close to the agora, so that we can see the whole thing from her roof garden."

Bedar had been listening to this with less than his full attention; most of it he had heard from others already. What had caught his eye, and held it, was the activity on the steps of the temple of Kerialos. The people who had been in the temple porch had begun to process out, leading flower-wreathed Horned Beasts, blowing strange double flutes and shaking metal rattles which could be heard from across the great open marketplace. They were carrying something else, which they hoisted up above their shoulders as they descended the steps, so that by the time they reached level ground there could be no mistaking what it was. It was a wooden figure of a pot-bellied man, carved, painted, and jointed so that its arms and legs could be moved independently, with poles held by the people walking below. So too could another part of its anatomy, which had been grotesquely enlarged so that it was nearly as long as the pot-bellied man was tall.

He became aware that Tysistrate had said something else and was waiting for an answer.

"I beg your pardon, my lady," he said. "I fear I was distracted for a moment."

"Oh, I was only saying that my sister-in-law's house is just here, in this side street."

He accompanied her to the door, and thanked her for wishing him luck in the continued quest of the blue silk purse.

"Oh, and—" She turned back for a moment from the door which a slave was holding open for her. "Psobos send you your desire tonight, of course. I hope you won't think it too rude of me not to offer to meet you myself, as you have been terribly charming, and I *do* think you are quite sweet—but I always try to find Ari on the night of the Psobion. It's one night at least that I can make him forget that girl in Temple Walk." She smiled.

Bedar had heard one of the ambassador's aides repeat a rumour that the Psobion ended in a night of general debauchery, with Boukossians tumbling into bed (or just into a convenient corner) with anyone they could lay their hands on. Of course he had not believed it. But then, he had not believed Smar's story about the puppets, either.

CHAPTER V

MARZANA KNEW WHAT he was getting into when he set off for the Boukossian customs house. He and his fellow Zashians had been through it a week ago when their ship docked at the island. There had been hours of standing around and explaining the same things over and over again to officials who all told you that you needed to speak to someone else—usually the person you had just finished speaking to. Marzana had been required to give one official a record of his name, occupation, place of origin, date of birth, current place of residence, address in Boukos, intended duration of visit, and height, in order to be told which other official he would have to speak to about not having his sword confiscated. He was glad it had not occurred to him that he would ever have occasion to go back to the place, because if it had, he might have taken a vow not to, and he would have disliked to have to break it.

It was a long walk to the harbour, where the customs house was. The clouds which had gathered by this time began to shed a little weak rain onto the pale streets, but this seemed only to make the festival crowds more determined in their celebrations. Marzana found this strangely cheering. He did not fully understand what it was that they were celebrating, and wasn't sure that he could have sympathized particularly if he had, but he admired their defiance of the weather.

The capital of the Boukossians was peculiar for a coastal city, in that there were few places in it where one could actually see the water. It was built against a section of coast naturally fortified with high cliffs above a sandy harbour. Most of the city sloped upward toward the sea cliff, so that as one climbed the last stretch of any of the streets heading west, there was a sudden sense of the sky opening up before one, as the city fell away. Along the edge of the cliff itself there ran a shoulder-high wall of white stone, with guard-posts which, as Marzana had noticed on his arrival, were not manned. A street of shops and two-storey apartment houses faced this boundary wall. The residents of the upper floors of these buildings, Marzana thought, must have been the only city-dwellers on Boukos to have a view of the sea.

He leaned against a conveniently-placed statue under the eaves of one of these houses, to take the weight off his bad leg and stay out of the rain for a moment. On the opposite corner of the street that he had climbed to reach the cliff there was a sweet shop. He knew that was what it was because on either side of the Pseuchaian inscription over the storefront there were brightly-coloured pictures, for the convenience of the illiterate, displaying piping hot buns and mounds of every sort of intriguing foreign confection. But the storefront was securely shuttered, and hung with a little notice which presumably explained that it was closed, or when it might reopen. Marzana contemplated the pictures sadly. He was very fond of sweets.

The rain had reduced itself to little more than a fine mist by now, and he could see clear sky out beyond the cliff wall, which boded well. He took off his hat to shake off the beaded raindrops; it was good thick felt, essentially waterproof. He looked at the statue he had been leaning against. It was one of the weird pieces of sculpture that were scattered about Boukos: a man's head, bearded and smiling, set on a square, uncarved post. He had first noticed them in the marketplace, when he accompanied the ambassador on his tour of the city; there the sculptures were very old, their features worn almost into shapelessness. He had supposed that they were some relic of the Boukossians' warlike past, meant to represent the severed heads of conquered enemies, set on poles as tokens of triumph. The worn lumps sticking out halfway down the posts he had noticed, but not been able to account for. The sculpture he had been leaning against, however, was a newer one, freshly carved and crisp-featured, and he could see quite clearly what the things halfway down the post were. Evidently the Boukossians, in their warlike past, had severed and displayed more pieces of their conquered enemies than just their heads. Interesting. He could not quite imagine the modern Boukossians making real trophies like this, but perhaps that was why they had resorted to the marble versions.

A gate in the boundary wall, with painted statues of indecent goddesses on either side, gave access to the paved ramp that zigzagged down the cliff face. By the time he reached the harbour at the bottom, Marzana was limping quite obviously, which always put him into an irritable mood. He found the customs house, a long, pink-brick building with a columned porch for people to queue in. There was not much activity in the harbour, but the porch of the customs house was crammed with people. Most of them were Pseuchaians, with heavy seafaring cloaks wrapped around them, but there was a scattering of foreign faces as well: a couple of shaven-headed, coppery-skinned Glifians, looking cold; a fat Shandian merchant with a large ring of keys; and a suntanned Pyrian, in a long blue tunic and ivory bracelets, who leaned against the wall near one of the customs-house doors, eating nuts and looking serene and patient. Marzana wondered what his secret was, and wished he could share it. There were of course no other Zashians in the queue. Zash did not yet have a trade alliance with any Pseuchaian state.

The wait was as long as it had looked. It was slightly enlivened by watching the Glifians quarrelling elaborately with several different officials, through their beleaguered interpreter, and the Shandian throwing up his hands, with what could only have been an invocation of some Shandian deity, when he was told that he would have to wait even longer to speak to someone who had gone out of the office on an errand.

Finally it was Marzana's turn to approach the marble counter behind which the customs officials held bored and leisurely court. There were not many of them; Marzana guessed that most of the staff had been given the day off for the festival, and those that remained felt hard done by and were determined not to do too much work too quickly.

A youngish, fair-haired Pseuchaian was ticking off items on a list in a wax tablet when Marzana came up to the counter, and continued to do so, with a lordly manner, for some time while Marzana stood in front of him. Finally he looked up, and did his best to appear completely nonplussed at the sight of a bearded Zashian on the other side of the counter.

"Yes?" he said. "May I help you?"

"I hope so," said Marzana. "I am the captain of the guard for the diplomatic mission from Zash."

"Yes, right," said the official, as if Marzana had said it so that he could confirm it.

"You will understand that the security of the mission is my responsibility."

"Yes—and?" he prompted irritably.

"I require information about certain Ariatans staying in Boukos."

He had intended to say more—in Zash, to be polite usually meant to be elaborate—but the young man behind the counter irritated him into brusqueness. Further explanation was scarcely needed, anyway; no doubt anyone could guess why a Zashian diplomat might want to know if Ariatans were in the vicinity. In their preliminary correspondence with the king of Zash, the Boukossian ministers had offered, as a special security measure for the duration of the ambassador's stay, to close the island to all Ariatans and deport any who were already there. His Radiancy had been quick to dismiss this offer as entirely unnecessary. There was no war between Zash and Ariata now, and no need to provoke a new one. It was a shame, Marzana thought, that he had to make it look as though the ambassador and his staff were worried about Ariatans after all. But it couldn't be helped. The truth was that the ambassador was missing, Ariatans had been seen hanging about him, behaving suspiciously, and Marzana *was* worried.

"Right … " said the official, looking back down at his list, stylus poised, and pursing his lips for a moment. "That shouldn't be a problem. Aryballos can help you with that. Aryballos!"

A balding person with several rings on each hand—a dandyish affectation in a Pseuchaian—came sidling along the counter to peer pleasantly at the first official. "You called?"

"Deal with this gentleman, will you, Aryballos? I have to finish up with this." He picked up his list and retreated to a desk behind the counter.

The dandyish person smiled at Marzana and adjusted one of his larger rings. "May I help you?"

"I hope so," said Marzana again, less truthfully than before. Hope was beginning to ebb.

He explained himself a second time—more fully, since Aryballos seemed content to listen until he had entirely finished talking. When this point was reached, however, Aryballos shook his head with a slightly reproving smile, like a parent smiling at a child which asks permission for something patently absurd.

"I'm afraid we can't give you that information, sir," he said.

"I see," said Marzana, hoping it sounded more like a polite remark than a growl. "The man to whom I spoke just now said that it would not be a problem."

The dandyish man gave him the sort of look that one parent would give the same child on being told that the other parent had consented to the absurd request. Since, however, Marzana was not a child, but rather a large man, with a sword, the look gradually melted off the official's face, and he turned, with a studied carelessness, to look back at his colleague at the desk.

"Psisteus?" he said, looking back at Marzana. "Psisteus told you that there should be no problem?"

"That man at the desk, yes. He is the one who told me that."

"That's Psisteus. I'll just go speak to him, then, and see what the confusion is. I won't be a moment."

And he wasn't. He was several minutes, leaning on the corner of Psisteus's desk and chatting pleasantly, both of them glancing occasionally at Marzana, who stood with his arms folded, to prevent himself from toying with the hilt of his sword, which was what he felt like doing.

Bedar would have done a better job of this, he reflected. Bedar would have spun them a web of impeccable Zashian politeness, shot through if necessary with fearless, calculated lies, and before they knew it he would have got what he came for, painlessly and elegantly, and be gone.

Aryballos came strolling back, fiddling with his rings again. He flashed Marzana a smile and pulled a writing tablet neatly across the counter towards himself. Then he began looking for a stylus, and disappeared under the counter for a moment before emerging with one.

"Now," he said. "Phemians, you said?"

"I beg your pardon?"

"What it is you're looking for."

"Ariatans. Your records of what Ariatans are in the city."

"Right! Of course—you people don't get on with the Ariatans at all, do you? Ancient enemies and all that—*Anaxandrides and the Fearless Band*, and that sort of thing, eh?"

Bedar, Marzana reflected, would probably know what on earth the man was talking about. Some dreadful Pseuchaian poem, perhaps, about Ariatans fighting to the last man for no particularly good reason. On the other hand, he doubted if even Bedar read that kind of thing.

"I am concerned that certain Ariatans may pose a security risk to His Excellency the ambassador," said Marzana levelly. He had explained this before, in some detail, but this man seemed to have cheesecloth for a brain.

"Right. Suspicious Ariatans." He wrote something down on his tablet: two words, probably *suspicious Ariatans*. "Good. Shouldn't be a problem. May I ask you a question? Is that natural?"

"I beg your pardon?"

"Your beard. Is that natural?"

Marzana stared at him for a moment. *Yes!* he was on the point of saying. *It grows out of your face!* Luckily he realized in time what the man meant.

"No," he said, leadenly. "It's henna."

"Mm?"

"Henna. It's a dye." *There is a queue behind me, you idiot—*

and you're asking me what I use to dye my beard? The man didn't even have a beard of his own to dye—*or* very much hair, for that matter.

"Interesting. I've never heard of it." He smiled again, as if to indicate that out of pure goodwill he would take it on faith that Marzana was right, even though *he* had never heard of it. He wrote something more down in his tablet—possibly *henna.* "Well. I'll just go see about getting you this information. You *will* probably have to speak to someone else, as it's not my department."

"Of course," said Marzana. *I've only spoken to two idiots so far. I would be disappointed if there weren't more.*

Aryballos folded up his tablet, took the stylus with him, and disappeared through a door next to Psisteus's desk—though not, of course, before stopping to lean on the desk for a minute and exchange pleasantries with Psisteus.

Someone else emerged from the inner room quite soon after this, and Marzana, who had begun to settle into a bored stupor in preparation for a long wait, roused himself quickly as he saw this new person heading straight for the section of counter where he stood.

This official was a brisk, dark man, who had brought his own tablet and stylus; the former he snapped briskly open on the counter, holding the latter like a knife raised for a sacrifice.

"Yes?" he said, looking up at Marzana with small, ferocious eyes.

"I have already spoken to someone," said Marzana. "I am waiting—"

"Yes, yes. How many bales?"

"I beg your pardon?"

Marzana doubted if even Bedar would have been able to make sense of this.

After a pause during which he scratched down something ferociously on his tablet, the new official looked up again and said, "You're here about a load of rugs."

"No." Marzana did not trust himself to attempt saying more than this without bursting into either laughter or, quite possibly, tears.

"You're a Sasian, aren't you?"

"Yes."

"You're not here about a load of Sasian rugs?"

"No."

"You told Aryballos you were here about a load of rugs."

"No, I assure I did not. I am here—"

The official made a peremptory slicing motion with his stylus. "*Why* did Aryballos tell me there was someone here about a load of Sasian rugs?"

"I have not the slightest idea, but it is certainly not my fault."

"I don't see any other Sasians here."

"That is true, but that still does not make it my fault. I came here to inquire about some Ariatans. I have nothing to do with rugs."

Aryballos had reappeared by this time. The ferocious man turned to him.

"He says he doesn't know anything about any rugs."

Aryballos looked at Marzana with mild surprise. "Oh, are you connected with the Kandian ship as well? You didn't say so."

"I am not connected with the Kandian ship. I am connected with the Zashian ambassador. I asked you about the records of Ariatans entering Boukos. You told me that 'it would be no problem.'" Was that an idiomatic expression, Marzana wondered, that actually meant something quite different?

"Yes, you see—he's not with the Kandians. He doesn't have anything to do with the rugs."

"But they're Sasian rugs, aren't they?"

"Yes, but they're imported on a Kandian ship. What did I do with that report?"

Aryballos disappeared under the counter again, leaving the ferocious man to stare up at Marzana.

"Do you have a permit for that sword?" he asked abruptly.

Aryballos's voice emanated from under the counter, just in time. "The Kandian is over there, by the door—the big, red-faced man."

"What Kandian?"

"The one with the Sasian rugs. He's the one you want to talk to. Ah, here it is."

He emerged from under the counter as the ferocious man stalked off to find the Kandian—the *Shandian*, in fact, it turned out—whose load of rugs had no doubt come off the black market from Satasparsa, since the Shand did not have a legitimate trade alliance with Zash. Marzana looked hopefully at the rolled-up document which Aryballos had brought up with him from beneath the counter. Aryballos perused it for a moment, then rolled it back up again and looked at Marzana with an expression of pleasant regret.

"You'll have to come back tomorrow—maybe the day after. You need to talk to Trikanos—he has the list. He's not here today, because of the festival."

With another flash of smile, he began to unroll his parchment again.

"I see," said Marzana. "He has this list at home with him?"

"No, of course not." Aryballos seemed offended by the idea. "It's confidential customs-house business—we're not allowed to take that kind of thing home."

"Oh, I see. So the *list* is in fact here, but Trikanos is not."

"That's right."

"And Trikanos is the only one who can read this list."

Aryballos had gone back to his rolled-up document again, but he looked up at this, with a pinched, unamused expression.

Marzana elaborated. "There is something special about this list, which means that only Trikanos can decipher it."

"Look," said Aryballos, in a voice as pinched as his expression, "I'm telling you, you have to come back the day after tomorrow, and talk to Trikanos."

"I am trying to understand why. I require information which is on a list which is in this building, which you could read … I do not fully comprehend why I have to wait for Trikanos."

Aryballos looked around for a moment, as if he expected to see the answer to this apparently painfully stupid question written somewhere on the counter. "Trikanos," he said finally, in clipped syllables, "is authorized to give out that kind of information." He went back to unrolling his parchment.

Marzana leaned on the counter. At that moment, to know how Bedar would have dealt with this, he would almost have been willing to *be* Bedar, not just mentally, but physically as well.

He took a conversational tone. "I am a soldier," he said. "I will tell you how things work in our army." Aryballos looked up from his parchment, although he kept it unrolled in front of him. "In our army there is a general, and he has authority over his corps. Then, in our army, there are the banner officers, and they takes orders from their general—that is, so long as the general is in a position to give orders. Should the general fall in battle, or for some other reason be absent from the field, the first banner officer assumes control. The important principle is that on the battlefield, *someone* must be in charge. Now, it seems to me that in this office, you are like the first banner officer—would that seem fair to you?"

"Well … " In fact, it seemed like a gross piece of flattery to Marzana, but Aryballos appeared to consider it reasonable.

"But no—pardon me, it is not fair, because this office is not the army." Marzana shook his head and gave the office in general a slow, critical scan.

"Look … Psisteus did say that it would be all right for you to get the information, because you're part of an official embassy."

"Yes. That is what he said to me."

"Well, I can't show you the whole list, of course—but I could look at it for you, and tell you what you need to know."

"Could you? That would be very accommodating of you."

Aryballos acknowledged with a tolerant smile that he knew this. "Next time you really will have to come when Trikanos is in the office, you know—but for now, I'll make an exception."

"Thank you." *It will spare me the trouble,* Marzana thought, *of hacking off your head and your private parts and decorating a post with you, in the antique Boukossian fashion.*

CHAPTER VI

BEDAR STOOD ON the edge of the square where he and Marzana had parted ways, contemplating a couple of greasy, leaf-wrapped parcels strung onto a wooden skewer. Feeling recklessly hungry, he had just bought them at a cart which had been so crowded with festival customers that he had not been able to ask the proprietor what exactly was in the parcels she was selling. Quite possibly, he thought, it was unclean meat. Of course, if you believed the Vanian theologians, there was no such thing. And he was very hungry. He slid one of the parcels gingerly to the end of the skewer and took a bite.

His teeth squeaked on something unexpectedly firm and fishy-tasting. He had no idea what it was, and almost spat it out, but it was delicious, flavoured with fragrant herbs and juicy with butter. He chewed, swallowed, and took another bite, and another.

It had stopped raining now, but it was still cold, in a damp way that Bedar was not used to, and found somehow worse, more insidious, than the sharp, dry mountain cold that he knew better. He caught a glimpse of the sun, as the clouds shifted overhead, and saw that it was nearly noon, the time that he and Marzana had appointed to meet. Fed now, and feeling slightly less desperate because of it, he set off to walk back to the house where the ambassador and his entourage were lodged.

Feeling that he should be well dressed for the festival, he had worn the red coat with the winged lions again today, and the red felt hat that went with it. He was not sure whether he regretted this or not. Before he left for Boukos, a friend at court, who had come to "help him pack" (actually to lean out his window and toss bits of stale almond cookies to the palace doves while Bedar packed), had wondered whether it was wise to bring such a flashy garment to a foreign country. "I expect I shall be stared at no matter what I wear," Bedar had said. "I should at least like to create a good impression."

The truth was, he had not thought he minded being stared at. In Suna, eyes followed him in the street or down a passage in the palace regularly, and he always took it as a compliment. He liked to dress well, and he was striking and did not try to hide it. He would have been disappointed if people had not stared at him occasionally. But after a week in Boukos, the constant display of Pseuchaian eyes popping wide at the sight of him, and the elbow-nudging and whispering and bold pointing in the street, were beginning to wear on his nerves. Pretty soon, he feared, his patience was going to give out, and he would either burst into tears or sink his teeth into somebody. He didn't know which would be worse.

In the courtyard of the ambassador's house, the boy who had been sent by Sosikles was sitting on the steps, forlornly scratching the ears of a lean, unnecessary hunting dog that one of the ambassador's aides had brought from Zash. The jug of wine which had formed the rest of the present still sat beside the boy. Perhaps he had been instructed to deliver it to the ambassador in person, and did not want to give it up to anyone else. He looked up as Bedar crossed the courtyard, watching him approach as if he really believed that this barbarian in his white trousers and his embroidered coat might intend to eat him, raw. Bedar tried to give him a reassuring look as he passed, but felt sadly that it had not made much of an impact.

There was no sign of Marzana in the front of the house, though a sundial in the courtyard had been registering the seventh hour when he passed, meaning, as far as he understood Pseuchaian time-keeping, that it was past noon. The atrium was deserted; the guards, when Bedar questioned them, said that neither their captain nor the ambassador had come in the door that morning. He thought about going to his room to change, but decided that there would be a certain shame in letting these Pseuchaians with their poor manners bully him out of wearing his favourite coat. He loitered in the atrium anxiously, twisting and untwisting a strand of his hair around one finger, a nervous habit he thought he had conquered years ago.

Jadresh, one of the youngest and least useful of the ambassador's aides, appeared on the stairs, the long, thickly-embroidered skirt of his coat dragging on the steps behind him.

"Bedar!" he said, spotting him as he was halfway down the stairs. "Have you just come in?"

"Yes, sir." Bedar released the strand of hair he had been twisting.

"Then you have positively missed all the fun." Jadresh leaned on the railing, looking over it into the atrium. "There was a Horned Beast in here. With flowers around its neck. Apparently it's a barbarian custom." He shrugged expansively, eyes rolling ceilingward. "A whole delegation of savages arrived at the door with the thing, and quite insisted on bringing it in—*to bless the house*, if you can believe it. Utterly ghastly, I don't need to tell you. Smar screamed."

"Did he?" said Bedar, trying to look interested.

"Absolutely. Like a girl. Then he took to his room. But now that I come to think of it, he did say that he had been looking for you. You should go see what he wants."

"Yes, sir. I shall do so directly."

"Oh, and did you know that His Excellency is still out? We think he must have been dragged off to attend this heathen festival. You were at the party last night, weren't you?"

"Yes, sir."

"Was it dreadful? Must have been. These people are really barely civilized. But they do have some very fine women—though I don't suppose you've been able to sample that particular local specialty."

"Sir." He had always thought it particularly vulgar when men discussed women as one would wine or sausages.

"I mean, His Excellency must be keeping you pretty busy." Jadresh smiled.

Of course that is what you mean. Bedar did not smile back.

"Oh, another thing, Bedar. There's a barbarian child of some sort kicking about the house today—I don't know how he got in. He's made off with one of my dogs. You haven't seen him, have you?"

"No, sir."

"Let me know if you do."

"Indeed, sir."

Jadresh finished his descent of the stairs and strolled through to the garden, patting around his garments and poking his hands into his sash in search of something. "Now what did I do with that purse?" he muttered.

Bedar retreated respectfully as Jadresh passed him, and turned to bolt for the front door as soon as he was gone. Continuing to wait for Marzana, who was nearly an hour late, seemed the least productive thing he could do just now, and he had no desire to encounter Smar again before the ambassador was safely back where he belonged.

On his way out, he stopped in the porch, where the gift-boy was still sitting with Jadresh's hunting dog. Bedar looked down at the boy.

"I should warn you," he said, "that dog belongs to a stupid man about twice my size, and he is looking for it. There's a passage around the side of the house back to the kitchen." He pointed. "That would probably be a good place to hide."

The boy looked at Bedar in astonishment for a moment, then got up, hoisting his painted wine jug by the handle, and tugging on the dog's collar.

"Thank you," he said, in a little mumble that Bedar could barely hear.

It began to drizzle again as Bedar went out through the courtyard gate, ignoring the curious look of the guard who closed it behind him. He could see no help for it. He would have to go to Temple Walk.

He seized upon a friendly-looking young man in the street to ask directions, and was given them cheerfully, along with a festival blessing of a far more graphic nature than the one Aristygion's wife had offered. He wondered fleetingly if this meant that his informant could guess exactly what address he was headed for in Temple Walk. He did not really like to think about it.

He had never actually been inside a brothel, but in Satasparsa, a city which he remembered like a bad dream, he had known where one was. Where, but not precisely what. He used to walk past it quite often, on errands for his first master: a low, ugly building with an entrance below the level of the street, and furtive-looking, unwashed men coming and going. In Zashian there was no euphemism for such a place, just a crude word which, at the age he had been when he lived in Satasparsa, he had only imperfectly understood. Pseuchaians, he knew, had a subtle array of terms to describe different subcategories of the things; he had heard some of them, but did not really know what they denoted. Thinking about this, he found himself gripped, as if by a sickness, by an almost physical memory of the part of his life that he had spent in Satasparsa. He felt, as he had been in those days, small and helpless and sunk inextricably in misery. He knew it was a bad way to be feeling in a foreign city, with an important task to be doing, but he could not shake it off just by wanting to. He tried to think about something else as he made his way through the busy streets.

There was nothing like hearing your own sentiments in the mouth of someone you disliked to make you rethink your views. Jadresh calling the Boukossians barbarians and "barely civilized" had made Bedar want to come to their defence. It had also made him realize that he had been letting the minor inconveniences of life in a foreign city blind him—temporarily, anyway—to all the things about the Pseuchaians that he knew were worthy of admiration. Their love of letters and learning, their democracy, their cosmopolitan ideals: all of that he had read and heard of hungrily at home in Zash, and it was what had made him devote himself to learning their language and their writing. And here he was at last in one of their cities—not one of the greatest, of course, not Kos or Pheme, but a fine enough place in its own right—and he was sulking because people gave him curious looks in the street? He felt ashamed of himself.

He arrived at Temple Walk. It was a short, broad street, paved in some white stone that glittered faintly even under the cloud-heavy sky, with a row of small flowering trees down its centre. At one end was a round, pink brick building that looked to Bedar like a lady's jewellery box expanded to monumental size. Presumably this was the temple in question. A colourful crowd of women with mantles pulled over their heads occupied its steps and choked the street in front of it, while the rest of Temple Walk was deserted. A soft sound of chanting and singing from the crowd reached the end of the street. Bedar ran his eye along the fronts of the buildings as he walked down next to the row of trees. They looked prosperous, even elegant. That they were shops of some sort and not residences he guessed from the fact that all the windows were shuttered, as if they were closed to business. But he saw no signs advertising what was sold, only some typical Boukossian paintings of naked or flimsily clothed women flanking some of the doors, and here and there an inscription which seemed only to be a woman's name. He had reached the middle of the street, and was looking past the row of trees to observe that the other side was much the same, before it occurred to him what all of this meant. Temple Walk was not a street with a brothel in it; it was a street *of* brothels.

It could all hardly have been less like the squalid building of his memories, but somehow the alien elegance of the whole place made him feel even smaller and more ill at ease. He looked at all the closed shutters, and back towards the crowd of women in front of the temple. Was it remotely possible that Boukossian prostitutes had a guild, like cheese-makers or tailors, and that they were holding some official function, in honour of the Psobion?

While he was standing there, listening to the lilting sound of the women's voices and turning over this absurd thought, he realized that he had been observed by a couple of bulky young men who had been lounging in a doorway a little further up the street. They had come out now and were strolling down towards him. Three more from the other side of the street emerged to join them. They formed a sort of loose barricade across the street in front of him, smiling and planting their large feet, in stout sandals, wide on the wet stones. A couple of them had light cudgels thrust through their belts.

"No customers today!" said the red-faced young man who stood directly in front of Bedar. "Better try Chimney Row or Pigeon Street."

Bedar looked up at them; they were tall, as well as thickly built, and he was neither. It took some effort to prevent himself ducking humbly and retreating, especially since he had no great desire to remain here. He thought enviously of Marzana, who would have been able to look these men in the eye and plant a hand on the hilt of his sword.

"Dear me," said Bedar, in his most languidly sexless voice. "I am *not* a customer."

The young men gave snorts of laughter, and the two nearest the one who had spoken first slapped him on the back. The crowd at the end of the street began to clap in time to their song.

"I'll just bet you're not, sweetheart!" said the largest of the group, with a genial leer in Bedar's direction.

"It was the trousers that confused me," said the red-faced one defensively. "I didn't know women wore them too."

"He's not a woman," said one of the others, who had not laughed with the rest. "He's a Sasian whatyoucall." His companions looked at him. "*You* know."

Evidently they did. A couple of them looked at Bedar as though they thought it might be contagious. Just then, he heartily wished it were.

"Well, I guess you *couldn't* be a customer, then," said the red-faced one, evidently contemplating the idea with horror.

Bedar said nothing, but gave a little shrug, expressive, he hoped, of a wistful regret.

"Then if you didn't come here for the girls," said the one

who had not laughed, "and you couldn't have come here for the girls, what did you come here for?"

"An errand for my master. He left something here last night—a purse, which he believes he may have dropped by accident."

"Which house was he in?" the mirthless one asked.

Bedar winced apologetically. "He recalls only that it had a painting of a woman by the door. He did, however, describe to me the woman whom he … met there. A brunette, he said. Also he mentioned that she was fair-complexioned, and of small stature."

"That's not much help!"

As it was a vague description of most of the women in the streets of Boukos, Bedar had not thought it would be.

"Perhaps you recall seeing my master here yourselves?" he suggested.

"Maybe. What's he look like?"

"Trousers," said Bedar. "And a beard."

"Sure, there was a foreigner like that here last night," said a bushy-haired young man who had not spoken so far. "I think he went into Oinchoe's."

"How fortunate that you remember!" Bedar needed little effort to counterfeit gratitude. "And Oinchoe—would I find her here today?"

"You would, but she's officiating in the temple, and men aren't allowed in."

They looked at him for a moment, evidently trying to decide whether he qualified for the prohibition or not.

"They'll be done in there eventually," said the bushy-haired young man to his companions. "He could go talk to the girls in the meantime—they might know which one had the foreigner last night."

"Sure," said the red-faced leader of the pack. "Go ahead."

The crowd of singing women was no longer clapping, but they were tightly packed onto the temple steps, and swayed a little with the rhythm of their song. A pair on the edge of the crowd, who were whispering to one another rather than singing, spotted Bedar as he approached, and turned to stare at him in fascination. He smiled at them, relieved to have escaped from the scrutiny of the men to something more pleasant. They were both young, and very prettily fit the vague description he had given the guards. One had a blue mantle over her head, the other a yellow scarf; both glittered with inexpensive-looking jewellery and were more elegantly painted than the average Boukossian matron.

"What is it one says?" Bedar asked, as he came up to them. "Psobos bless something or other? I am afraid I am not yet well versed in your customs."

"Psobos be buggered!" one of the women said merrily, and it sounded to Bedar like it might actually be a ritual exclamation. "Men aren't allowed here, you know—but we'll make an exception for you."

"You are *too* kind!" He assumed it was a joke, and that they realized he wasn't a man.

"And you are too cute, you barbarian, with your trousers," said the other woman, tucking her arm through Bedar's. The way she said *barbarian*, it sounded like an endearment.

"We do wear them especially to impress foreign ladies."

The first woman laid claim to Bedar's other arm. "Look, Rhoias, he paints his eyes, like the boys from the Horses! Have you ever seen anything so cunning? You don't suppose he *is* one, do you?"

"What? One of us? That would make it all right, then, wouldn't it?"

"Shouldn't you two be singing?" Bedar asked, looking innocently from one to the other.

"You wouldn't ask that if you'd heard us sing! Tell us what you're doing here, barbarian."

"First tell me to whom this temple belongs."

"Orante, of course—the goddess of love and the mother of the world. We're all her acolytes, you know."

"We're not like the common girls in Pigeon Street."

"Of course not! Who could think it? But explain something else to me, of your kindness. I do not understand why you are worshipping at this temple of your love goddess on the day that everyone tells me is sacred to Psobos."

"Oh, that's simple. Psobos is a little, silly god, you know, who follows about in the train of the great god Kerialos, getting into mischief—why do you stare at me like that?"

"Surely it is blasphemy to speak that way about one of your gods, lady?"

They both laughed. "Don't you barbarians have any silly gods?

"No—though we do have some sects with silly opinions. But do go on. This Kerialos is your god of wine, I think?"

"Yes, he gave the knowledge of the vine to mortals—he travels around with panthers and things, and Psobos is one of his companions."

"We have a festival of Kerialos in the autumn, when the grapes are ripe. It's quite different—the women take over the city for the day."

"That sounds to me like a delightful custom."

"Oh, wait until you see it! You might be surprised!"

"But we haven't answered your question. We're doing a ceremony for Orante so that she'll give us her blessing, even though we are celebrating the Psobion—because, you know, Orante is a much greater goddess than Psobos is a god. And then we're going to draw names to choose who gets to be the nymph Amphia in the Kerialos Play. I don't suppose you know the story of the Kerialos Play."

"I confess I do not, lady."

"We'll tell you. Kerialos had a nymph named Amphia for his mistress, and Psobos wanted her—well, you've seen the puppets, I guess, you know how it was. Anyway, he thought of a way to trick Kerialos so that he could get at Amphia."

"He started flattering Kerialos, and saying that Kerialos had given men the greatest gift of all the immortals, and so on, and begged Kerialos to teach him the secret of how to make the vine grow, as only he could. Finally Kerialos gave in and taught him—"

"And then Psobos waited until Kerialos was very drunk—"

"And he made the vine grow up all around Kerialos, and trapped him there all night."

"Leaving Psobos free to spend the night with Amphia."

"And did Amphia approve of this?" Bedar inquired.

"Oh, that's part of the fun of it. We do the play every year, you see, in the agora just before the lamps are lit. It's always an actor from the theatre who plays Psobos, because he has speeches to say and everything—and Kerialos they just choose out of the crowd, depending on who looks drunkest. But we get to choose a new Amphia every year—it's been a custom since this temple was built, and back then there weren't even any houses in Temple Walk, just girls who'd meet you on the steps of the temple—very primitive." They giggled at the idea. "Anyway, it's up to that year's Amphia whether she approves or not. People make bets."

"One year, in my mother's time, the Amphia actually got away."

"Yes, but that doesn't usually happen. I heard that was because the actor doing Psobos had given one of her friends the pox. Usually Psobos catches her—or she'll throw herself at him, sometimes. That's usually the longest odds."

"And … then what?"

"Oh, then everybody goes at it, of course, like Psobos and Amphia. That's when *we* want to have somebody lined up already, otherwise we'll end up back here, with the pitiful men who couldn't catch anyone."

"Are *you* busy tonight?"

"Not fair—I was just about to ask!"

"Sadly, I must disappoint you both. I have other plans." He sketched them out wistfully in his mind as he said this, so it was not quite a lie.

"Some girl is lucky, then."

"Or some boy. Mm?"

"That would be telling. And I am always discreet." Actually, his plans involved a cup of spiced wine and his bed, with nobody in it but himself. He feared they would prove pure fantasy.

"Well, fine. But you haven't told us yet what you've come here for, if it wasn't to pick up one of us."

"Of course. You have distracted me terribly from my mission. I am here because I find I need to speak to someone named Oinchoe. Do you know who she is?"

"Naturally. She runs one of the best houses here. But you can't speak to her now, barbarian—she's inside the temple."

An outburst of cheering and hand-clapping arose near the front of the crowd, and Bedar looked up to see that the temple doors had been opened from inside, and a pair of women with large baskets had emerged. The singing stopped now, and a hum of conversation moved through the assembled women.

"What happens now?" he asked his companions. "Is the ceremony over?"

"Yes, the first part. Now comes the part where we put in our names for Amphia, like we told you."

"Come along, barbarian—we must get you a ballot to put down your name."

Bedar felt something like a stab of panic. "But—you do realize I'm not—"

"Not a woman?" They laughed, hauling playfully on his arms. "Yes, yes, but you're quite a pretty boy, you know—you'd do marvellously."

"But what if I were found out?"

"Well, you would be, of course. Then it would be the joke of the decade! Come *along*!"

They began to push through the crowd, more or less dragging Bedar along with them. The women who had come out of the temple were descending among the crowd, passing out something from their baskets—presumably the ballots for the selection of that evening's nymph. The woman in the yellow scarf, who had hold of Bedar's right hand, left him in the charge of her companion and wriggled away through the crowd to get ballots for all three of them. She returned shortly, yellow scarf askew, triumphantly holding out three irregular shards of earthenware.

"Here we are! Now, take one and write down your name, barbarian. No arguments."

"What do I write with?" Bedar asked resignedly.

The young woman who still had hold of his elbow tossed her mantle back from her face and extracted a long metal pin from her elaborately knotted-up hair. "With this. It's traditional." She handed the hair-pin to Bedar. "Go on, write your name."

"Oh, and don't write it in Sasiasan or whatever you call your language, or the head priest will never be able to read it when she pulls it out."

"*If* she pulls it out."
"Yes, right—*if*. Go *on*!"

CHAPTER VII

MARZANA STOOD IN a narrow street in what he was sure was a bad part of town, going over in his mind what he knew of Ariatans. He had never met one, but he had read about their system of government, and of course he knew something of the history of their conflicts with Zash.

In Ariata, according to what he had read, to be free meant to be a warrior—or, for a woman, a mother of warriors. The city governed a large swath of mainland Pseuchaia, whose farmers and workers and artisans all belonged to an unfree peasant class. The free Ariatans trained their children up in barracks, with every form of inhumane severity, to the end of making them tough, uncompromising automatons of the state. Their ethic seemed to promote an unappealing mixture of self-sufficiency and slavish obedience to authority, or to some abstract idea of the Public Good. They fancied themselves a democracy, loathed the idea of kings, and had regular assemblies of all the heads of free households, at which they voted on important issues and elected officials, not with the elaborate secret ballot mechanisms of Pheme or Boukos, but by the simple expedient of shouting "Yes!" or "No!" They were officially anti-aesthetes, and had no time for any of the arts. They committed suicide, apparently, on the slightest provocation.

Zash had first tangled with the Ariatans more than three centuries ago, when the kingdom reached its westernmost limit, engulfing the Deshan Coast and annexing three small Pseuchaian colonies: Seleos, Xia, and Phiros. The three cities had belonged to Kos originally, but the Kossians, after a single disastrous sea-battle, had decided to cut their losses, and left the colonies to Zash. The Ariatans, whose standing feud with Kos apparently went back to the mythic origins of both cities, weren't having it. They had arrived on the Deshan Coast with a force so absurdly small that the king of Zash had made jokes about it in his court at Suna, and they had captured Xia and Phiros for themselves. The series of naval battles and sieges that followed was known in Zash as the First Pseuchaian War. It ended with Xia and Phiros in Zashian hands once more, but only after four years of bloodshed. And Zash had been fighting with the Ariatans over those cities on and off ever since.

The last Pseuchaian War, seven years ago, had been a short affair compared to the first: a matter of months rather than years. It had begun, like the first war, with an Ariatan strike on Xia and Phiros, which had succeeded once again in recapturing both cities. The Zashian king, Kurzandana IX, had retaliated promptly by besieging Ariata. Being fanatics, Ariatans were hard to wear down with a siege; but Kurzandana IX had been a ruthless king, and was prepared to wait. There was a whole series of jokes at the Zashian court, in very poor taste, about what the Ariatans had been eating as that siege wore on. In the end, what lifted it was not the surrender of the Ariatans themselves but the defection of the governors of Xia and Phiros, who offered to return their cities to Zashian control in order to end the war and rescue their compatriots.

In the ever-shifting pattern of allegiances between the

Pseuchaian states and their neighbours, Boukos had been from time to time aligned with the Ariatans, and had occasionally gone to war alongside them. The last of these occasions, a little more than thirty years ago, had ended very badly for the Boukossians, who had cut their ties with Ariata soon afterwards. It was the last battle of that war, a disastrous defeat for the Pseuchaians, that the old men in Fish Street remembered so bitterly. It was in that battle that Marzana's father had fallen.

Since then, the ruthless Kurzandana had been replaced by his more peaceable son, and much else had changed. Yet here Marzana was, hunting down Ariatans, the enemies of his father and his father's father before him, as if all the old patterns must necessarily reassert themselves.

He considered whether he might be overreacting. Even a nation of fanatics could produce innocent tourists, and people did come from other parts of Pseuchaia to see the Psobion; perhaps that was all these men were doing. Perhaps they had spoken to the ambassador out of benign curiosity, having never met a Zashian and wondering what they were really like. Perhaps the fact that they left Gorgion's just after he did was merest coincidence. Though they had not been drinking, that in itself need not seem suspicious. Perhaps they simply did not care for Boukossian wine.

And yet. Stamnos at Gorgion's had spoken of four men (as far as he remembered) with Ariatan accents and Ariatan clothes. Aryballos at the customs house had eventually been persuaded to reveal that four Ariatan men had arrived in Boukos eight days ago—that is, the day before the Zashian delegation landed. It might not mean anything. But Marzana had an unpleasant feeling that it did.

While he was a soldier on active duty, and even since he had taken up his present job, there had been occasions when his good guesses had saved people's lives. Now, he feared that if he had guessed correctly, he was going to be too late for that.

Aryballos had not been able to give him an address, since the Ariatans had not been required to provide one at the customs house, but the Pyrian sailor whom he had seen lounging outside had told him about a street of rooming houses, not far from the harbour, which was frequented by foreigners. By the time he left the customs house, it was past noon, so he had decided to make straight for that street, rather than taking the time to return to the ambassador's house, where Bedar might have given up on waiting for him anyway.

It was an ugly, depressing street, with puddles of dirty water in the places where the paving stones were broken, and tall, grimy buildings on either side which must have kept it in shadow even in broad daylight. There were people about, in doorways and on covered balconies, staying out of the rain, looking like they were waiting for something, though they might not themselves have known what. A lone shop window was hung with dusty foreign trinkets: strings of cheap Glifian glass beads, tin figurines from the Shand, scraps of cloth woven with some unidentifiable floral pattern.

The shop appeared to be open, and Marzana thought that, in this neighbourhood of suspicious gazes, it might be a good place to start asking questions. He pushed past the heavy curtain that covered the door, and stood frozen for a moment on the threshold, assailed by a scent from the past.

It was incense; the air of the shop was blue with it, thick with a sharp, sweet, unmistakeable smell of resin from trees that grew in the forests of Smerdin, beyond Zash, so far to the east that in Pseuchaia it was barely a rumour. How it had found its way to a shop full of cheap trinkets in a bad neighbourhood in Boukos, Marzana could not guess, but it was the same incense that had burned in the tent of the daughter of the lord of Arakesh, on her journey down from the mountains to Apasana five years ago. He had been often enough in that tent to remember the smell vividly.

He let the curtain swing back over the door and stepped out into the street again. There had to be a better way of finding out what he needed than that. He stood looking down at the surface of a puddle, speckled with tiny, cold drops of rain, remembering Parmatya's voice, the way her fingers used to tuck strands of her soft black hair back underneath her veil, things he thought he had succeeded in burying under the weight of years. It felt like a violation of something to be thinking of her here, in this dirty, foreign street. Yet he could not help wondering, for a futile moment, where she had been when she last thought of him—and when was that?

Foolishness. He crossed the street briskly, the heels of his boots splashing in the puddles, and began knocking on doors.

He found the place he was looking for on the third try; the landlady was not in, but a young man sitting in the grubby stairwell of the house told him that he had heard some Ari-atans talking on the second floor landing a few days ago. Marzana climbed the stairs. There were two doors on the second floor landing, and one was open onto a chaotic scene of dirty children. Marzana turned to the other door and knocked on it.

There was no answer. He pounded harder, and tried to listen, above the noise of the dirty children, but could not hear any movement or voices within. He considered the possibility of knocking the door down. If he had known for certain that the men he sought had been or were still within—if indeed he had known that the men he sought were the men he should be seeking—he would have done it without hesitation. But all he had to go on were his suspicions. He turned back to the stairs and found himself confronted with two of the children from the other room, who stood staring up at him with enormous eyes and open mouths. Between them, another, very different pair of eyes also looked up at Marzana: small, yellow eyes with horizontal slits for pupils. In their grubby hands, the children held a rope that was tied loosely around the neck of a shaggy, knobby-kneed black Horned Beast.

Marzana stared at the group for a moment in speechless horror. They had probably touched the thing, which was bad enough—but then they had actually brought it into a dwelling, which was far worse. The place would need to be purified. The parents of these children should be informed; someone should send for a priest immediately. He paused in this illogical train of thought. They ate these things here, and drank their milk. Perhaps they also kept them as pets.

"Do you live here, mister?" One of the children was the first to work up the courage to speak.

"I? No."

"Do you know who does?" the other child spoke up. "We knocked, but nobody answered. We've got to take Lalia in to bless their house, for the Psobion."

It was stranger even than he had imagined. The thing was not a pet; it was some sort of ritual device. But the children holding it, with their huge eyes and dirty tunics, were hard to resist.

"I will check to see if the door is unlocked for you," Marzana offered.

He reached for the latch and found, rather to his surprise, that it lifted, and the door swung inwards. The room beyond the door was dim, its single small window closed with peeling shutters. It was unoccupied, empty except for a cushionless couch and some rolled-up blankets in one corner. Marzana stepped inside, and the children with their Horned Beast came through the door after him. He turned, thinking to ask them what they needed to do with the animal in order to bless this squalid place, but something caught his eye. There was an inner door, closed, in the darkest corner of the room, and on the dusty floor beside it, like a pool of spilt wine, lay a deep purple coat, embroidered with gold knots, rubies winking around the button holes.

Marzana did not remember what the ambassador had been wearing when he left for Sosikles's house, but he had seen him in that coat before. He crossed the room in two strides and picked up the coat. Underneath it lay a blue felt hat, slightly crushed, with a red feather, which Marzana also recognized, a silver-hilted dagger in its sheath, and a lamb-skin purse, still heavy with coins. He held up the coat to inspect it, but could see no sign of bloodstains.

One of the children had come to look over Marzana's shoulder at the goods on the floor.

"Did they steal that stuff from you, mister?" the child asked astutely.

Marzana straightened up. "Yes." He looked down at the children. "It is not a wise thing, to steal from me."

They looked as though they readily believed it.

The door in the corner was unlocked, like the front door, but it stuck, and had to be forced open. Marzana looked for a moment into the small inner room, then turned sharply back to the children, pulling the door shut behind him, so that they should not see what was beyond it.

"You have the … what do you call it? the public watchmen in this city, yes?"

The children looked at one another uneasily, across the Horned Beast, then back at Marzana.

"Yes," one of them said finally.

"You could find them now?"

"What for?"

"They are needed. There has been an ill deed done here."

With the children and their animal gone, Marzana gathered up the ambassador's belongings from the floor. The purse and dagger he tucked into his own sash. He wrapped the coat and hat up in one of the old blankets from the other corner, and, opening the shutters, he leaned out and dropped the bundle into the narrow alley between this building and the next. It landed in a puddle, between a broken clay jar and an abandoned sedan chair. He pulled the shutters closed and leaned against the windowsill, trying to make sense of this.

There were two dead men in the inner room, but neither of them was the one Marzana had feared (and half expected) to find here; neither of them had ever worn the coat that he had just dropped into the alley. They were strangers to him, Pseuchaians with sandy hair and plain white tunics, like servants. Their throats had been cut; he guessed that they had been dead since last night. The ambassador himself, from the look of things, had not been killed, only robbed. Was that what it amounted to? These Ariatans were thieves, and the two men who lay dead in their lodging were merely some underworld acquaintances who had got in their way? But that did not explain why His Excellency had not returned home the night before.

CHAPTER VIII

"WHAT EXACTLY ARE you doing here?"

Bedar looked up. A tall, silver-haired woman in a red gown and gold jewellery of a priestly style stood over him where he was seated on the temple steps.

"Explain yourself," she demanded.

The young woman in the yellow scarf, whose name was Leires, leapt to Bedar's defence. "He's writing our names for us, Holy Mother. Look, you see he does the prettiest writing imaginable." She picked up a clay ballot to show the priest a specimen of Bedar's careful Pseuchaian lettering. "All the girls want him to do their names now, you see. And he is being such a dear obliging thing—isn't he?"

There was a chorus of agreement from the surrounding crowd of women. Bedar eyed the priest warily, but she was looking at the ballot with an expression of grudging admiration.

"Very nice," she said, returning it to Leires, and her gaze to Bedar. "But I don't suppose you came here to do this—did you?"

"No, he didn't." Rhoias, Leires's friend, spoke up. "He came here to speak to Oinchoe."

Bedar did not mind that his companions had taken it upon themselves to speak for him. In fact, he thought it might have been for the best. As he understood it, this Orante was a goddess of fertility, and he was fairly sure it would constitute some sort of blasphemy for him to be even sitting on the steps of her temple. He preferred to keep a low profile.

"Well, he may speak to Oinchoe, then," said the priest, continuing to talk about Bedar rather than to him, "and after that he may be on his way."

She looked at Bedar for a moment, and he looked innocently back. Pursing her lips, she turned away into the crowd of women. She reappeared a few moments later, bringing with her another woman of about the same age, this one shorter, with a soft, round face and bleached curls piled on top of her head.

Bedar got to his feet, nerving himself to tell the ridiculous blue-silk-purse story one more time. Oinchoe listened with a solicitous expression, her small hands clasped just below her chin.

"Dear me," she said, when Bedar had finished. "I'm afraid I didn't have any foreigners in my house last night."

"Ah," said Bedar, marvelling inwardly at his own calm. "Perhaps there has been some mistake."

The priest had pursed her lips again, and looked as though she was coming to the conclusion that Bedar had made the whole thing up. Oinchoe, on the other hand, looked disappointed at not being able to help.

"It must have been one of the other houses," she said. "I'll tell you what—I can ask some of the other ladies for you." She beamed at Bedar. "We will get to the bottom of this, my dear. We must get your employer back his property."

"You are a flowing spring of kindness, my lady," said Bedar, his mind filled with unpleasant images of hunting under dirty cushions in brothel bedrooms for a purse that did not exist.

The priest said something to Oinchoe about chasing pigeons, which Bedar supposed was idiomatic, and then mercifully was called away to attend to something. Oinchoe beckoned for Bedar to come with her. He looked around for Rhoias, to return her hair-pin, but she had disappeared into the crowd of women. He handed the pin back to Leires instead, and apologized for not being able to stay and write any more names for her friends.

"Oh well," she said, with a shrug. "Duty calls, I guess. Psobos bless your 'other plans,' barbarian."

"And yours, lady. And yours."

Asking the other ladies proved a lengthy process of following Oinchoe around as she wove through the crowd looking for her friends, and listening to her retell the story of the bearded foreigner and his lost purse, with little variations and elaborations about how Bedar was a dear foreign boy and they must help him find what he was looking for. All the women canvassed, who were mostly of Oinchoe's generation, listened to the full story, nodding attentively, before admitting that they had neither seen nor heard of any Zashian the night before. One of them gave a long account of two Glifians who had come to her house a week ago, but did eventually confess that this probably had no bearing on Bedar's investigation. Several offered to help by asking their friends, and one of these eventually came bustling up to Oinchoe and Bedar, looking very pleased with herself, and followed by a dark-haired, Phemian-looking woman in a green gown.

"You're the one looking for the foreigner, I suppose?" said the Phemian woman.

"Yes, he's a dear boy who works for him," Oinchoe supplied, "and he's looking—"

"For a purse. Iresia has just told me. Well, he was at my

house last night. A tall, dark man, with a beard and outland-
ish clothes. That's the one you're looking for?"

"Indeed, my lady. I am overjoyed to have located the right
house at last."

"Your employer ought to have remembered the name,"
the Phemian woman said haughtily. "It is written over the
door. Eudia's. That is not *my* name—it is the name of the
woman who ran the house before me. I keep it, since I took
over, because it is well known."

"Oh, indeed," said Oinchoe. "Quite well known. Eudia
was a great lady in her time."

"I am sure that my master would not have chosen your establishment if he had not known it to be of the finest quality,
my lady," said Bedar. "Alas, the name over your door would
have been of little service to him, as he is not able to read your
language." This was no slander; His Excellency did not even
know the names of the Pseuchaian letters. Few Zashians did.

"Well!" said the woman who was not Eudia. "I had heard
it said that barbarians did not know how to read—but I took
it for an ignorant falsehood."

"I'm sure they know how to read in Sasi—Sasasi—in their
own language, you know," said Oinchoe. "But never mind
that now. The important thing is, the dear boy's employer
was at your house last night."

"Yes, he was. He left at the fifth hour, I remember dis-
tinctly. He paid me sixteen nummoi, which was generous
of him. He just dumped the coins out onto the table, which
I thought peculiar, and he wouldn't pick up one that fell on
the floor."

"Indeed, my lady," said Bedar.

Sixteen nummoi was a princely sum in Boukossian currency, but the ambassador and his entourage were operating
on a vast budget provided by the Zashian king, and part of

their mandate was to spend lavishly, to impress the Boukossians. What puzzled Bedar was not the large sum of money, nor the ambassador's reluctance to touch the coins, but the time that the woman had quoted. Sosikles had said the ambassador and his companions left his house at the fourth hour, which did not give them much time at Gorgion's, for the "few games" that Kottabos had mentioned, before His Excellency had arrived in Temple Walk. Bedar wondered if he was misunderstanding Pseuchaian timekeeping again, or if someone else had made a mistake.

"Which of your girls did he see?" Oinchoe asked, delicately putting a question which Bedar had not been sure how to phrase.

"Pelike," the Phemian woman replied. "She's just over there, if you'd like to speak with her." She pointed.

"I'll go and fetch her!" Oinchoe scurried off.

The young woman she brought back with her was truly beautiful: tall and willowy, with an extremely fair complexion and dark brown hair in long, glossy ringlets.

"It's about the foreigner who came to see you last night," Oinchoe was saying.

The beautiful Pelike gave first Oinchoe and then Bedar a look of most disappointing vacuousness.

"Oh, he was *so* charming!" she gushed, wide blue eyes fixed on Bedar. "He told me his name, but I couldn't pronounce it, because of the funny foreign sounds. And he hardly spoke any Pseuchaian at all, you know, but that was all right."

This struck Bedar as a little unfair; the ambassador's Pseuchaian was not as good as his, to be sure, but it was certainly passable. Perhaps this silly woman had simply not been able to understand his accent.

"He did tell me he would send me a present today, you know," Pelike was saying, "so I *was* rather expecting you."

Bedar had his hands behind his back, in the pose of a respectful Zashian servant, which now struck him as fortunate. The fingers of his left hand quickly sought the clasp of a bracelet on the other wrist. He wished he had been wearing a different one; this one had been a gift, on an anniversary which would no longer be celebrated, and he disliked the thought of parting with it. The clasp stuck a little.

"Oh, he hasn't come to *give* you anything," the woman who was not Eudia said, in the moment before Bedar had got the bracelet unfastened. "He's come to pick up something your charming Sasian left behind."

Bedar cursed her mentally. The catch of the bracelet was still sticking, and Pelike was already beginning to pout.

"Is that true?" she asked.

"My dear lady, the gift which His Excellency has in mind to give you is not the sort which can be procured at a moment's notice. I conveyed his instructions to the jeweller this morning, and he assured me that they could not be carried out in less than a week."

The woman who was not Eudia snorted as Pelike's eyes grew wide again. "You're not going to believe that, you goose. He came here to ask about some blue silk purse that your dashing foreigner dropped."

"Oh, *that*," said Pelike, to Bedar's astonishment. "It wasn't blue, it was purple, and he can't have it back because I got rid of it. Well, you see, I didn't know what was in it—some sort of foreign witchery, one of my friends said. Dried up bits of grass and a pebble and a *dead beetle*. I threw it away. You can tell him so."

"My lady," said Bedar, with a neat bow.

In his mind, several things had just fit together, maddeningly: Pelike's Zashian leaving at the fifth hour, and hardly speaking any Pseuchaian; Jadresh praising the local women in vilely gastronomic terms, and hunting in his clothes for a missing purse as he went out into the garden. It was probably a charm against impotence.

"I daresay he hasn't given you a second thought, you know," the dour Phemian woman was saying to Pelike. "Why, he probably has half a dozen wives at home." She looked at Bedar. "All lovely as the dawn, no doubt."

"His Excellency has twenty-seven wives," Bedar said neutrally. This was true, of the ambassador; he doubted Jadresh was married. "However, as to their beauty, I regret that I can tell you nothing, as *I* am not employed in such a capacity in his household as to have seen them."

This was not strictly true; His Excellency did not keep his women in seclusion like some sort of jealous merchant in a popular tale. And the point of his retort was almost certainly lost on the women anyway. But Bedar was too angry to care.

Well, Jadresh, he thought, as he left the crowd of women on the temple steps, *you may eat and drink in safety. But if I had given away Vakshathra's bracelet to your Pseuchaian one-night-stand, may the hounds of the Dark Valley devour me if I should not have had my revenge one way or the other.*

He had passed by the place where the bulky young men were lounging without noticing them, but a voice hailed him before he had got much further. He stopped, but did not turn.

"Hey! Come here a minute! We need you to settle a bet for us!"

He turned with a sinking feeling.

CHAPTER IX

THE SHADOWS WERE long, and the evening light was slanting dazzlingly out of a cloudless sky by the time Marzana arrived, with the officers of the Boukossian public watch, at their headquarters on the edge of the agora. They came in through a side entrance, to avoid the crowds that could be heard cheering in the square.

"What is going on out there?" Marzana asked, nodding in the direction of the noise.

"The Kerialos Play now, most likely," said one of the younger watchmen. "The athletic contests would be all over by this time." He sighed. "Last year I took a prize in sprinting, you know. But of course I couldn't compete this year, seeing that I'm serving in the watch and all that. I'll bet that good-for-nothing Korphos won—and I was a spear's throw ahead of him last year."

"Oh, dry up!" the watch captain barked. "You have to do your civic duty like everyone else—there's nothing special about it. And festival days are busier than most, when it comes to crime and disorder. Do you know, last year on the day of the Psobion we had two accidental deaths *and* an armed robbery in one of the boy brothels."

They had gone down a tiled hallway, and emerged in a room lined with benches, where uniformed watchmen were sitting, waiting their turn to report on their day's activities in their superior's office. The three duty watchmen of Marzana's party sat down on one bench, while Marzana and the watch captain took another.

"Boy brothels?" Marzana repeated. "There are brothels just for boys?" Did the prostitutes offer lessons or something, like the temple-girls in Kakuma?

The watch captain looked as if he was trying to decide whether or not the foreigner was mocking him. "Not *for* boys. Of boys—full of boys. For men who like boys."

"Oh," said Marzana. "Yes, of course."

That morning, he would probably have shuddered and thought, "Barbarians!" That evening, it was not so simple. Certainly they had tastes in Boukos which he would never share, customs of which he could never approve. But the Boukossians themselves were interesting people; their tastes differed, and not all of them approved of their own customs.

"Personally, I think they should all be shut down," said the watch captain, as if he had heard Marzana's thought.

They gave their report to the chief of the watch. It was lengthy and detailed, but did not really amount to much. The watchmen had spent the afternoon questioning people in the neighbourhood where the murdered men were found, trying to find out more about the Ariatans who had probably killed them. Marzana had accompanied them, in what the captain of the watch, who had been very impressed with the Zashian's professional approach, chose to call a "spirit of co-operation." Marzana had contented himself with explaining that he viewed the Ariatans as a possible security threat to the ambassador, and had taken as many opportunities as arose to ask questions of his own of the locals. If the Boukossian watch had demonstrated much of an ability to track down people or information, Marzana might have reconsidered his decision to conceal the ambassador's disappearance from them. But the watchmen, though well-meaning, were civilian volunteers to a man, and acted it. They made small talk with witnesses, wasted time chasing down vague rumours, accepted hearsay unquestioningly because the person offering it was someone's sister-in-law's freedwoman's step-daughter. Their captain was really no better, in spite of his attempt at military-style discipline. He was enthusiastic about his job, but he was not a professional.

It was not that it was hard to get reports from the locals of having seen Ariatans. Indeed, it was too easy. The four men lodged in the street of rooming-houses were not, as Marzana knew from his visit to the customs house, the only Ariatan citizens in the Boukos that week. There was a large family visiting relatives for a wedding in the cloth-merchants' district, a young couple whom Aryballos had suspected of being on the run from disapproving parents, and three other men who had arrived independently at different times, "on business." And aside from the people who might have seen any of these, there were the people who, when asked whether they had seen any Ariatans, would say, "Yes," and then tell a story about someone who turned out to have lived in Boukos for twenty years, or whose mother was suspected of having been an Ariatan because of the way she wore her hair. None of the people Marzana had been able to speak to privately had seen a Zashian, or anyone who could be mistaken for one.

The names of the four men under suspicion were Thereus, Karestes, Nunnios and Orgion, but knowing this had not been much of a help, as they did not seem to have done anything since passing through the customs house that had required them to give their names to anyone. Instead, along with the details that their landlady had been able to supply when she returned home, what the watch had amassed amounted to a list of places where people had seen Ariatan men throughout the day, which seemed to have no sense to it at all. This the captain dutifully related to the chief of the watch, along with an admiring report of how helpful Marzana had been in their investigation. The chief of the watch, a small, grey-haired man in an immaculate white tunic, regarded Marzana with interest, and asked him to stay for a moment after he had dismissed the others.

"If there is anything I can do to assist you," he said seriously, leaning on his desk, "I hope you will feel free to speak. I am very sensible of the importance of your ambassador's mission. I will have the record of today's investigations copied for you, of course."

"Thank you, sir," said Marzana, though he was not sure that there was anything in there that would be of any use to him, even if he could have read it.

"You have heard about Minister Lekythos, I suppose?"

"Sir?"

"One of your chief supporters in the assembly, I understand. He died this morning."

"I am sorry. Is there suspicion of foul play?"

"Apparently not. It seems to have been an accident—but the sort that looks … well, looks like it might have been more than that. He tripped and fell downstairs while his house was being purified for the festival. I'm afraid it may be an omen that the opposition could use as further leverage against the alliance."

This struck Marzana as something that was going to cause headaches for Bedar. He wondered whether it had come to his attention yet.

In due course, the copy of the report was presented to him, written out on a small roll of expensive Glifian paper, which was probably meant as a respectful gesture. He thanked the chief of the watch and left the building by the side door through which he had entered, having no particular desire to fight his way through a crowd of play-watching Boukossians.

The sun was going down, by this time, in a blaze of orange and purple gaudier than the ambassador's coat. Marzana tucked the roll of paper in his sash and stood by the curb, arms folded, looking down the street and wondering what, if anything, to do now.

A woman was coming down the shadowed side of the street, a slim figure wrapped in a pale cloak. Marzana watched her progress, his gaze following her in search of some relief from his own thoughts. She was carrying some round, heavy-looking bundle, but she walked quickly along the dark side of the street.

Should he return home now, or was there something more he could still accomplish tonight? Was it possible that Bedar had found His Excellency by now? Of course it was *possible*; Marzana still had no idea what had become of him. He might have been anywhere, for Bedar to find. Or anywhere else, where Bedar had not looked.

A narrow side-street that the solitary woman had just passed disgorged a little knot of revellers on their way to the agora. Arms linked and draped over each other's shoulders, they swayed along, brightly-coloured cloaks tossed carelessly back, jars of wine in hand, wreaths of flowers on their heads.

"Aiee Psobos!" they shouted, more or less together, a tumult of male voices.

"Widow! Oi, Widow!" one of them sang out. "Psobos send you a new ploughman, with a strong plough and a sturdy team!"

The others cheered and whooped, monkeylike. The woman's cream-coloured mantle must have been a sign, Marzana thought, that she was a widow. How the revellers happened to know that she needed a ploughman, on the other hand … Marzana considered, with distaste, the possibility that this was a metaphor of some sort.

The woman looked back over her shoulder briefly at the men, and then walked on, ignoring them. But one of them seemed to have recognized her.

"Widow Chereia! It's Widow Chereia!"

"Coming to the play, Widow?" another called.

"Do you have anyone picked for the night, Widow? You could have any of us for the asking! Especially me!"

"Especially *me*! Pick me, Widow Chereia, pick me!"

Marzana knew, by this time, what the custom of the Psobion night was; it was one of those that he did not think anything could ever bring him to countenance. It angered him to see these unmannerly young men mocking a poor widow with it.

They had nearly caught up with her by this time, and were making little swaying lunges forward to try to grab hold of her mantle. Abruptly she stopped and turned on them, stepping out into the sunset-lit half of the street as she did so. Her pale cloak glowed pink and orange in the light. The revellers tumbled to a halt around her.

"If you have something to say, say it to my face." Her voice was clear and ringing.

The men seemed daunted for a moment, but then one of them, drunker than the rest, plucked up his courage.

"I'll say it to your face, Widow—pick me, or I'll just pick you!"

The man made an unsteady grab at her, and she swung her bundle, thumping it soundly against his chest.

"Leave her alone. All of you. Now."

Marzana had strode out into the middle of the street. The orange light of the sunset flashed on his drawn sword.

The revellers stared in open-mouthed terror. The woman froze too. Her bundle bounced heavily on the pavement and rolled, shedding its cloth wrapping on the stones. The men stumbled back a few steps, then turned and pelted off down the street, losing garlands and splashing wine and tripping over cloaks in their haste.

The woman turned to look behind her. She stood now with the slanting sunset light on her face. The fold of the pale mantle that had covered her head had fallen back. For a moment she and Marzana (sword drawn, silhouetted in all his foreignness against the orange and purple sky) stared at one another. What he saw was that the revellers had not, as he had for some reason imagined, been mocking her. They really had wanted her to pick one of them for the Psobion night.

She was young, and she was lovely. Her hair, straight and smooth and richly brown like polished wood, was caught back in a simple twist from a fair oval of a face, with straight black brows and hazel eyes.

"I am sorry if I frightened you," said Marzana. He slid his sword back into its sheath.

"Well," she said after a moment, "I think that you frightened those men more."

"Good." He made her a solemn, irrelevant bow, and wondered what on earth to say next.

"Do you know," she said, looking at him with a curious and beautiful intensity, "I saw a painting of a Sasian once, when I was a little girl. He looked just like you. But then … I don't think I believed he was real. There was a painting of women with fish tails just next to him."

"Zash is full of men who look like me," Marzana said, then

found himself adding, absurdly: "The women with fish tails are harder to find."

She laughed, radiant with relief. "I will bear that in mind. Thank you for your help. Those goons probably did not mean any harm—it is quite customary to behave like that on the Psobion night. But it *is* lovely to be rescued."

"I am glad to have served you."

He crossed a stretch of pavement to pick up the round thing that she had dropped. It was a dense, heavy object the size and shape of a large melon, or a man's head. The pale yellowish surface was rough to the touch, imprinted with the weave of the bag in which it had been aged. It was a cheese.

There was nothing for it; he had the thing in his hands before he had realized what it was. He picked up the cloth that had fallen away as it rolled. A delicious smell assailed him as he did so, and he realized suddenly that he was very hungry. And he was terribly fond of cheese.

"I am afraid it has got dirty," he observed.

"That's all right—it's only the rind."

"Of course." He rewrapped the cheese carefully. "Do you have far to go, before you are home?"

"Yes, rather. All the way to the sea-wall. You're not going that way yourself, are you?"

"Perhaps I am. Is it likely that you may meet with more drunk young men on the way there?"

"Tonight?" She smiled. "Quite likely."

"Then I find that my way does lead me toward the sea-wall. If you like, I can carry your cheese for you."

"Thank you."

For a moment longer they stood fixed in their spots in the street, looking at one another. She was probably still remembering the painting from her childhood. No woman, as far as he knew, had ever looked at him in quite that way:

as if he were a marvel, a fascinating, otherworldly thing of which she was only slightly afraid.

"Well. It's this way."

"Of course. Please lead on."

She did, drawing her pale cloak in graceful folds about her shoulders. When she observed that he had fallen a step or two behind her, she slowed her pace.

After a day of trudging around Boukos, up and down steep streets, back and forth through badly-paved neighbourhoods to inquire about Ariatans, Marzana's hip ached fiercely, and he was limping as if newly injured and had given up trying to hide it. He had dropped back not so much because he could not keep us as because he thought it respectful, but there did not seem to be any point in insisting on this.

"I hope you are not in a hurry," he said wryly.

She smiled. "Not at all. It is a very nice night."

"It is."

"May I ask your name?"

"Forgive me. I had forgotten that it is the custom here to give one's name. It is Marzana." Somehow that didn't seem enough, so he added formally, "Son of Sorgana son of Utapesh of the clan Tamun." Then he felt embarrassingly presumptuous. He would never have introduced himself in such a grandiose style at home.

She was silent for a moment, as if listening to a distant phrase of music.

"Say it again?"

He did.

"Marzana … " She pronounced it carefully. "Is that right?"

"Yes."

"It's not as hard to say as it might be, then. Is that what people call you—I mean, is it what *I* should call you, having only just met you?"

"If you wish."

She gave him a slightly curious look. "Well, my name is Chereia. But of course you heard the goons shouting it."

"Yes. Were they ... acquaintances?"

"Customers. I keep a shop. What do you do?"

"Guard people."

"Oh, really? All the time?"

"I am a captain in the Royal Guard of Zash. We are responsible for the king's residences and the safety of the royal family. I have been charged with guarding the trade delegation to Boukos. That is why I am here."

"I see! I am honoured to have such a distinguished escort." She sounded serious. "I'm for it, you know—the trade alliance."

"Ah. I see." He did not quite know what to make of this. Zashian women did not say things like this.

"Everyone is divided," Chereia went on. "There are the people who are for it, and the people who aren't—I mean, of the people who are interested in politics. I am, of course. When you keep a shop, it is hard not to get interested in politics—people come in and talk about it all the time. Anyway, I'm for the alliance. And not just because I want to buy Sasian perfume, or anything. I think it could be the beginning of a new peace between Sasia and Pseuchaia, because once *we* have an alliance, Pheme is going to want one too, pretty quickly. I should think the Phemians are watching with great interest to see what happens here. They haven't amassed the power they have now by being reckless—they're the sorts to let another state try the waters before they get involved—but once they see it working for us, they'll want in. Kos probably will too—if it tends towards peace, the Kossians are likely to be in favour of it. And that will leave the stupid, war-mongering Ariatans out in the cold, and deal a good slap in the face to all the old fools who go around muttering that the gods put Sasians on the earth for Pseuchaians to fight, and there can never be peace with men who wear trousers, and twaddle like that. So you see, I'm for it. Quite decidedly. I suppose you are, too—or are you? You're a soldier, you would do your duty whether you like it or not."

"I would," he agreed. "It was enough for me to know that our king wished his subjects to trade freely with the Pseuchaians. Yet, having been part of the delegation, all the things I have heard—I see the reasons why His Radiancy desires the alliance, and I think him wise. I see that Boukos has much to offer Zash beyond trade goods. But I had not seen all that you describe. I only hope that there are enough men in your city's assembly who see the matter as clearly as you do."

"Oh. Well." She seemed embarrassed by this praise. "I'm sure I'll like to buy Sasian"—she paused, and attempted the unfamiliar sounds—"Zzasshhian perfume, too."

"Yes, and Parkan rugs that haven't been brought in on the black market by unscrupulous Shandians."

"I have heard about this! It's true, isn't it, that all the Sasian rugs that you can buy in Pseuchaia are actually stolen?"

"They are technically 'spoils of war'—taken by raiders in the Parkan Mountains, which is the only place they actually make the rugs that everyone here thinks of as Zashian. You can of course buy them legally, in Zash, from the people who make them, but only the stolen ones end up exported to the Shand and to Pseuchaia. I have an acquaintance—a friend—from the Parkan, who has told me all about this. He is also 'for it,' as you say."

"Of course—it would benefit these people too. And do you know who else I think it would be good for?"

"Perhaps I can guess. The Pseuchaian colonies on the Deshan coast."

"Exactly! Phiros and Xia. They wouldn't be cut off from the rest of Pseuchaia any more—nor we from them. And Pheme would stand in the way if the Ariatans got any ideas about taking them back again. You had thought of this too, no doubt?"

"Well … " Marzana felt an impulse to be quite truthful. "Actually it is something else I have heard said by the same friend."

She smiled. "I just listen to gossip in my shop, and piece together my own opinions out of that—don't worry!"

They walked on in silence for a moment or two. Marzana was formulating something that he wanted to say.

"I did not see a painting, as you did, but … I had heard that in Pseuchaia there were beautiful women who walked about the streets barefaced and talked politics with men who were not of their own family—and I do not think I believed that was real, either."

She gave a low laugh. "Did you not, indeed? Well, thank you."

Somewhere in Marzana's mind a sharp, cynical sliver of his conscience jabbed him in a place that he had not know was still sore. What did he think he was doing, paying compliments to this Pseuchaian woman? He remembered the smell of incense in the shop that afternoon, the pattern of the carpets in Parmatya's tent, the flicker of the lamp-flames in the evening; these details came back to him reproachfully, as if to ask how, having once been there, he could now be here. But he could no longer smell that incense now—only the tantalizing aroma of the unclean cheese he was carrying.

Feeling the need to speak, he asked, somewhat abruptly: "What was the Zashian in that painting doing?"

"Fighting Ariatans. I think it was a picture of Anaxandrides and the last stand at Dardania."

"Anaxandrides? I have heard that name earlier today." One of the fools in the customs' house had mentioned it, he recalled.

"He was a famous Ariatan general."

"Famous for fighting at Dardania?"

"Yes, I think so, mostly. You've heard of the battle, then, but not the general?"

"Of course. Dardania was one of the early victories of Taksharesh the Undefeated. The Ariatans were massacred. It is not surprising that no one in Zash remembers the name of their general. In Zash, people are famous for winning things. I do not think I will ever understand the Ariatans."

Chereia laughed again. "Does anyone? But I didn't know King Tak—Taka—what did you call him?"

"Taksharesh. You would say … Tagares, I think."

"Yes, I would. I didn't know he was called the Undefeated. Was he really? Undefeated, I mean."

"Oh, yes. If you do not count that he was murdered at thirty, by one of his wives. We generally do not. It was not thought to have been a fair fight."

He had to admit that it he found it gratifying to make her laugh.

"I will tell you something that you will find hard to believe," he said, by and by.

"Yes?"

"It would not be easy to guess, from looking at me, but some of my ancestors are Kossian."

"Truly?"

"Yes. My father's family comes from Zeleush, which used to be a Pseuchaian colony."

"Yes, of course—Seleos."

Marzana nodded. "His people were descended from some of the colonists."

"Does your ancestry have anything to do with your speaking Pseuchaian?"

"Something, yes. I was raised in part by my uncles, who still live in Zeleush. There it is quite common to learn Pseuchaian, and there are many good teachers. So I received instruction at an early age. But I do not think that any of my family could have foreseen the use that I would put it to. My uncles imagined, I suppose, that it would be useful for me some day on campaign to speak the language of the enemy."

"They had it decided from the beginning that you would become a soldier?"

"My father was a soldier. Actually, it was my mother who was determined that I should follow him, not her brothers— they are both merchants. In the event, I have never fought Pseuchaians. But when I was on campaign in Smerdin, it would have stood me in very good stead to have spoken the language of that land. At the time, I cursed my uncles for having had me taught Pseuchaian instead. Now, I am grateful to them."

"I guess it would be hard for you to do your job here without being able to speak to the locals."

He had not been thinking of his job, and for a moment was on the point of saying so. Then he remembered, for no particular reason, a haunting run of quick notes in a piece that Parmatya had been trying to learn on the sampan, and he could see her delicate fingers moving over the strings, and he said nothing.

As if music had come into both their heads at the same moment, Chereia just then began to hum something softly: a pretty, lilting tune.

She stopped. "What is your opinion of Pseuchaian music?"

"I am afraid I have not heard enough to form one yet."

"Oh! Well—I apologize, then, but I shall have to remedy that."

And she sang aloud the same tune, with two short verses about spring and birds singing in the trees.

"That was lovely," said Marzana afterwards, because it had been.

Parmatya used to sing, of course, as she accompanied herself on the sampan. He had heard all her repertoire over half a dozen times during that summer. Of course, it was difficult to compare two women's voices, when the styles of singing were so different.

"I don't know much of anything about Sasian music," said Chereia.

"I do not imagine that you would have any reason to."

They walked on in silence for a few moments, while Marzana thought about what to sing for her. They were climbing one of the hills towards the sea-wall, and it was rather hard going. They reached a cross-street which formed a slight plateau in the steep ascent. There was a stone bench set into the wall of one of the corner buildings, like the place where Marzana had seen the two old men sitting that morning.

"I think I need to sit down for a moment," said Chereia abruptly.

Marzana looked at her. She showed no sign of being tired.

"You don't mind, do you?" she asked cheerfully.

"No, not at all. Indeed, I would be grateful for the chance to sit down."

She did not say, "That's what I thought." She said, "Oh, good."

They sat on the bench, with the wrapped bundle of the

cheese between them. Marzana had recalled a song that he thought would do, since the text was about neither love nor religion. He had at first intended to just begin singing, but found somehow that was not quite going to work.

"Would you like to hear a Zashian song?" he asked, somewhat woodenly.

"Oh … if you don't mind. I didn't mean to put you on the spot."

"I don't mind. It should be sung to an accompaniment, but—I hope it will sound acceptable without it."

She was silent for so long after he finished singing that he wondered if he had chosen badly. Perhaps a country dance song would have been easier for foreign ears to appreciate.

"I am sorry if it bored you," he said. Then he looked at her, and saw that she had not been bored, and felt he needed to explain himself. "Zashian art music is difficult to appreciate—a lot of Zashians don't like it."

"Well … I think a lot of Zasians must not have heard you sing."

"Thank you. I did have lessons, as a boy. There is a famous music school in Zeleush. No—truly, there is!" He laughed, because it was beginning to sound like he had acquired every skill under the sun in Zeleush, and because she was laughing too.

"Your uncles certainly prepared you well," she said.

"I am becoming more and more grateful to them."

She adjusted the folds of her cloak for a moment and looked at the ground. The sun had disappeared behind the row of houses across the street, and the sky was becoming dark. They sat in silence for a little while. By and by Chereia looked at the bundle on the bench beside her.

"You must think it strange that I have been out buying cheese on the night of the Psobion."

"Yes."

"Well, in fact I was not buying it."

"That is, if anything, more strange still."

She laughed. "My brother-in-law gave it to me. He has just recently bought a place in the country, and is very proud of it. He also likes to feel that he is helping me out. You know, his poor little brother's destitute widow." She shrugged. "I just hope the cheese is good. He gave me some olive oil last year that turned out to be rancid. I really don't think he knew, and I didn't quite have the heart to tell him."

Marzana wondered if she had children. It seemed rather a lot of cheese for one woman. But he thought it would be impolite to ask.

"Do you feel rested enough?" he asked presently.

She looked at him with a slight smile and nodded. "Shall we walk on?"

He nodded.

At the next intersection, down a cross-street they caught a glimpse of a torch-lit square, hung with garlands, where musicians and food vendors looked as though they were preparing for a crowd.

"Is there dancing, then?" Marzana asked. "At night, in the streets?"

"Oh yes." She turned to look back down the street that they had climbed. "They're starting to come up from the agora already. Not everyone dances, of course."

"No—some are like those ... what did you call them?"

"Goons?"

"Exactly."

"Well. Some of them might have wanted to dance, I suppose. Anyway, I'm a hopeless dancer."

"I was never very good myself—even before I unfitted myself for dancing entirely."

They had turned back and were climbing the hill again.

"That seems an unfair way of putting it," she said. "Especially since you are a soldier. Surely someone else did it for you."

"Not exactly. I fell off of a citadel wall. Well—I was pushed off."

"Oh! Poor thing. It wasn't—was it very … " She looked like she did not entirely want to know.

"It was fairly high. I was lucky not to have been more badly hurt. But I was reckless to be climbing up there in the first place. We were besieging some rebels in Smerdin, and I was impatient with just starving them out, so I led an attack … My commanding officer was not impressed. I was promoted to the Royal Guard after I recovered, though, rather than being disciplined—for in fact my men had taken the citadel."

"Good for you!"

He had to admit that it was also pleasant when she made *him* laugh.

They walked on, and she asked him what the war in Smerdin had been about, and he tried to explain. She seemed fascinated, and slightly scandalized, by how little he actually knew about the causes of this war that he had fought in. He reminded her that in Zash, soldiers were expected to fight for their king, whether or not they approved of his politics, so it really did not matter whether they knew anything about them or not. She found it hard to believe that they would not still want to know what they were fighting over. Finally he admitted that five years ago, when he fought in Smerdin, he had been thinking of other things than politics. She asked what they were, and he realized that he was probably going to tell her.

That was when the vanguard of the crowd from the agora

approached near enough behind them to make out Chereia's white cloak and Marzana's foreign clothes.

"Hey! Widow!"

"Not this again," Marzana growled. Chereia stifled laughter behind her hand.

They both turned, and the light from the torches carried by the new batch of revellers fell on their faces. The crowd was mixed this time: almost as many women as men, and everyone arm-in-arm with at least one other person. It was a woman's voice that shouted next.

"Nice catch, Widow!"

There were whistles and cheers of agreement.

"Psobos send you a good night!"

"Psobos bless the plough!"

And so on.

"Oh, come on," said Chereia hastily. "Let's take this street and get away from these fools."

They turned into a side street, and Chereia slowed her pace, which Marzana had found difficult to keep up with.

"I hope you don't think—" she began, and then stopped. They looked at one another, and Marzana could tell that she was wondering what she actually meant to say. She did not finish the sentence.

"It is not our custom," he said carefully. This seemed safest.

She looked relieved. "It's not *my* custom either. I am a widow—you know that. I am dressed in mourning—that is what this undyed cloth means, here. Widows usually wear it for six months. My husband died four years ago. I did love him, and I miss him still—but I am not really in mourning now. I only wear this on the Psobion night, if I have to go out, because *some* men are decent enough not to bother a woman in a white cloak. And falling into bed with any stranger who happens to have a stiffy, just because it's the Psobion night and everyone else is doing it, isn't my idea of sensible behaviour."

Marzana did not reply. He hoped she did not think this was because he was shocked by her frankness; of course he was, but not nearly as much as he might have expected to be.

At length, to break the silence, she said: "Widows must not be such solitary creatures in Zasia. I mean because when a man dies, he wouldn't leave just one wife."

"Well, a widow goes back to her family, usually."

"Oh, yes—so do they here. I just chose to do something different."

He roused himself to answer her properly. "It is only the noblemen in Zash who have very many wives. A man of a lower rank may have only one wife, and perhaps keep a few concubines, if he can afford to. But I believe that can happen here too, can it not?"

She made a face. "Oh, well, it can, but a man has to do it outside his own home, you know—and it isn't a good idea to flaunt it in his wife's face." After a moment she said, "What about you, though? How many wives do you have waiting for you at home?"

"I am no nobleman. My family is of middle rank." But that did not answer her question either. "I am not married. The only woman waiting for me at home is my mother. She was left a widow at about your age, with two small sons. I am the younger—I was born a month after my father's death."

"I am sorry."

They turned out of the cross-street into another that climbed towards the city's edge.

"I have realized something," Marzana said finally, "about my own folly."

"What is it?"

"For me it has been five years, but if I were to show it

according to your custom as it is in my heart, I would be in undyed cloth from head to foot every day of the year."

She drew in her breath. "I am sorry. I am so sorry. That is not folly at all."

"No, no, it is. The folly is, she was not my wife. And she is not dead."

He knew that what he had just done was shocking; but he had known, all the same, that he was going to do it. He could imagine every female of his acquaintance (there were not many of them) gaping in horror at the very idea of a respectable man revealing the secrets of his heart in this way to any woman, never mind an immodest Pseuchaian woman whom he had only just met, who hit people with cheeses and talked about sex in the street.

"Oh … " she said. "You had your heart broken. I *am* sorry."

He tried to imagine how Parmatya would react, if she could know of this betrayal. He supposed it *was* a betrayal in some way. But what he had to admit to himself then, at last, was that he could not quite imagine this, for one rather good reason. He could not conjure in his mind a clear enough image of Parmatya's face. He felt a strange, guilty sense of relief.

CHAPTER X

BEDAR ARRIVED IN Old Pottery Street just as the sun sank out of the sky. He was soul-crushingly tired, his dinner had consisted of a small wedge of sticky cake eaten hastily on a street corner, and the trail of the missing ambassador was by now very, very cold. But he had not heard from Marzana all day, and he felt the need to be doing *something*, if only to take his mind off the grim contemplation of what was going to happen to him when he returned to Zash without his master.

He had spent the afternoon lying to people. It was as he was leaving Temple Walk that the news had reached him, in the form of gossip overheard in the street, that Minister Lekythos, one of the champions of the Zashian alliance, had died that morning. He had returned to the ambassador's house, rightly guessing that when this news arrived there, it would mean trouble. It had been worse than he imagined. Shortly after he had left for Temple Walk, apparently, a deputation of the Zashians' more tentative supporters had arrived at the house with the news, wishing to see the ambassador and talk about how to recover from this setback. The ambassador's aides, not knowing where he was, had improvised idiotically, saying that His Excellency was closeted in his room and refused to descend on account of the Boukossian festival, which offended him. Evidently Smar had chimed in with some irrelevant squealing about people bringing unclean animals into houses. The tentative supporters had been offended themselves, and left in a state of great indignation. Tracking them all to their homes and convincing them that His Excellency had actually gone out early that morning, unbeknownst to his staff, to enjoy the Boukossian festival, had been the work of tedious hours, and required all of Bedar's resources of tactful deceit.

Old Pottery Street did not seem so aptly named as Temple Walk; there was no sign of any old pottery that Bedar could see. The street lay just outside the city's walls, in what was now an old and built-up suburb at the eastern edge of the city. It had been difficult to find, but now that Bedar was here, he could not tell what it was he had spent so much time looking for. The buildings on either side of the street were wide-fronted and low, in the sprawling, suburban style, and had a look of restrained gentility. There were no paintings around the doors or windows, no rows of potted trees. The street was thinly populated at this hour, and its scant traffic seemed to consist entirely of solitary men, most of them in a hurry.

About halfway down the street, a building with a low, columned porch was distinguished from the other staid facades by a pair of white plaster horses, reared on their hind legs, which flanked the entrance. It looked like it might well represent the pinnacle of whatever this neighbourhood had to offer. As Bedar stood watching from the street's end, he saw three men enter, and two more leave—far more than were coming and going from the other buildings.

"Pardon me, sir," he said to a man who was passing close by him. "Can you tell me what is that building with the horses in front of it?"

The man looked down the street at the statues, then back at Bedar. "That's the Horses," he said, and walked on.

"Thank you so much," said Bedar to thin air.

The doors between the plaster horses stood open, and light from within pooled on the white pavement. Bedar walked in. The entry hall was high-ceilinged and decorated in stylish black-and-white mosaics, the central design of which showed a chubby Psobos, done in much the same style as the puppets. Stairs on either side of the hall led up to an inner gallery, and through an arch in the far wall Bedar could see what lay below the gallery, at the heart of the building: a glimmer of water and the pale forms of naked Boukossians. It was a bath-house.

Though this was bad enough, he had been half-expecting worse. He had been in one of these places already today, in his quest for one of the ministers. He had been obliged to have a long conversation with the man (who had been mercifully wrapped in a towel) in a room full of steam and naked youths; he had then slipped on the wet floor going out, and been helped up by someone who was not wrapped in a towel. His clothes had been damp from the steam for an hour after.

A big, fair-haired man in a gilt-edged tunic had swept up out of nowhere while Bedar stood for a moment inside the door. His eyes flickered appraisingly over the embroidery on Bedar's coat.

"May I be of assistance, honoured sir?" he inquired, separating his syllables carefully for the foreigner's benefit. "My name is Skyphos. My humble establishment is at your service."

"Thank you," said Bedar wearily. "I am looking for someone." Whom he heartily doubted he would find any news of here.

The big man held up a finger knowingly. "Ah. Say no more. You are looking for Pheres."

Bedar looked at him. "I am?"

"You are a Sasian gentleman, are you not?"

"I am, uh, Sasian, yes."

"Then it is Pheres that you are looking for." The man beamed. "Take the stairs on your left. You will find that it is the fourth door at the top."

Bedar paused uncertainly. Was it possible that the ambassador *had* come here, and that this Pheres knew something about him? This struck him as the only explanation for the man's peculiar words.

"Thank you," he said finally. He took the stairs to the left.

The gallery ran around the outside of the main bath, with an elegant parapet overlooking the splashing, laughing bathers below. The outside walls were lined with doors, closely spaced as though they led to narrow rooms all around the outside of the upper storey. A few doors were ajar, but as Bedar arrived at the top of the stairs, only one was wide open. A slender, pink-and-white youth stood in the doorway, wearing a couple of bracelets, a purple hair-ribbon, and nothing else.

He had been leaning against the doorpost, looking out over the bath, but at the sound of someone coming up the stairs he looked around in that direction, eyes narrowed between pale lashes. For a moment, before the boy's expression became more guarded, Bedar caught the weight of a leaden contempt. It was gone so quickly that he could almost have believed he had imagined it, if he had not understood pretty well what its cause was. It had nothing to do with him, personally; it was just the way that this boy felt about any man coming up those stairs and heading for his door.

He remembered now that he had heard someone mention the Horses earlier that day. *He paints his eyes*, one of the girls in Temple Walk had said, *like the boys from the Horses*. The pale eyes of the youth in the doorway were indeed heavily made-up. *You don't suppose he is one?* the girl had said. *One of us …* It had not made sense to Bedar at the time, and he had heard it without giving it much thought. Now he understood, and the only thing he could think of was how fast he could get out of this place. The girls in Temple Walk had seemed to enjoy their work. For all he knew they might even have been free. Nothing could be more certain than that the boy in that doorway was a slave, and hated it.

But the boy was no longer looking at Bedar with contempt; his expression had changed to a kind of cool curiosity. And before Bedar had quite turned to escape down the stairs, the boy spoke, in a voice a shade deeper than Bedar's own.

"Sir, may I ask you a question?"

Bedar stood where he was, half turned away, and waited for some new piece of the usual Boukossian idiocy.

"You're a Zashian," said the boy, "I can tell that from your clothes. But you don't have a beard. Are you a eunuch?"

Bedar looked back at him, frankly startled. No strange euphemisms, no prurient giggling or blushing or hand-waving? Just a straightforward question. It was oddly refreshing.

"Yes," he said. "That's right."

"Hah. Fancy that." The boy looked faintly, reservedly pleased with himself for having guessed. After a moment he added diffidently, "I never met one before, that's all."

"No," said Bedar. "I suppose not." He imagined the boy probably wanted to hear his voice—it was one of those things—and he didn't mind obliging. With his best Suna court accent, he said, "No one here seems to know what I am, but where I come from, we are as common as … "

"As whores in Boukos?"

"Well. Almost."

The boy didn't exactly laugh, but he smiled slightly, and his bare shoulders twitched. He was leaning against the door-post with one hand, the other poised on the pale angle of his hip.

They stood an uncertain moment longer. The boy must have been wondering what Bedar was doing there. Bedar was wondering it himself. He couldn't recall now which door the man downstairs had directed him to, but there were painted inscriptions above each one, and sure enough, the one where the boy stood was marked PHERES • 12 n. "You are looking for Pheres," the doorman had said, and all that meant was, "You will be satisfied with Pheres—he is pretty and expensive and will do whatever you want." The thought made Bedar's stomach turn over queasily. The boy was certainly attractive, but there was nothing Bedar wanted that he could do.

"Did you come here by mistake, sir?" Pheres suggested.

"Yes," said Bedar readily. "Or no. Ah. You've heard that one before."

Pheres rolled his eyes. "All. The. Time."

It was Bedar's turn to not quite laugh. "Listen," he said, on impulse, "Would you—"

He checked the impulse abruptly. He had been about to ask if the boy wanted company. He remembered what the girls in Temple Walk had said about the men they got on the Psobion night, and he had been about to offer himself as an alternative to whatever dregs-of-humanity customer might turn up any moment now. He had realized in time that such an offer would probably be too vague to be immediately understood, or too odd to be trusted—or, worse, maybe prostitutes heard that sort of thing all the time, too. *I just want a little conversation, I'm not like those other nasty men, I really care about you* ... with the unspoken understanding that sex acts would be performed after that in a spirit of gratitude, real or feigned.

So he said instead, "Do you do … what is the word? It is a Pseuchaian science, I believe, for relieving stiff muscles … " He put a hand illustratively to his shoulder, which was indeed painfully tense. He knew the term, in fact, but thought this mild pretence would make sense of his hesitation.

"Massage?" Pheres supplied. "Yeah, I can do that." He paused, eyes narrowed appraisingly. "I mean, for what you're talking about, probably you should go to the healers at the temple of Petteia. But they're closed now. And I'm pretty good."

"I rejoice to hear it."

The boy's lips twitched with another faint smile. "There's tables downstairs."

That brought Bedar up short. "Tables?" he repeated blankly.

"Massage tables. Downstairs by the bath. Yeah … that's probably a bit too Pseuchaian for you, huh?"

"I fear it might be."

"Well, you can come in here and be private, but even if you *really* only want a massage? If we do it in my room, it'll cost you twelve nummoi. That's just the price to spend time with me. So. Just to let you know."

"I understand," said Bedar.

Part of him wanted to take the opportunity the boy was offering him to shrug regretfully and leave, pretending that money was an obstacle. The situation was already slightly embarrassing, and threatened to become more so. He didn't entirely know what he might be getting himself into, except that it was going to involve spending a large sum of his master's money. Taking pity on unhappy prostitutes was in no way part of the Zashian mission in Boukos. He should continue on his search for the ambassador, even if by now it seemed pointless. He couldn't make himself do it.

"Well, then," said the boy, after a moment. He stepped aside, with a languid motion, from the open door. He looked a little uncertain himself, as if he didn't know quite what was being asked of him either. "Come in."

Bedar came in. The room beyond the door was airy and genteelly painted like the rest of the building, with a shuttered window at the far end, a lit lamp on a stand, and a few pieces of furniture. It looked comfortable, not like a prison cell. Maybe, Bedar thought, if he hadn't caught that glimpse of the look in the boy's eyes when he first came up, he would not have expected anything different.

Pheres closed the door quietly behind them. Bedar looked at him.

He was as beautiful as one of the Boukossians' statues: long-limbed and clear-skinned, with the physique of a young athlete and elegantly proportioned features. But he was made up in a style that did not suit him at all. The delicacy of his pink-and-white complexion had been dampened to a chalky white with a heavy dusting of powder, the gentle recurve of his lips stained red, his eyes smeared thickly with blue and black. His hair, which was a shining, rosy gold, had been tortured into rows of short, crisp ringlets held in place by a fussily tied ribbon. It almost looked like a deliberate attempt to hide his real beauty.

"May I take your coat, sir?" He stood in front of Bedar, and his eyes dropped to the buttons that fastened the coat at the shoulder.

Bedar unfastened the buttons himself and shrugged the coat off. Pheres took it from him, then reached out and took Bedar's hat as well. The boy was about Bedar's height, perhaps slightly taller. He wore a scent that was surprisingly complex and appealing, much more sophisticated than his makeup. He laid coat and hat on a stool beside the bed. Bedar tugged his purse of money out of his sash and added it to the pile.

"Does your tunic have buttons too?"

"My—my shirt?" It did—two small buttons at the neck— and Bedar covered them reflexively with his hand. He realized too late that this must have made him look like some kind of blushing maiden. That was by no means what he was, but the message had already been sent.

"You don't want to take it off?" Pheres said neutrally. His expression showed no hint of what he thought of that, whether it surprised or puzzled or amused him.

"It, ah, is what one would normally do, I suppose."

Pheres shrugged. "Yeah, normally. But it's all right. This isn't about making you do things you don't want to do."

We're both trying to take pity on each other, Bedar thought. He didn't know whether it was ridiculous or strangely touching.

"I'm sure we both have enough experience of that," he said.

Pheres frowned slightly, studying Bedar for a moment. "Yeah, I guess so, huh?"

He turned away toward a chest by the foot of the bed with some crumpled cloth draped over it. Extracting a length, he shook it out to reveal a shapeless Pseuchaian garment. He tossed one end over his shoulder and wrapped the other around his waist, tweaking the folds so that it hung as well as something with no tailoring that had been wadded up in a ball could be expected to do. Bedar wasn't sure whether to say, "Thank you," or "You didn't need to," or in some other way acknowledge that he knew the garment had been put on for his sake. In the end he said nothing, but sat on the end of the bed and reached down for his boots.

"I'll do that, sir," said Pheres, dropping to his knees. "Hah, buttons on your boots, too." It took him a moment to work them free. He looked up at Bedar from where he knelt. "Want to lie down, sir? On your stomach, and I'll work on your back."

"Thank you."

Bedar stretched out on the couch and turned to lie face-down, pillowing his head on his folded arms. The sheet covering the bed smelled surprisingly clean. Well, it was an expensive place, and that was probably the sort of thing you paid for.

He felt the mattress shift as Pheres got up on the bed and moved to straddle his thighs. "It's better if you put your arms down to the sides. Yeah, like that." He adjusted a cushion. "Comfortable?"

"Yes." In fact, he was tenser than ever.

"It should go without saying, sir, but if I do anything you don't like, just tell me to stop."

"Of course."

The boy gently tugged the hem of Bedar's shirt free from his sash and pushed it up a little. There was a pause as he slipped off one of his bracelets and reached something down from a shelf. Out of the corner of his eye, Bedar saw him dripping oil from a little flask into the palm of one hand.

"Don't worry, sir, I won't use much. It won't get on your clothes."

"You know you need not call me 'sir.'"

"No?" He nudged Bedar's shirt up further with the back of his hand, and pressed his oiled palms flat on Bedar's back, leaning firmly down into the tight muscles. It felt wonderful. Bedar let an appreciative moan escape his lips.

"How come?" said Pheres.

"How … come what?" Bedar's voice came out muffled by the cushion.

"How come you don't want me to call you 'sir'?"

"I … didn't say that. I said you need not. It is what you call a man, and I am not one."

Pheres was silent for a moment, his hands working over Bedar's back. "You're an adult, though—right? And you're not a woman, so … what is the respectful thing to call you?"

Bedar blew at a lock of hair that had fallen across his face. "I don't know," he admitted. "I don't know what would do in Pseuchaian."

"What is it in Zashian?"

"There is no such term in Zashian. It is not necessary."

"Oh." And after a moment, "Well, nobody calls me 'sir' either, s—uh, and probably nobody ever will. How is this? Good?"

"Extremely. May God bring you swiftly to the day when you are called 'sir' as you deserve."

The boys hands stilled for a moment. "That's a classy thing to say." Bedar thought he sounded genuinely moved, and was trying to hide it. He ran his thumbs slowly down either side of Bedar's spine. "If I'm not going to call you 'sir,' then maybe you should tell me your name?"

"Oh. I haven't, have I? Forgive me."

"That's all right. I know Zashians don't introduce themselves."

"Not to other Zashians, no—but to Pseuchaians we should, as it is your custom. My name is Bedar."

"That's all?"

Bedar laughed softly. "Yes, that's it."

"It sounds like it's missing something."

Bedar looked over his shoulder, as best he could, and arched an eyebrow at the boy. "Oh, yes?"

Pheres opened his mouth and closed it again very quickly. Beneath the thick coat of powder on his face, he was clearly blushing, and it suited him.

"I'm sorry," he said.

"Don't be. It is a staple of Zashian humour. Not at all anything to be ashamed of."

"What I meant," Pheres said, with emphasis, "is that your name sounds like it's missing some syllables. Some sh-djuh-zz stuff that Pseuchaians can't pronounce properly." The sounds seemed to give him no difficulty. "For a Zashian name, it seems too easy."

"It's not a Zashian name, really. It's a Parkan name. That's … " He tried to muster the energy to explain his origins, but it was hard when he was so relaxed.

"The mountains in the south-east, right? I thought you looked like you might be from there."

"You did?"

"Mm-hm. It's the shape of your eyes, mostly. They're very pretty."

"Thank you."

Pheres smoothed his hands lightly down Bedar's back one last time, and drew his shirt back down. "I think that's as much as I can do without making you take any more clothes off. How does it feel?"

"Wonderful."

"Don't get up. There's no rush." The boy moved to sit on the bed between Bedar and the wall. "You know, it's all right if you decide you want something more, s—um—Bedar. That's what I'm here for."

Bedar turned on his side to look at him, tucking his hair back behind his ear. Pheres sat with his knees drawn up under his crumpled mantle, one arm hooked around both legs, his gold bracelet catching the lamplight with a warm gleam.

"I don't really think it would be all right," Bedar said. "But out of curiosity, what do you imagine you might do for me?"

"What do I imagine … " Pheres frowned. "Well, I'm sure I could do something. You're a Zashian eunuch, right? It's only in Samerdin that they cut off *everything*."

Bedar gave him a wide-eyed look. "You really are terribly well-informed."

"I'm right, then."

"You are, yes. I must confess it is refreshing. I have been taken for a woman several times since I arrived here, and for a child at least as often, and earlier today I was asked to settle a bet about whether I am able to relieve myself standing up, or not."

Pheres made a disgusted noise. "People are so stupid." After a moment he added, "But you said it wouldn't be all right. Am I just not your type, or is there a taboo in Zash? I wondered about that."

"You are very lovely, but too young for … for anything that I would expect—or wish—to do with a lover. And it is thought deplorable in Zash for the act of love to be exchanged for money. It is what you would call a taboo, I suppose."

"Oh, I see. That's not what I thought. Boys are all right, just so long as you don't pay?"

"It is more complicated than that, but … that is not inaccurate."

"Right. I mean, it's not *respectable* to pay for boys even here. Because a love affair with a boy is supposed to be all Kossian, you know—high ideals and poetry and honour and stuff. Not that Boukossians generally take it that seriously, but you wouldn't necessarily want your political rivals to hear about it if you were a regular at the Horses, you know? So it's more complicated here too, I guess." He fell silent with a wry expression. "Sorry. I'm talking too much."

"Not in the least. I came in here for—" He stopped in his turn.

"For a massage," Pheres supplied after a moment. "Not to listen to me talk about the theory of loving boys. Right?"

Bedar rolled over fully to lie on his back, pushing his fingers up into his hair. He felt relaxed and comfortable.

"Your thoughts are as interesting to me as your hands are skilled," he said.

Pheres sat looking at him for a long moment in the lamplight.

"So you feel better now?" he said presently.

"Much. Thank you."

"You were very tense."

"I have had a fairly awful day. Psobos, you might say, does not appear to smile on me."

"But I suppose … the disdain is mutual?"

Bedar laughed. "You suppose correctly—indeed, eloquently."

A smile tugged at the boy's lips again. His smiles always seemed to start and never to reach the halfway mark. "May I ask you something? You're part of the trade delegation?"

"Yes. I am the ambassador's secretary."

"And why does Zash want a trade alliance with Boukos?"

"Ah. Well, there are many reasons." Bedar linked his hands behind his head and rearranged himself on the cushion. "None in itself definitive, but taken together, compelling. Boukos is, in a sense, the low-hanging fruit of the Pseuchaian League—your city already does more trade with Glif and the Shand than do Pheme or Kos, so it is not impossible to imagine trade with Zash too. And then, His Radiancy the king of Zash is young, and wants to do things differently from his father—and his father would never have made an alliance with any Pseuchaian state. And he is looking to strengthen his alliances to the west because the eastern border is threatened by the new regime in Smerdin. This is a small beginning, but it is something."

"You sound knowledgeable. Are you in the inner circle at court?"

"I? No, of course not. But I have served men who are, and you hear things."

"You do."

Bedar smiled. "We're lucky, now—we have a good king. A just and compassionate king. It makes all the difference at court. Everyone breathes easier. I first visited the court with my master under the last king, and in those days you couldn't trust anyone—it was all intrigue and backstabbing. The atmosphere was poisonous. There are still some of the old guard left, but they have lost most of their power. The court is a different place altogether. Now I am talking too much."

"No! I could listen to you all night. If you didn't have anywhere else to be, of course."

"Indeed. I understand that this is a night when everyone in the city wishes to have somewhere to be." A rather dangerous topic; he wondered why he had raised it.

"You know about the Psobion night? Have you had invitations?" Pheres's tone was arch. "I'll bet you have."

"I have. Several."

"So Psobos doesn't smile on you so much as leer at you."

Bedar laughed. "Surely men come here sometimes and simply pay for your conversation?"

The boy looked diffident. "You are very sweet. No, they don't, not really. Some of them pretend to, but … "

"Ah. I thought they might do that. How tedious."

"Yeah, that's a good word for it. Though I guess … sometimes it just takes them a while to ask for what they really want."

"Are you yet convinced that is not what I am doing?"

"I think I am."

"I hope so."

Pheres frowned. "I don't know what you *are* doing, though. I mean, you had the idea of asking for a massage out there in the gallery—you didn't come here for that. In fact, you were about to leave when I spoke to you. You really did come in by accident, didn't you? You thought the Horses was something else."

"I didn't know what it was," Bedar admitted. "Then I thought it was a bath-house, and I asked the doorman a question which he misinterpreted, and he sent me upstairs."

"What did you—" Pheres started to say when he was interrupted by a crash and a shout from the room next door. He broke off and started up from the bed.

More noises followed: a man's voice raised in anger, and a boy's voice protesting or apologizing, the sound of a slap, and then of a falling body.

"Excuse me, sir," said Pheres perfunctorily. He was already across the room and yanking open the door.

Bedar rolled off the bed and took the time to put on his boots before following, so that by the time he looked out into the gallery, Pheres was in the room next door. Bedar could hear him shouting at someone. Soon after, a dark-haired young man with his mantle clutched clumsily around him and his sandals in his hand stalked out of the room, started and grimaced horribly when he saw Bedar, and made his way down the gallery, walking with the exaggerated care of someone who was drunker than he thought he was.

Bedar looked around the doorway into the second room. "Is there anything I can do?"

Pheres was kneeling on the floor by a tipped-over chair, gathering up shards of a smashed wine-cup. On the bed sat a smaller, prettier boy with brown curls and tears streaking his eye-makeup down his cheeks. He looked up at Bedar, and his eyes went wide.

"Holy Orante, Pheres! Another Sasian? Is he yours?"

"Shh, Nenni, that's not … " Pheres looked embarrassed, but he turned to Bedar. "Could you check that Makron—the goat-fucker who just left—that he's really leaving, and not trying to bother somebody else?"

"Of course."

The dark-haired young man had disappeared down the stairs by this time, and Bedar caught up with him in the entrance hall, where he was trying to put on his sandals while telling the doorman he wouldn't pay because a boy had tried to bite him.

"I'm afraid there must have been some misunderstanding," the doorman replied coolly. "None of our boys bite."

He ushered the young man out the door, and Bedar returned upstairs to report that he was gone. He found Pheres and Nenni sitting side-by-side on the bed, the broken cup cleared away, and the chair righted.

"Thank you," said Pheres. He moved to get up from the bed, patting his friend on the shoulder.

"May I ask," said Bedar, addressing the younger boy before Pheres could make his excuses and leave, "what you meant just now when you said, 'another Sasian'?"

"Oh, yes, sir!" Nenni looked pleased to be able to explain. "Pheres had a Sasian last night too, sir."

"Nenni … " Pheres looked pained. "I know he asked, but—you really shouldn't say that sort of thing."

"What sort of thing?" The little boy looked confused.

"You shouldn't talk about the other men who come here—it's … it's like they all like to pretend they don't exist, or that we don't notice who they are."

"Oh," said Nenni, still looking uncertain.

"Anyway," said Pheres, "that's sorted. Makron won't be back—Skyphos won't let him in if he does come—and you can just shut your door and take the rest of the night off. It's late, the busy period's over, and you've earned a rest. That fucking swine—I can't believe he tried that with you."

"Are you sure it's all right for me to shut my door?"

"I'm sure. If Skyphos asks about it—which he won't—tell him I told you to do it."

"Pheres! I don't want to get you in trouble!"

"Skyphos likes me. And he won't even ask. He likes you, too. Anyway, I've got to go."

At this, Bedar thought it would be polite to retreat to Pheres's room. He stood there, contemplating his coat on the chair by the bed, wondering whether to put it back on. Within a minute, before he had decided, Pheres followed him in.

"Sorry about that," Pheres said.

"Not at all." Bedar looked up. "It was good of you to go to your friend's aid."

Pheres shrugged. "That's how I was brought up. That's one good thing we learned, I guess. Older boys should look out for younger ones."

There was an awkward moment's silence. It struck Bedar that either he needed to say it was time for him to go, or Pheres needed to come up with a reason for them to go back to the bed, otherwise they would just go on standing there.

"That kind of thing doesn't happen here all that often," Pheres said, nodding toward Nenni's room. "Most of the men are well-behaved, really. But on the Psobion night, you get a lot of assholes—they've had too much to drink, or they're just feeling sorry for themselves, and want to take it out on somebody."

"I have heard," said Bedar.

Pheres gave him a sharp look. "Have you?"

"Earlier today, when I was speaking with some women in Temple Walk."

"I see."

Bedar tucked a strand of hair behind his ear. "Please believe that I have a good reason to ask this, Pheres—and if I did not, I would not. Was there really another Zashian here last night?"

"Oh. Yes, there was. It's all right—I don't mind talking about it." He gave another of his unfinished smiles. "He was very different from you."

"I imagine he must have been. He was not, by any chance, a tall man with curly hair and a long, curled beard, dyed nearly red? Wearing a purple coat, and exhibiting an astonishing facility for not listening to anything one says?"

"Yes, sir. As I said, very different from you."

Bedar felt sick. "And did he … when he discovered the nature of this place to which he had come, no doubt, unwittingly—did he leave immediately?"

Ever so slightly, Pheres shook his head.

"I see," said Bedar quietly.

"Is he … You seem upset. Is he your … "

"Faithless lover? Merciful God, no! No, he is my master. He has disappeared—he did not come home last night—and I have been looking for him. If he was here, you are the last person I know of who saw him."

Pheres stared. "Blessed gods! Disappeared? No wonder you said you've had a bad day. If your employer—you mean 'employer,' right, not 'master'? 'Master' is the word we use for someone who owns a slave … "

"Yes, that is the word I meant." Bedar felt suddenly cold with shame and embarrassment. "I'm sorry, I did not mean to mislead you—it did not occur to me, since you knew I was a eunuch, that you would not realize I was a slave. I am of course a slave. In Zashian law, there is no such thing as a free eunuch."

Pheres did not seem to care that he had been misled into calling a slave "sir."

"You mean … they did that to you, and now you can never be free?" The boy's expression looked like pure outrage.

"No, in law and in absolute truth, no—but in practice, in the world, I have a great deal more freedom than you might think. As a servant of the court, there are places I can go, privileges I enjoy, that are barred to most free men. And, truly, I have been what I am for so long that I have learned to think of it as if it could never have been otherwise."

"Blessed gods," Pheres repeated. "And here I am feeling sorry for myself." His gaze had dropped to the floor, but now he smiled up at Bedar, a wry, beautiful, sidelong smile.

"No doubt it's always better not to feel sorry for oneself, but what you have had to endure here … I can only imagine … "

"You came in here because you were looking for your master, but you stayed because of what you'd heard about the kind of customers we get on the Psobion night, didn't you?"

"I may have. I'm not a very obedient servant—is that what you were thinking?"

"No, it isn't at all." The smile came up and faced forward, breathtakingly. "Anyway! Your master is missing, and I'm the last person who saw him—or not the last person, but the last person that you've found so far. Sit down. Let me think what I can remember that might be helpful."

They sat on the bed again. Pheres turned and reached across the bed to unfasten the shutters, letting in moonlight and a gentle breeze. He leaned on the windowsill, his head propped on his hand. He caught his lower lip in his white teeth, and bit on it thoughtfully for a moment. Bedar had to stop himself from telling the boy not to do that. It was like watching someone manhandle a piece of art; but they *were* his lips, and it would seem hard that he should not be allowed to chew on them if he wanted to.

Bedar sat on the edge of the bed without removing his boots. He felt a little stunned in the aftermath of that smile. He tried to remind himself that Pheres was too young, not his type—but it had been a surprisingly grown-up smile. And then he thought about the fact that His Excellency had been here, last night, and his mind snapped shut like a trap.

"Zukohashkra," Pheres said at length, precisely. "Is that something like his name?"

"Exactly like," said Bedar, who had forgotten what they had been talking about.

"He didn't tell me his name, but he happened to mention it, in a story he was telling about himself. He talked quite a lot, but … I will have to try to remember if he said anything that could be helpful. It was only last night—but you know, you don't remember these things if you don't think they are going to be important."

"I would not wish you to have to dwell on anything disagreeable." He didn't want to have to dwell on it himself, though he knew he was going to.

The boy laughed briefly. "You *are* sweet. It wasn't bad. He'd been drinking pretty hard—he wasn't up to much." He winced. "I beg you forgive my coarseness, sir. Gods. I'm *still* calling you 'sir,' like an idiot."

"Please do not trouble yourself about it."

"It's a hard habit to break—and you're very … very sir-like." He spread his pale fingers on the blanket, whose stripes were muted in the bluish light, and looked thoughtful for a moment, but without chewing on his lip. "Oh! I've remembered. He had to leave—he stayed quite a long time, but in the end he left in a hurry, because he was meeting some men who had invited him somewhere. He didn't explain it very well, but I *think* they had invited him to see the consecrating of the streets. It would have been about the right time for that."

"Thank you—that is very helpful. What is the consecrating of the streets?"

"It's a sort of pre-Psobion ceremony. I've never seen it—I don't know exactly what they do. But they start off at each of the gates of the city. If he was going to see the consecrating, and I'm pretty sure he was, he probably would have arranged to meet these men at one of the gates. The Eastern Gate is quite near here—though that's not necessarily the one he was headed for."

"The men he was meeting—I suppose they were some of the ministers of the Basileon?"

"Would they have been? I don't know."

"I would imagine so." Bedar explained about the party, and how he had left early, and the ministers had taken the ambassador out to "lengthen the night" with them. It was a relief to tell it all just as it had happened, rather than weaving more elaborate lies.

"No," said Pheres, when the explanation was finished. "In that case I don't think it *was* the ministers he was meeting. I saw a couple of them—they came in with him, and Skyphos was hovering around being obsequious. But when he said he had to go out, it sounded like he was meeting different people. He couldn't quite remember their names—I got the impression they were men he had only just met, and that he found them sort of … quaint? I mean, he seemed to find everything here quaint, but there was something a little different about these men. Like they were some kind of curiosity. I know that's not much help."

"On the contrary, I think it may be. It would explain why His Excellency did not return with any of the ministers last night."

"Yeah … he ditched them. At any rate, I think he did. So Zukohashkra is the ambassador, then?"

"Indeed. He did not boast to you of his own importance? That surprises me."

"Well, actually—he said something about being a relative of the king of Zash. Not a *close* relative, is he?"

"First cousin. His Excellency Zukohashkra son of Zukoshakthra son of Zohanaza the Eighth."

"Immortal gods," said Pheres dryly. "Royalty."

"He has disgraced his royal house with what he did, coming to a place like this. In Zash, no respectable man would stoop so low."

"This is not Zash." Pheres shrugged. "When you come here, you speak Pseuchaian, you drink the local wine, you adapt to the customs. You make love to the local boys."

"Certainly. To those that are willing."

"Sir. I am always willing. That is why one comes to a place like this."

"No. That is why one *doesn't*."

Pheres smiled again, wistfully.

"Forgive me," said Bedar, getting hold of himself again. "That kind of thing is not helpful, I know."

Pheres shrugged. "Maybe not. Sometimes it's nice, though. What are you going to do now?"

"I do not know. I cannot see that there would be much use in going around to the city gates, and I have no idea where else I could pick up any trace of His Excellency or these men that he was meeting."

"It might be a good idea to go to the gates, actually. They

have little tiny temples there, with priests. They might have noticed Zuko—I'm assuming his friends call him Zuko?"

"I don't think so, but please do not let that stop you."

"Well, the priests might have noticed him waiting around there last night—I mean, he is quite noticeable. I don't know if the priests would be … busy, because of the Psobion night—they might be, I don't know what the custom is. But you could go to the South Gate at least—it's worth a try."

"Yes … yes, you are quite right. It is worth a try."

"I know there are six gates to the city, and I think they're quite easy to find, because they're at the ends of the main streets. So you just find the main streets, and follow them to either end—right? And dodge all the people who'll try to throw themselves at you, even if they'd got somebody lined up for the night already."

"You are too kind."

"Hah. If you stay in the main streets, you won't have to worry about anything worse than that—like anyone trying to actually drag you into his house or something. It's pretty lively, I think … there are people dancing, and things."

"I must confess," said Bedar, after a moment, "that I get lost easily. Do you think you could come with me?"

"No, I'm sorry, I couldn't."

"One is not allowed to … to take you home, for instance, for the evening?"

"Well, yes, men do that sometimes. But it's very expensive."

"How much, exactly?"

"Thirty-six nummoi." Pheres made an apologetic face. "So … like I said, very expensive. Kind of ridiculous, really."

Bedar got up from the bed, and unfolded his coat on the clothes stool. He found the purse of Pseuchaian money which he had taken out of his sash and untied it.

"Would you like to come?" he asked, looking back at Pheres.

"Yes, certainly. I mean, utterly—of course. But—"

Bedar poured the contents of the purse out onto the striped blanket on the bed. It was a small heap of coins, but they were in very large denominations. Pheres looked impressed. Pulling the sleeve of his shirt down over his hand, Bedar sorted through the coins. It was hard to see the numerals in the darkness, and he was not used to the different shapes and sizes of Boukossian currency.

"These large ones I believe are worth ten nummoi?" The boy nodded. "That makes thirty-six, then—and I owe twelve more, I suppose. Oh, enough of this." He pulled his sleeve back up and plucked the rest of the coins out of the heap with his bare hand, in spite of the sinisterly grinning horned heads that were stamped on each one.

"Oh!" said Pheres, who had been looking puzzled. "You have a thing about goats, don't you?"

"Yes. Yes, we have a 'thing' about goats."

"You don't eat them, or drink their milk or anything, do you?"

"We do not like to so much as *look* at them—we certainly do not eat them."

"Nice." When Bedar looked surprised, he explained: "Oh, they taste foul. Everything about them tastes foul. You're not missing *anything*."

"I am delighted to hear it. So there you are—forty-eight nummoi."

"That's not your money, is it?"

"No, indeed. My savings are not so great. This is money with which my master was provided, by the court bursar, in order that he and his staff might spend lavishly and make a favourable impression in Boukos."

"Oh, good. I wouldn't want you to spend so much of your own money just to take me out. I mean," he added, after a moment, "if you really do want me to show you around the city, you should know that I've only lived here as a slave—I don't really know my way around that well."

"Your first guess was better," said Bedar with a smile.

Pheres nodded. "I'll get ready—it'll only take a moment."

It took more than a moment, but he was quick all the same. He yanked the ribbon out of his hair and combed through the curls viciously with his fingers to loosen and disarrange them. He splashed water on his face and scrubbed it with a towel, efficiently taking off most of his makeup. Then he shed the crumpled mantle and wriggled into a much neater plain white tunic, which he belted at the waist. He slipped off his remaining bracelet and stepped into a pair of light sandals.

"There," he said, looking up at Bedar and giving his hair another rake-through. "I'm ready."

"So you are."

"I, uh, don't like going out with paint on. I hope it's all right."

"Of course."

"I do like the way you do your eyes, though. It's different. Suits you."

Unquestionably it suited Pheres better to be without makeup. He looked older, handsomer: a young man rather than a boy.

"Thank you," Bedar said belatedly. "I could show you how to do it if you like."

Pheres's eyebrows went up. "That would be nice," he said politely.

It was hard to think when they might have the opportunity for that. It had been a stupid thing to offer.

Out in the gallery, Bedar slung his coat over one shoulder, and Pheres slipped his arm through Bedar's, his pale hand resting lightly on the black fabric of Bedar's sleeve. His face had returned to the guarded neutrality which must have been all that most of his customers ever saw. But without the unflattering paint, even that was more beautiful.

They went down the stairs and were met by the smirking, gold-braid-encrusted Skyphos in the lobby. Bedar was bracing himself to put on a lordly air and pass himself off as a discerning foreigner, a man of expensive tastes who had been impressed by some of the brothel's merchandise, not a presumptuous eunuch spending his master's money. He saw Skyphos's eyes flicking over Pheres's state of dress, and the smirk fading, replaced by an altogether more human expression. Skyphos sighed.

"You know I can't let you go out, Pheres, unless—"

"He's good for it," Pheres cut in.

He nudged Bedar, and Bedar produced his purse full of coins, casually poured out a handful, and tipped it into Skyphos's palm.

"Is that about right?"

Skyphos closed his hand around the coins. "Thank you, sir. Enjoy your evening."

"You can let go of my arm now," Bedar said when they were outside in the street, between the white plaster horses.

"Sir." He did. The place where his hand had been felt cold. "It's this way—the South Gate." He tipped his head in that direction.

They walked to the end of the dark suburban street in silence, and Bedar began to wonder if he had made a mistake, perhaps several mistakes. They turned into the street that ended in the tall, white columns of the South Gate.

"I left my hat in your room," said Bedar.

"I hid it, so you'd have to come back for it."

"Really?"

"No. That would've been kind of weird."

"Yes."

"Do you want to go back and get it now?"

"No, it is not really necessary. No one here wears hats. I suppose that is why I forgot it. In Zash, one does not go out without a hat."

He looked at Pheres and wondered whether he was cold in his short-sleeved tunic. The night air was fresh.

"Would you like my coat?" he asked, swinging it off his shoulder and offering it.

Pheres looked at it for a moment, then up into Bedar's face. "Are you sure? You don't need it?"

"I don't need it."

"Thank you." He took the coat, almost gingerly, and then had some difficulty getting it on. "I've never worn anything with long sleeves before," he confessed, as Bedar helped him into it.

"Nor buttons, I suppose. Shall I do them up for you?"

"Thanks."

"This is my favourite coat," Bedar remarked, as he buttoned it.

"It's the most beautiful thing I've ever worn." Pheres ran his fingers over the embroidered winged lions. "By far."

Bedar stepped back and looked at him. He stood in the light of a nearby window, which gleamed on the gold embroidery and his reddish fair hair. The coat fit him quite well, and would have suited him, but with bare legs and his short tunic hidden under the coat's hem, it gave him the look of someone who had half-dressed hastily to escape a house-fire or a jealous husband.

"You really ought to have trousers," Bedar said critically.

"Perish the thought!" said Pheres, and they both laughed.

What was this? Bedar wondered. What was he—what were they both—doing? There could be no future in this. After tonight, Pheres would go back to entertaining lecherous men at the Horses, and Bedar would go back to serving one of those very men. Nothing would change, except that Bedar would now always look at his master with contempt, and possibly, he acknowledged with a queasy honesty, with a kind of envy.

CHAPTER XI

"YOU KNOW," SAID Chereia, leaning forward a little to look past a painted column and down the street, "the goats are long gone."

"Oh. Yes, they are."

"Not that it matters, of course."

"Indeed no. We have this cheese. We could probably hold out here for a considerable time."

They were sitting on the steps of a temple, in a quiet street, where they had taken refuge upon being overtaken by a procession of boys leading garlanded goats. Marzana had nearly tripped in his haste to get out of their path, necessitating an embarrassing explanation about the significance of the Horned Beast, to which Chereia had listened very respectfully. Sitting down on the temple steps after that had been her idea. The moon had risen now, and the goats were, as Chereia had pointed out, long gone, but they were still sitting on the steps. Marzana had told her about the ambassador's disappearance and his own afternoon of hunting Ariatans. He had even shown her the list of Ariatan sightings which the chief of the watch had given him, but the moon was a thin, new one that kept darting behind heavy clouds, so there was not enough light to read by.

"But would you really eat that cheese?" she asked.

Marzana looked down at it. "I might, if I were hungry enough," he admitted. He very nearly was. "It does smell delicious."

"Of course it is important to observe the customs of your people, but I can't help feeling that it is a shame you don't eat goat cheese."

"It is a very ancient tradition in Zash, the avoidance of the Horned Beast. Many people do not take it seriously any more, but I was raised in an old-fashioned family. It is often debated whether the thrice-holy Vaksha, who brought the worship of the Almighty to Zash, approved of the custom or not. The Vanians believe that he did not—and I suppose they may well be right. They are a modern sect which is popular at court. I do not belong to it myself, but I know several excellent people who do. I belong to the Kamahashan sect. It was founded by the holy Kamahash, who had a vision of the Almighty in the rays of the sun, which is why we represent the sun on our temples … " He trailed off, feeling an idiot for talking so much, and about religion, of all awkward things.

Chereia seemed to be waiting for a moment to see if he would say more. She had an interesting smile on her face; Marzana wished there were more light for him to see it better.

"Look up," she said finally, pointing to the decorated eaves of the temple above them.

He looked up, into an elaborate carving of a sun, surrounded by rays painted in bright yellows and reds and gilded so that they gleamed slightly even in the darkness.

"This is the temple of Hesperion, our sun god. I am one of his followers, as it happens, though only since I bought my shop. Everyone in my trade worships Hesperion."

"Ah! So then … do you not worship the other gods?"

"Oh, no, I do. But people have their own cults that they belong to, depending on their profession, or where they live—there is one god that we regard as particularly *ours*, to whom we offer special sacrifices, and whose holy days we keep. Sometimes there are mysteries to be inducted into. Hesperion doesn't have mysteries, though—he is quite an open, above-board sort of god." She turned around to look back into the dark porch of the temple. "The doors are closed now, of course, or I would take you inside and show you the statues. You can do that sort of thing in a temple of Hesperion—I mean, take in someone who isn't of the cult, though a foreigner who doesn't even believe in the gods of Pseuchaia might be stretching a point. But you can see some of the carvings out here. Would you like to go and look?"

"Certainly."

The moon slid out from behind a cloud for a moment. He rose from his seat on the steps and offered her his hand. As she took it, her mantle slipped down briefly from her shoulders. Her gown, which was pale blue, was clasped on each shoulder with a row of tiny silver brooches, and the delicate fabric pulled apart a little between each, so that her creamy skin showed through. She tossed her mantle back around herself and released his hand, smiling.

"This temple is quite old," she said. "You can see that from the style of the carvings."

"Ah," he said. "Yes." Her hand had been slim and warm in his.

"It's too bad there isn't more moonlight, though."

"Yes. That is unfortunate."

When he did finally turn his attention to the carvings on the temple facade, he noticed something surprising. They were flatter and stiffer than most Pseuchaian stonework, shallow carvings of men and women walking sideways, looking stern, their hair falling in carefully chiselled waves over their shoulders, their garments draped in crisp stone folds. They reminded him of Zashian carvings.

"They are beautiful," he said.

"Yes, I think so. Some people don't think much of this style any more, but I think it is quite … dignified."

She pointed out the carvings which illustrated particular episodes in the the sun god's career. Marzana followed her down the length of the temple porch, listening to her explanations and watching her face as she described certain scenes of which she was particularly fond.

She said, "Hesperion isn't one of these gods who has a lot of embarrassing stories about chasing boys who don't want to be chased and stealing mortal men's wives while disguised as animals and that sort of thing."

"You must be proud to have such a respectable god for your own." He had heard some of the boy-chasing, wife-stealing stories, which were popular in Zash as anecdotes illustrative of Pseuchaian barbarity, and he had been greatly relieved when none of the stories of Hesperion seemed to be tending in that direction.

Chereia laughed. "I suppose I am. I hadn't really thought about it that way."

"So this … this business of having a personal god, is it the same as Psobos being the patron god of Boukos?"

"Yes, in a way. Except that he's *not* the personal god for everyone in Boukos—I mean, I don't have a shrine to Psobos in my house, even though I've lived here all my life. But all the Pseuchaian states have their patron gods. For Kos it is Anaxe, for Pheme, Amphiaraos, the sea god, and for Ariata, Hymestos and Dion, the Twins. We acknowledge all of them too, of course, but Psobos is our own in particular."

She stood with her back to the carving of Hesperion presiding over the first festival in his honour, lines of suppliants leading goats and carrying baskets sideways across a dark blue ground marching past behind her shoulders. He felt the need to ask more questions, lest she should remember that they were supposed to be returning to her shop, where they would have to part ways. He launched unwisely into the first thing that came to mind.

"Is that why this city has so many ... I am afraid I do not remember the Pseuchaian word. Never mind." In fact, he did remember the word, but it had occurred to him in time that it was not a polite thing to mention, even to a Boukossian woman, and he was shocked that he had intended it.

"Brothels?" Chereia supplied cheerfully.

"Ah. Yes. That is what I was trying to think of."

She laughed. "It's the other way around, actually. We have a sex god as our patron because of the brothels. The Psobion was begun five hundred years ago, because there were so many brothel-keepers and prostitutes in the city that they wanted to have their own festival. Psobos was their particular god, who had been imported from the east—I don't know where, exactly, but they say he had always had rites quite like the Psobion, only on a smaller scale. Anyway, it caught on quickly—as you can imagine, since it was just an excuse for people to behave badly for a night—and the first of the Psobioles went up soon after, and Psobos became our patron. Before that, the city had no patron deity, but the biggest festival was in honour of Xereus, king of the gods. At least that's what they say. Every so often somebody will get up in the Basileon and give a speech about how we should return to the old ways and make the other cities of the Pseuchaian League take us seriously." She shrugged.

"You do not agree."

"I'm proud of my city the way it is. Our government is better run than Pheme's, and we are a real democracy. We don't have much crime, either, compared to the other Pseuchaian states. We have a good public watch. Well—they are considered to be good. What did you think?"

"They are civilian volunteers. They seemed to me to be well-organized, but to be in need of some true expertise."

"Fair enough. You are probably right."

She was looking off down the length of the temple porch, and he was afraid she was thinking that they should be leaving. He searched anxiously for something more to say, feeling as stiff and shallow as the carvings on the temple wall.

"Would you like to go up onto the gallery?" she asked, before he had thought of anything. "The stairs are just down there." She pointed. "It is a bit of a climb—it's up to you whether you'd like to give it a try—but the view of the city from up there is wonderful."

"Yes—yes, I would like that very much." He could scarcely believe his good fortune.

The stairway was spiralling and dark, except for a few small windows let into the thick walls. They went up slowly, hands brushing the cool stones of the walls, Chereia looking back over her shoulder every so often, always with a smile, no doubt to make sure that he was not falling behind, though she never said so. In the light from the little windows he noticed how her pale mantle clung in close folds to the curves of her hips, and how the hem of her gown, which she had gathered up a little in front to climb the stairs, would swing around her slender, bare ankles, just above the crisscrossed ribbons of her sandals.

They emerged on a sort of windy ledge, bounded by a low, columned parapet, at the top of the temple's painted facade. The view of the clustered pale rooftops of the city, running downhill into the darkness, punctuated here and there by a flickering glow where revellers were burning torches, was well worth the climb. But, Marzana observed with disappointment, they were not alone on the gallery. A pair of young men stood leaning on the railing a short distance from the stairs' head, admiring the view and talking quietly with their arms tucked around each other's waists. Chereia turned back towards Marzana and made a face, screwing up her nose in an expression of comical annoyance.

So. She too had hoped that they would be alone up here above the city, under the black vault of the heavens. He tried to imagine Parmatya screwing up her nose like that, and failed. In fact, the thought made him want to laugh.

The pair by the railing had realized that their solitude had been disturbed, and were looking over their shoulders. One of them was a youth of perhaps twenty, and the other was a boy, with large, dark, childish eyes.

"Hello, Widow Chereia," the boy said, politely.

"Hello," said Chereia. "We seem to have had the same clever idea. It is a nice night to be up here."

"It is," said the elder half of the couple. "Psobos give you joy."

"And you."

"Did you see the Kerialos Play?" the boy asked. It seemed this was probably a usual topic for casual conversation on the Psobion night. The youth looked slightly impatient with it.

"I'm afraid not," Chereia replied.

"Oh, that's too bad. It was a very good one this year. The Kerialos was wonderful—you would not believe how he looked the part!"

"I see," said Chereia, smiling. "And did the Amphia put up a fight this year?"

"Barely! Gnossos Terpheros was Psobos, so she hadn't much cause." The boy looked at Marzana for a moment. "Is he a real Sasian?"

"Dymnos!" the youth said in a reproving undertone.

"Yes," said Chereia, "he is."

"Oh!"

"We should perhaps … " Chereia made a motion towards the stairs.

"No, no," said the youth. "We were just going. Weren't we?"

"Sure," said the boy, smiling up at his companion. "Let's go."

They invoked Psobos once more, with a refreshing vagueness, and went off down the stairs together.

Chereia met Marzana's gaze when the pair had disappeared down the stairway. "It makes me feel old," she remarked.

"Old?"

She took a few small steps towards the stone parapet and laid a hand on it carefully. The wind tugged at her mantle, and she pulled it closer about her shoulders with the other hand.

"Old," she repeated. "That boy used to come into my shop all the time, on his way home from school, a few years ago, when I had first opened. He seemed a little child. And now look at him—he has a lover to look at the stars with on the Psobion night. I didn't think any time at all had passed."

Marzana leaned with folded arms on the parapet and looked down, past the temple facade, which dropped away in a sheer, painted cliff, into the street far below. He smiled.

"I do not think that you noticed how that young man looked at you," he said. He could see the pair emerging from the columned porch below, still wound around one another, walking slowly in the direction of wherever they were going to spend the night.

"Looked at me? How?"

"With jealousy. I do not think you seemed to him to be

old—he looked at you with a jealous eye, because you were distracting for a moment the attention of his … his private friend, as we would call it in Zash—we are very circumspect about these things in Zash."

She laughed. "You flatter me—and you're wrong, anyway. I think he was looking at *you*."

Marzana opened his mouth to say that this was ridiculous, and then thought that perhaps it wasn't. "It may be that he was looking at both of us. But it seemed to me that he did not have any need for jealousy."

"No, indeed. It looked to me like his work was done."

Marzana looked down into the street again. "Even from above, you can see that everyone is walking around with linked arms—look."

She cast a brief glance downward, then drew in her breath and took a small step back from the parapet.

"I will have to take your word for it," she said.

Marzana looked at her, and felt an upwelling of warm affection. She was afraid of heights—evidently very afraid, since this gallery was not terribly high—yet it had been her idea to climb up here, so that he could enjoy the view. He looked back out over the vista of rooftops and thought about how many couples the city was divided into tonight under them. Four years ago, he thought, the woman beside him would have been half of one of them.

"It must be difficult to be alone," he said, "after having … known a different life."

Chereia nodded. She had taken up a station at a small, safe distance from the railing and was looking out at the horizon. "For a while after Stratos died I worried that I might find myself falling for the first man who came along, out of simple loneliness, and that it would be a terrible mistake. By now, I have lived on my own for long enough to come to enjoy my independence, and I think if I fell for a man now, it would not be out of desperation. Do you find that an amusing expression—to fall for someone? Or do you have something like that in Zasian?"

"Something equivalent, I suppose. We say that one 'catches love'—as if it were an illness."

"Very nice."

"I suppose. People have such negative metaphors all over the world, it seems. Falling and being ill … "

"What do you think? Are they warranted? For my own part, I have never experienced that sort of involuntary love. I loved my husband, for most of the three years we were married—but he was chosen for me by my parents, and when I came to love him, it was more or less by my own choice, because he was my man, and a good one. So I really do not know about the falling or the catching, although I am twenty-four, and one would think I should be wise in the ways of the world."

"But what you have just said seems to me very wise, indeed. You had excellent cause to love your husband, I think, and you should not be ashamed of it." He watched a point of torchlight moving down a street that showed only as a black line between sloping rooftops. "Also," he said, "I am eight years your senior—you should not speak to me of feeling old."

"You're right, I should not. We are both young."

He looked down at his own embroidered sleeves on the white stone parapet, and then up at her, a graceful Pseuchaian shape silhouetted against the dark sky, of a piece with the whole landscape. Yet she stood there, waiting for him to tell her the secrets of his foreign heart; and he had a feeling that whatever he said, she was going to understand.

"My own experience of falling, which I think is the right word, was … one of the happiest seasons of my life, but then, for a short while, I was foolish enough to believe it could become my whole life—and it could not, and the whole happiness was destroyed."

"Because she left you?" He dark brows contracted.

"Indeed, no. Because her father would not let us marry. She was … what is the expression that you use—beyond my circle?"

"Out of your sphere."

"Yes. Her father is the lord of Arakesh, and was commander of the army corps in which I served five years ago. I met her when her father's household—the women and children and slaves—had to flee from a peasant uprising, and my division escorted them to safety, to join him in Apasana. On the way down she and I had occasion to talk, sometimes. I was banner officer of the division, and I went to see her in her tent first to reassure her, after we were on the road. Of course we were never alone together. There were always others present—her maids and her eunuchs usually, and sometimes her sisters and her father's younger wives and their children. It was a pleasure for me in those days simply to be in her presence. A Zashian man does not have many opportunities to enjoy the company of women of good breeding. It did not matter very much to me how we passed the time, but usually it was with trifles. We would sit together and talk of little things, and eat rose-water candy—they make some of the best rose-water candy in the region around Arakesh. They have a certain recipe … Often I would listen to her play on the sampan—that is an instrument that you do not have here, quite different from your lyres. It has a flat body, and the strings run across it, and you pluck them like this … " He ran his fingers across the surface of the railing to illustrate. "At any rate, I visited her often, because I suppose our feelings were clear to each other almost from the beginning.

Probably they were clear to the maids and the eunuchs and her father's younger wives as well. We did not speak of it for a long time. I suppose it was in my mind all along that we could not be together, but I did not dwell on it. Then finally we spoke of it—in a few moments when the one eunuch who had been attending her had stepped out for some water—and she told me that she would persuade her father to let us marry, which was truly more than I had dared to hope for. We had reached Apasana by this time, and I lived there in hope for nearly two months. Yet in the end, he said no, and that was all. I never saw her again after the day she told me that. I heard later that she was married to the governor of a province. That would have been a much better match for her, though he will of course have other wives."

"Which you would not have done."

"No."

She nodded, and appeared to be studying the roof of a nearby house with concentration.

"You were in Apasana for two months?" she said finally.

"Yes. My division was garrisoned there."

"Yes, but you were there for two months before she told you her father had refused? Did it take her two months to ask him? Or two months to decide to tell you he'd turned you down?"

"I don't know," Marzana admitted.

She shrugged. "Perhaps she was trying to wear him down with continual pestering. That may be it. What was—I mean, what is her name?"

"Shamshi. That was her public name, but within the family she was called ... something else, much prettier. It is a custom in her clan—in all that part of Zash—to give girls one name for public use, and another that is only used in private."

"Hm. Interesting. You know the other name, though? The family one?"

"Yes. It is how I think of her."

"Oh, good. You're just not saying it, because it's private. That's fair, I suppose." She leaned tentatively against the railing, but without looking down. "My husband's name was Stratos Psistiades. 'Son of Psisteus.' He intended to name our first son Psisteus—or he intended to *try*. But we never had any children, so it never came to that."

He did not know what it would have been appropriate to say in response. He felt that perhaps he should have said, "I am sorry," but then, he was not sure that would have been true.

"I met a man in the customs house this afternoon named Psisteus," he said instead. "He was remarkably unhelpful."

"Oh, do tell! Complaining about the customs house is a popular pastime in Boukos, you know."

Marzana readily provided all the absurd details of his visit to the customs house; he found it a relief to learn that Boukossians were able to laugh at their own institutions. He had glossed over the customs house in his previous account of his afternoon, not wishing to sound like a snobbish foreigner complaining about the local government.

"Have you any similar stories?" he asked when he had finished.

"Oh, I do, but I could not tell them as well as you just did. My stories all involve the courts. I have a case that has been wasting my time, and draining my income, for several years."

"Do you have to bribe many people?" Marzana asked sympathetically, remembering the experiences of one of his uncles who had tried to take somebody to court in Zeleush once.

Chereia looked shocked, something he had never expected to see. "Is that what honest people do in Zasia?"

"Yes—yes, as a matter of course. You don't … That is not the way things are done here, then?"

"No, indeed." She smiled, and he felt weak with relief. "I only meant that it is costing me money to pay a good lawyer to argue my case for me. It is against my late husband's creditors. Stratos was a spice merchant, but he was nearly bankrupt when he died. He was killed in an accident in the street—he was only forty, so he had not made any provision for me in the event of his death. I knew the state of his finances, though—or thought I did. What I did not realize, until some time after his death, was how far in debt he had been. If he had declared bankruptcy before he died, all might still have been well. But he hadn't—instead he was deep in debt for equipping a couple of ships which he hoped would restore his fortunes. It's no wonder he didn't tell me about that, as I would hardly have approved. At any rate, after his death I sold the house, which was bigger and grander than I needed, and paid off the debts that I knew about. With what remained, and with my dowry—which was a large sum, since he'd been rich when my parents married me to him—I bought my shop and the rooms above it, where I live.

"Then the ships that were supposed to remake Stratos's fortune sank, of course—this was the first I had heard of them—and creditors began coming out of the woodwork wanting to be paid. But of course I hadn't the money to pay them—only my shop, and half of that was bought with my own money. So I refused to sell it to pay them, and they took me to court, where we have been ever since. I have just engaged the services of a good lawyer, who thinks he can finally sort the matter out—two others have only managed to stall for a little while. But now this one seems to have broken down on me, or thrown a shoe, or whatever metaphor you like. This afternoon one of my neighbours, who delights to be the bearer of bad tidings, put her head in my door to tell me that he—my lawyer—has got himself involved in a scandal."

"Oh, dear. What did he do?"

"Apparently he propositioned a minister's wife at a pre-Psobion party, after having too much to drink. You'll say it doesn't sound like the sort of thing that would cause a stir in a place like Boukos, but the fact is, a man's wife is a man's wife, even in Boukos—visiting prostitutes is one thing, but adultery we don't tolerate. This is the sort of thing that can ruin a man's reputation. As soon as I heard about it I went out—when you met me I had just come from his house. I was hoping to catch him before he takes his razor into the bath with him or anything. But he wasn't home—only his young wife, wringing her hands, saying he was out at the local temple taking part in the festival, putting a brave face on it all. So I left a present, and a consolatory note, and told her to hide the sharp objects." She shrugged. "What more can one do, really?"

"Indeed," said Marzana, wondering what exactly the lawyer would have intended to do with his razor in the bath. He had an uneasy suspicion it would be better not to ask.

"Oh!" said Chereia suddenly. She looked at Marzana with that superb intensity over which she seemed to have a perfect command, and leaned a little closer to him along the railing. "Do you know, I have just remembered something. I think your Ariatans might have come to my shop this evening."

"Oh," said Marzana. He had been hoping for something rather better, though he could not have said what. He turned to face her, leaning on one hand on the railing, doing his best to look interested.

"I was closed all day, you see," she said, "but they happened to come when I was going out the door, and they thought I was only just closing, so they wanted me to open up again so they could get something. It was around the twelfth hour, as I was leaving for my lawyer's. There were four of them, just like the ones you were looking for. Three of them stood in the street, looking sort of tense, and I didn't get a good look at them—it was just the fourth one who talked to me, and he did sound Ariatan, and look Ariatan. You know, fair hair cropped very short, and a plain tunic, and that sort of twangy Ariatan accent. I noticed that his friends had short hair and plain tunics too. I do think they might have been your men. I'll tell you what—when we go back to my house, where there's light, you should let me take a look at that list, since you can't read it, and I will see where my sighting fits in with the others."

"Yes, I suppose we should do that." He had to admit that he had all but lost interest in that whole business now. He roused himself to ask a useful question. "Did you reopen the shop for them?"

"No—they were quite rude and insistent, but I was in a hurry. If I had known that it was going to be a matter of some importance tonight, I should have stayed to talk to them longer—my errand was nearly pointless anyway. But I didn't know, of course. I told them to try somewhere else, some-where that was open. I suppose they did, because they left."

"What was it that they wanted to buy? You have not yet told me what you sell in your shop."

"No, I haven't, have I?" She stepped back from the railing. "Well, if you come home with me now, I'll show you. I think that it may be something you'll like."

CHAPTER XII

"THESE ARE DELICIOUS."

"Mm-hm. One hundred percent goat-free."

"Really?"

"Yep. Imported sheep cheese from Kos. Only because this is a good restaurant. Look, it's written up on the wall."

Pheres pointed with his half-eaten cheese pastry, and Bedar saw that there was indeed a neat red inscription over the takeout-food counter at the front of the restaurant: *Genuine Kossian Telema Cheese Served Here.* He dipped another of the triangles of crisp pastry into the garlicky yogurt sauce that had come with them. Pheres stuffed the rest of his pastry in his mouth and reached for another olive.

"You might want to slow down a little," said Bedar. "I should be very sorry if you made yourself unwell."

Pheres nodded, and chewed deliberately for a moment. He swallowed. "We have to get on with our investigation, though. We may have better luck at one of the other gates."

"We may," said Bedar. "But that is no reason for you to give yourself indigestion."

"No, sir." Pheres nibbled gingerly on the olive. "I think our shrimp are coming—look."

Bedar looked. The waiter, in his bright red tunic and white

apron, was navigating between the crowded tables on his way from the kitchen, holding aloft a steaming plate.

"I can't believe you've never had them before," said Pheres.

The restaurant was a small one, tucked in between a bookstore and a barber's shop just inside the Eastern Gate of the city. They had stopped in, after inquiring fruitlessly at the gate shrine, because Pheres had heard from someone at the Horses that the food here was very good, and Bedar had decided that he needed to eat before taking another step. A proper meal, sitting down—which, interestingly, was the way you ate in Boukossian restaurants, although reclining on couches, which he found awkward, was the fashion in all private dining rooms.

The shrimp arrived, crisp and fried to perfection, with another kind of yogurt to dip them in, this one full of herbs which Pheres could not identify. Bedar discovered that he had in fact eaten shrimp before, just that morning, and Pheres was amused by his story of the mysterious leaf-wrapped parcels.

"Did you order anything else?" Bedar asked.

"Some grilled mushrooms and baked figs. That's all."

"It seems enough."

"I'll finish anything you can't eat. Not a cheap date, am I?"

"I hadn't noticed."

Pheres laughed. He seemed to be having a good time. He had got rather excited at the idea of going into a fine restaurant, and when Bedar had suggested that he order for them, he had considered the menu on the wall quite seriously and seemed to feel it an important responsibility to introduce Bedar to all the best Pseuchaian dishes.

"Do you know that there is a Zashian name almost the same as yours?" said Bedar. "Fereza. It comes from a western dialect. It means 'shepherd,' I think. 'Guardian of flocks.'"

"No, I didn't know that. It's interesting. My name means 'wolf.'"

"Ah. The opposite."

"Pretty much. 'Fereza,'" he repeated. "I like it."

"I thought you might."

"So what do you do, Bedar?" Pheres asked as Bedar re-filled their wine-cups. "What does a Zashian ambassador's secretary do?"

"I take care of His Excellency's correspondence, attend functions with him, and carry messages. His Excellency does not read Pseuchaian, so he brought me principally to look after any foreign writing that might require his attention. I was not his secretary in Zash—I was a clerk under the authority of his regular secretary, who does not have any Pseuchaian. Before that, for many years I served a different master, in Rataxa. I was attendant to one of his wives, who was the daughter of a Phemian merchant from Phiros. That was how I learned to speak Pseuchaian, and to read and write and to admire Pseuchaian learning. It may seem a luxury, but for me that learning was a matter of survival. There is always work for a eunuch who can read, even outside the women's quarters. I mean work that isn't … "

"On your back," Pheres supplied promptly. "Or on your knees. Yeah. You're way too pretty not to worry about that. I figured."

"They don't want you in the women's quarters after a certain age, either, unless you're sufficiently ugly."

"Speaking of that. How old are you?"

"How old do you think I am?"

"I have *no idea*, that's why I asked." He leaned back in his chair and considered the question, twiddling a half-eaten shrimp. "You look … twelve? Thirteen? And about forty. I mean, you don't *look* forty, but you definitely seem like you could be. You are, aren't you? That's why you're smiling. You're forty … forty-three."

"I'm twenty."

"No."

Bedar nodded. "I had to grow up quickly. And, in some ways, of course, I couldn't grow up at all. So."

Pheres stuffed the rest of the shrimp in his mouth. "I'm almost seventeen. You're *three years* older than me?"

"Apparently. I'd appreciate it if you'd keep it to yourself. I've been passing myself off as 'about forty' since I was … well, about your age. The time I left the women's quarters." He helped himself to another shrimp. "While we're on the subject, I'm a little shocked to learn you're almost seventeen."

"Oh, I know. I'm already too old for a lot of the customers at the Horses. Most of them would probably tell you they'd never go for a sixteen-year-old, but they assume I'm younger." He shrugged.

The unflattering paint made more sense in this light, since it had seemed somehow to make Pheres look younger. Bedar wondered what fate awaited him when he could no longer pass himself off as a young boy.

"*Twenty.*" Pheres shook his head. "No wonder you didn't want me to call you 'sir.'"

The waiter returned to their table with a dish of mushrooms and another of figs.

"So I have told you how I learned Pseuchaian, but you have not told me how you learned so much about Zash—why you don't say 'Sasia' like everyone else in Boukos, and you know all about eunuchs and so on."

Pheres rolled one of the mushrooms around in the oil at the bottom of the dish. "There were a lot of Zashians on the estate when I was small. Slaves. Prisoners of war. My mother died soon after I was born, so I was raised mostly by my father's slaves, until I was old enough to begin training."

"Training for what?"

"Have a mushroom," said Pheres. "They're good. Training for war. I was … My father is a general. My name—before I disgraced it—was Pheres Hesteanos Stesiphanis."

It was like hearing the person across the table from you say, "I come from the Dark Valley where the sky cannot be seen." For a moment Bedar felt a sharp, irrational stab of fear.

There was one cheese pastry left in the dish; Bedar pushed it across the table towards Pheres. "You don't have an Ariatan accent."

"No." Pheres picked up the last cheese pastry. "I never did when I lived in Ariata. I have a sort of nowhere-in-particular accent. My mother was from Kos—that may be why. Come to think of it, you don't have a Parkan accent yourself. At least not like the ones I've heard—though my father's Parkan slaves were all peasants."

"What do you imagine I was?"

Pheres stared. "Go *on*! Is there anything about you that is what it seems? I've had enough trouble believing you're a slave, you can't mean to tell me now that you were born a peasant?"

"Why not? You know already that I am not what I was born but what I have been made. You're right, I don't have a Parkan accent any more. But I was seven when I was taken away."

"Was it a war, then?"

"A sort of raid—part of a local skirmish that did not even make it into the records at Suna. I know because I looked it up once—I was quite depressed when I found it wasn't there. I cannot even say, 'I was captured in the war of Such-and-Such.' It does not even have a name."

Pheres made a sympathetic face. They attacked the dish of figs, which had been baked in honey and were wonderfully fragrant and sticky.

Bedar went on, "It was not a particularly successful raid. The raiders set fire to some dovecotes, and stole a few sheepdogs and one of the neighbours' sons, and me. I do not know what they did with the sheepdogs—kept them, in all probability. I and the neighbours' son were taken down to Satasparsa, with some female prisoners from another village, and sold at the market there. The neighbours' son did not survive."

"Was he wounded in the raid?"

"Did not survive being gelded, I mean. It's a wonder any-one ever does, in Satasparsa. It is the place in Zash where one goes to sell anything one has not come by legally. A dungheap of a city. But I did not have to live there long. I was sold to the nobleman in Rataxa with the Phemian wife when I was ten. I was fortunate. My first master was a hard man, but after him my lot improved. Sometimes I think of all the things I have done and seen and learned that I would never have known if I had stayed in the village where I was born, and I feel very fortunate. That may sound absurd … "

"No," said Pheres. "Not exactly."

"But your own history has been very different from mine, I believe."

"Yeah. Well, I've still got my … "

"Yes. I noticed."

Pheres laughed lightly. "In some ways I might as well not. If I were still in Ariata, I would be living in the barracks with the other boys, finishing my military training, which I started when I was seven. I know I wouldn't be happy—but at least I would not be ashamed. My father is a general, as I said, and his father was a general, and *his* father ruled Ariata for a while—he was elected, we don't have royalty, obviously you know that, but in a way, in Ariata, my father is about equal to Zukohashkra in Zash. His grandfather was a sort of king. He has Zashian prisoners-of-war to work his estate and serve in his house, and he married a beautiful Kossian woman, but she only gave him one son before she died, and that was me. I guess I must have seemed like enough—I was smart, and strong, and I looked like my mother. I had funny ideas about Zashians, but my father and I only ever fell out over that once. He gave me a lecture about barbarians, and how they were like beasts." Pheres shrugged disdainfully. "It didn't make sense to me even when I was a child.

"When I was twelve, my uncle, my mother's brother, invited me to come and stay with him in Kos, to see the theatre and things. My father didn't want to let me go—nobody in Ariata thinks anyone should want to go to Kos—but my uncle pestered him with letters until finally he allowed it. He said it might do me good to see how the degenerates in Kos lived—it would give me a sense of Ariatan superiority. Of course *that* didn't happen. I spent three months in Kos. I saw the plays at the theatre festival and listened to philosophers talking in the school where my uncle taught and visited the temples and saw all the best sculptures and paintings. If I got a sense of anything, it was *Kossian* superiority.

"Anyway … I'm making this into a longer story than it needs to be. One of my father's old political enemies was in exile in Kos, and met my uncle at a party and learned who I was, and he arranged to have me kidnapped on my way home from the exercise ground one day. I think his intention was to ask for a ransom, but my uncle couldn't pay, or took too long trying to raise the money, or something—and in the end, the men who were holding me decided to take me down the harbour and sell me to a Phemian slave-trader. He was on his way to Boukos. When we got here, I was bought by the owner of the Horses, and I've been there every since."

"I am sorry for you. What terrible misfortune to have suffered. But your father … surely … You have been speaking of him this while as though he is still alive … "

Pheres nodded. "As far as I know, he is."

"But surely he is a powerful man, and could do something to free you."

Pheres met his gaze for a moment, and his expression was almost apologetic. This, Bedar realized suddenly, was going to be the worst part of the story.

"For a free man's son in Ariata … there is almost no worse thing that could happen to him than what has happened to me. Well, I suppose what your people did to you—that would be worse." He gave him a slight, wry smile. "But like I said, it's almost the same, to an Ariatan. I did write to my father as soon as I could, so that he would know what had happened to me. I didn't ask him to send someone to Boukos to buy my freedom—that would have been disrespectful from a son—but I did hope that he would. I heard nothing for a long time—much longer than it should take for a letter to go to Ariata and a reply to come back. Then I had a letter from a man who lives on the street where we have our town house, who served with my father in the last war. He wrote to tell me that my father had received my letter, and what he'd done when he read it. He had sent for some of his people, the sort he could give orders like this, and he had ordered them to go to Kos and bring him back the heads of the men who had done this thing to me. He had ordered them to go to my uncle's house, and that for not keeping a better watch on me, my uncle should have his eyes put out. Then someone had asked him what should be done about his son, and he had said: 'I believe they have daggers in Boukos, and I pray that the boy has not so far forgotten his military training that he does not remember how to turn one on himself.' Then they all drank his health and called him a brave man and a good Ariatan."

Bedar swallowed dryly. "Pheres. Please tell me that you have never thought of this—this thing that your father wished for you, and that you never shall. It is the worst of sins."

"In Zash."

"No. In Zash we are *taught* that it is the worst of sins. It *is* that everywhere. I am not a dogmatic person, Pheres. I do not think there is much harm in worshipping a whole rabble of gods instead of the one Who is—but about this matter I cannot bring myself to be tolerant. This is not honour—it is despair and blasphemy. It is what the hounds of the Dark Valley would eat your heart for. Do not think of it—I beg you."

Pheres looked at him for a moment with his pale, quiet eyes, and Bedar thought he could guess his unspoken words: *Give me a better reason than your Zashian religion, which has nothing to do with me.*

But what he said was, "I do not think of it. Truly, I never did much. My father and I never saw eye to eye."

"Forgive me," said Bedar, feeling shaky with relief. "I had no right to presume so much. We are barely acquainted."

"Oh. No." Pheres looked surprised. "I suppose not, but … it doesn't feel that way, does it?"

"No," Bedar admitted. "I feel at ease with you. You make me feel … Hah. This will seem an insult, but I don't mean it to be. You're the closest thing I've encountered in Boukos to … to one of my own kind." He winced. "It *is* an insult, any way you look at it—please forgive me, I … "

"No, it isn't. You're lovely. I'm honoured." His genuine smile flashed out again, a little sad but still dazzling. "And

I know what you mean. I'm older than I look, and younger than I act, or something. Like you. I'm not quite a man."

"But you will be. Some day soon."

"Excuse me, boys." They looked up with a start. The waiter was standing over them, his tray clasped to his chest, looking apologetic. "I'm afraid you're going to have to go."

Bedar looked down at the dishes on the table. There were still several shrimp left, nearly half the mushrooms, and some of the olives too.

"We are not quite finished our food," he said, looking back at the waiter.

"We'll be quick," said Pheres, reaching for the shrimp dish.

The waiter glanced towards the kitchen, and his apologetic expression deepened. "I really think you're going to have to go *now*. I'm sorry. The owner told me to come tell you. Some of the other customers are complaining."

"Oh!" said Pheres and Bedar at the same time.

Bedar pushed back his chair and got up. "We will of course leave immediately. How much do we owe for the food?"

The waiter did a quick tally of the dishes. "Four nummoi. Oh, and you had the Kepherian red. That's six obioi more. I'm sorry you didn't get to finish it."

"You speak too soon," said Pheres, getting to his feet and picking up the wine carafe. He tipped back his head and drained the several cups' worth that had still been in it. He wiped his mouth on the back of his hand. "All right. Let's go."

Bedar paid the waiter, and he and Pheres left the restaurant under the gaze of most of the other diners, Pheres with a greasy handful of shrimp. Outside the restaurant door, they looked at each other, and both spoke at the same time.

"Pheres, I am—"

"Sorry for getting us kicked out."

"But … surely that was my fault. I am, after all, a foreigner, and a eunuch. They could hardly have objected to you. This city is fully of prostitutes."

"Yes, but we don't go into respectable restaurants." Pheres shrugged and took a bite of shrimp. "Maybe they just didn't like the way we're dressed."

"Here, I will teach you something useful. Do you know what this means, in Zash?" He made a gesture with his left hand, fingers spread, the back of his hand towards the restaurant.

"No, but I can guess," said Pheres, with a wicked grin, and he imitated the gesture.

"Let us be off, then."

"Mm." Pheres tossed a shrimp tail over his shoulder. "You know, you should have taken the rest of those olives."

They set off down one of the major streets, which Pheres thought would lead them to another of the city gates. It sloped uphill, so they went at a leisurely pace. The huge draught of wine that Pheres had taken made him talkative. He began telling Bedar long, vivid stories about his childhood in Ariata and all the things he had seen in Kos. Four or five times, Bedar caught himself wanting to suggest that they turn down some side street which looked like a more pleasant place to walk. He had to remind himself each time that he was supposed to be looking for his master, not just going for a walk with Pheres.

They walked through a torchlit square and heard the people who were still scattered about in knots discussing that afternoon's games. The Kerialos play had been good this year, they said. The Amphia had been one of the most beautiful in recent memory, and the Kerialos had looked just like a famous statue in Kos, which everyone knew was the spitting image of the god.

"I've seen that one," Pheres remarked. "He's great, as a

statue, I guess, but he's not really my type. Not how I picture Kerialos, I mean. I don't think I really have a 'type.'"

"I do not imagine that slaves in a mine daydream much about digging holes in their spare time."

"You are fabulously understanding, Bedar."

There were musicians playing at the far end of the square. An infectious drumbeat throbbed out under a twitter of flutes and strings, and a man's voice rose into a wail with some ludicrously straightforward lyrics about pining hearts. A small crowd stood listening, and a few people were dancing in the torchlight.

Pheres spun so that the heavy skirts of the red coat swung out around him. He raised his hands above his head, snapped his fingers, and executed a couple of fast, proficient dance steps, his sandals scuffing over the paving stones.

"Very nice!" said Bedar sincerely.

Pheres held out a hand with a little flourish, tipping his head to the side to look down the length of the embroidered sleeve at Bedar.

"What? No, I don't … know how to dance."

"I do not believe that." Pheres straightened up, keeping his hand held out, palm up. "I believe all the rest of it, even your age, but I do not believe you can't dance."

"I did not say *can't*—I said *don't know how*."

He took Pheres's hand, which was about the same size as his own, but stronger and bigger-boned. Pheres drew him close, danced smartly away from him, drew him close again. Bedar followed fumblingly. He had poise enough, and knew how to move gracefully in the mundane actions of his life. It wasn't that he lacked the necessary skills for dancing.

"I never found time," he said, as Pheres twined around him, stamping jauntily.

Pheres caught him by the waist and spun him. "Time for what?"

"Learning to dance."

"Fair enough. You were busy surviving. It doesn't matter. You're doing fine."

They linked arms and smiled into one another's eyes.

After a little while, the musicians began a slow, soft melody, and the dancers sat down to rest, most nestled together in pairs on doorsteps and benches around the square. Bedar and Pheres, who had by this time found their way into the heart of the crowd, sought out an empty doorstep and dropped down onto it. Pheres had unbuttoned Bedar's coat and shrugged it half off his shoulders. Bedar leaned back against the closed shop door behind them. The singer was crooning something about the moon.

"Back there in the restaurant," said Pheres, "you said that I'll be a man someday soon, and you're right. I can see that day coming, and I'm … I'm terrified of it."

Bedar looked at him, surprised. "Are you? Why? What will happen?"

"It's not so much what will happen, not like you're thinking. I'll probably be sold on from the Horses and end up a labourer or something—I think I'll be able to stand that. But I don't want to be a man. It disgusts me. I don't want to *want* anyone in the way the men at the Horses want me. I don't want to understand what that's like—and I'm afraid I will." After a moment he added, his voice low, "You can tell already, can't you? It's close."

Bedar thought about the way Pheres had drawn him into the dance. There had been moments when he had expected something more: strong hands on his body, pulling him closer, claiming him. He would not have been surprised to feel evidence of a grown man's desires if they had pressed against each other in the dance, but they had not.

"Yes," he said, "I think it is. I am sorry, for your sake." He realized that sentiment did not have the ring of truth. "It does not disgust me."

"No? If I *wanted* you, like a … like you were a boy … "

Bedar raised his eyebrows. "It would not be a problem. The *problem* is that you're not a man yet."

Pheres looked at Bedar in the dark and gave a breath of laughter. The musicians had ended their crooning tune and were pausing for a drink.

"We should—" Pheres started, getting his feet under himself and preparing to rise.

The musicians struck up something full of martial drums and energetic strumming. The audience whooped and began clapping in time. Some of them jumped up to dance again.

"How apt," Pheres murmured, and Bedar noticed that all the dancers were men. It was one of those virile dances with jumping and stamping and shouts of "Hey!" in time to the martial drums.

"Do you know this one?" he asked, looking at Pheres.

"I used to. They dance it at home." He got to his feet, let Bedar's coat slide down to his elbows, and swung it off like a cloak.

He appeared to remember the dance. He stamped and jumped and swung Bedar's coat around with panache. He moved like a man, the torchlight highlighting the elegant planes of his face and gleaming on his red-gold hair, which had nearly finished the transition from regimented curls to beautifully tousled mane.

The dance ended, and Pheres stood with hands on his hips, looking pleased with himself. Bedar got up from the doorstep. The music slowed to something gentler.

"Teach me this one," Bedar said, holding out both hands.

Pheres looked at him. "We shouldn't be doing this. We should be looking for Zuko."

Bedar dropped his hands and sighed hugely. "Must we?"

"Yes, Bedar. We have to find your ambassador, because if we don't, and you come back to Zash without him, your vicious countrymen may cut off something you really *need*. Like your head."

So they left the dancers in the square, and slogged on uphill until they reached the white wall above the sea that marked the western edge of the city. They found the gate, and the small shrine that stood just inside it, but it was unstaffed.

"I guess the priests here don't take vows of chastity," Pheres remarked.

"It would seem strange if anyone connected with the cult of Psobos did that. It would seem contrary to the whole spirit of the thing."

"Yeah, I suppose so."

Pheres had sat down on the steps of the shrine, draping Bedar's coat around his shoulders. Some distance down the street, Bedar noticed, there was a group of people standing about in the light of an open door, with cups of wine. He glimpsed a distinctive blue robe among them which he recognized from the first shrine they had visited, back before the restaurant and the dancing.

"I think I see where the priest has gone," he said. "I will go and find out what he knows. You stay here."

Pheres started to get up.

"No, sit. You look comfortable. I will not be long."

Pheres sat back down, stretching out his legs and crossing them at the ankle. He waved goodbye as Bedar walked away.

Bedar was gone longer than he intended. He found the priest, a white-haired, red-faced man, deep in conversation with a couple of elderly women, and it was some time before there was a long enough pause in the steady flow of talk to allow for an intrusion. Then the priest insisted on taking him inside the house to get a drink, which Bedar felt obliged to finish. It transpired that the priest had in fact seen a tall, dark-haired Zashian, but he couldn't remember when, or whether it had been at his temple or somewhere else. He was very grateful, however, for the interruption of his conversation with the tedious old women, and he wondered whether Bedar had any other plans for the night. Bedar, mercifully finished his drink by this time, said that he did, and made his escape.

At least he thought he had escaped. Then he found two tall young men blocking his path.

"Hello, sweetheart!" one said loudly.

"All on your own?" said the other.

Bedar was about to reply truthfully, as he had to the priest, but realized in time that he didn't want to involve Pheres in this.

"On my own but not, sadly, at liberty," he said. "If you will excuse me … "

They wouldn't. They loomed over him, arms linked, apparently helping each other stay upright. They had obviously had a lot to drink.

"Psobos give me strength," one of them intoned. The other one snickered.

"Oi!" came the shout from behind the young men. "He's with me."

They turned to look at Pheres, who was advancing quickly with Bedar's coat slung over his shoulder.

"Hey, I know you," said one of the young men. "You're from the Horses, aren't you?"

"Huh," said the other. "The one in trousers, too?"

"Move along," said Pheres. He brushed past them to reach

Bedar and slung a proprietary arm around Bedar's shoulders. "We're not working tonight."

"Aww … "

Pheres turned away, drawing Bedar with him. They had not taken more than a couple of steps when the two young men were joined by a third, who came staggering out of a doorway in Bedar and Pheres's path. He saw them, and his face twisted into an ugly expression. It was Makron, the man Pheres had chased out of Nenni's room at the Horses.

"They said they're not working!" his friends informed him. "May Psobos's balls drop off—right?"

Makron lurched toward Pheres with a growl. "You little fucker … gonna mess up your pretty face. You and your gods-cursed Sasian friend."

The three of them surrounded Pheres and Bedar by this time, moving in.

"Hey, hey, nothing wrong with the Sasian, Makron—leave him to us if you don't like him!"

Several things happened very quickly after that. Pheres was obliged to let go of Bedar in order to dodge away from Makron, at the same moment that one of the other young men caught hold of Bedar's arm. It wasn't a hard grip, and Bedar simply twisted out of it, but that put him directly in the path of Makron's lumbering attack. The man's fist was swinging toward him. Bedar heard Pheres, behind him, shout a warning. He swayed out of the way of Makron's attack, and without thinking swung back, kicked him soundly in the stomach with the heel of his boot, and drove the flat of his left hand into the man's nose, with a force that produced a disgusting crunch, a howl from Makron, and a spectacular spike of pain down Bedar's forearm.

"Run," Pheres advised.

They ran, pelting away up the street, in no particular

direction. At the mouth of a darkened alley, Pheres caught Bedar by the sleeve and pulled him into a network of back streets.

"You're not a dancer—you're a fighter!" Pheres gasped, half-laughing, as they ran. "I should have known!"

"I think I broke my hand."

"You definitely broke his nose."

At length they stopped, near the mouth of another alley that opened back onto the street that they had just quit. They could see the sea wall, white against the deep blue sky on the other side of the street. They leaned against the wall of a building to catch their breath.

"Huh," said Pheres. "I hoped this was going to take us somewhere else. I don't know my way around as well as I thought." He looked across at Bedar. "How's your hand?"

Bedar flexed it experimentally. "I suppose if I can move it at all, it must not be broken, but it certainly hurts."

Pheres winced sympathetically. "Poor thing. I'm going to look around the corner and see if I can figure out where we are."

He went to the mouth of the alley and looked out. After a moment he beckoned Bedar to join him.

"We're in luck. See that shop there, with the lit windows? I go there all the time, and the owner is nice. We'll go knock on the door, see if we can hide out there for a bit."

The shop on the corner had a woman's name over the door, like the houses in Temple Walk, but instead of paintings of naked women on either side of it, there were brightly-coloured pictures of heaps of candy and sweet pastries. It was a very welcoming facade, and the warm light that shone through the slats of the closed shutters was welcoming too. Pheres knocked on the door, and after a moment it was opened, and they both stared in surprise at the person in the doorway. He stared back.

"Bedar?"

"Marzana!"

CHAPTER XIII

THEY STARED AT one another speechlessly for a moment, and Marzana realized two things: that it had been quite some time since the disappearance of the ambassador had ceased to be uppermost in his mind; and that, to judge from Bedar's expression, he was thinking much the same thing.

"Pardon me, sir," said the boy who stood on the steps with Bedar. "Is Chereia in?"

"Ah. Yes." Marzana held the door open, and the boy and Bedar came inside. They looked as though they had been running, and Bedar was cradling one hand gingerly in the other. "What happened?"

"A slight altercation in the street … " Bedar looked embarrassed. He accepted the stool that Marzana shoved forward for him, and sank onto it gratefully.

"He hit someone in the nose," said the boy. "Quite hard. The fu—fellow deserved it."

"Did he," said Marzana. "And your hand? Not broken, is it?"

"I don't think so." He held it out and let Marzana confirm his diagnosis.

"Are you the captain of the guard, sir," said the boy, "who is also looking for Zukohashkra?"

Bedar winced at Marzana's touch on his wrist. It was

swollen but showed no evidence of serious damage. "I have *not* been going about the city telling everyone, Marzana, I assure you."

"Yes," said Marzana, "I am. You should ice that, or—since I don't suppose we can get ice here—put a cold cloth on it, at least. It's not broken."

"You haven't found old Zuko, have you?" the boy asked.

"His Excellency? No, I have not found him."

"Oh, b—well. That's too bad."

Marzana looked at the boy, who stood leaning with one hand against the wall, holding Bedar's coat slung over his shoulder. In his years of soldiering Marzana had had a good deal of experience dealing with adolescent boys, and he had never been able to understand how some men could find such beings adorable. In Zash, not very many men did; but in Pseuchaia it was apparently a regular fashion. This one was a slender, girlish creature—though not perhaps as girlish as Bedar, and he did have attractively regular features and an interesting colour of hair.

The boy looked over his shoulder towards the inner door of the shop.

"Hello, Chereia," he said.

She stood in the kitchen doorway, drying her hands on a towel. She had been shaping some sticky almond dough into cakes, in order to bake a fresh batch for Marzana to sample. He had been observing the process, and they had been discussing the relative merits of almonds and walnuts. She had been right when she guessed that he would be pleased to find out what she sold in her shop. They had eaten a simple dinner of bread and cheese in the kitchen hen they arrived. He had taken out the list of Ariatan sightings, the pretext for his coming into the shop, but they had not actually got so far as looking at it; that idea, which had never been particularly interesting to him, had been completely forgotten in favour of the much more appealing prospect of being shown around the inside of the tiny, beautifully appointed sweet shop and the large and impressive kitchen behind it, and sampling several kinds of sweets and making inquiries about their manufacture.

"Hello," she said. "What's going on out here?"

"We're taking refuge in your shop," said the boy. "I hope you don't mind."

"Of course I don't. Refuge from what? Oh, no, you don't need to answer that. There's always something or someone to take refuge from on the Psobion night, isn't there? Hello, you must be Marzana's friend, the secretary."

"Yes, my lady." His gaze flicked briefly between Chereia and Marzana, and Marzana fancied that he looked ever so slightly relieved.

"Come through into the kitchen. I'll get you a cold cloth for your hand—and both of you look as if you could use a drink."

All three of them offered Bedar a hand to help him to his feet, but the boy was fastest, tucking his hand neatly under Bedar's uninjured arm, and carefully taking it away again once Bedar was standing.

"It's Pheres, isn't it?" said Chereia to the boy, as they were going through to the kitchen.

He nodded, looking surprised. "I wouldn't have expected you to know."

"Well, you come in here quite often with all your friends, and I hear them saying, *Pheres, Pheres! Which kind should I get today? Should I get the sesame ones today, Pheres, or the fruit ones?* They're very loyal customers, your friends."

"Yeah. This is their favourite sweet shop in the whole city. And they're … pretty discerning."

Chereia laughed. "I am honoured!"

In the kitchen they stood around Chereia's worktable while she fetched a cloth for Bedar and wine cups for both him and Pheres. She refilled the cups that she and Marzana had drunk from earlier.

"How fortunate it is that we happened to find you here, Marzana," said Bedar, sipping his wine.

"Indeed."

For a moment the two of them looked at one another, and no one said anything. Marzana supposed he should really ask Bedar how his own hunt for the ambassador had been proceeding, and explain about the Ariatans and the coat and the dead men in the rooming house. But he had a strong feeling that Bedar was currently about as interested in all of that as he was himself—which was to say, he didn't want to hear a word of it. Then he thought that he should explain who Chereia was, and how he came to be in a closed sweet shop with a beautiful widow instead of out scouring the dark streets for His Excellency. And then he thought that perhaps he would wait and see if Bedar would broach the subject first, by explaining the presence of the red-haired boy.

The boy was at the moment standing with Bedar's coat folded around his arms, gazing about at the shadowy interior of the kitchen, making the same inspection that Marzana had when he first entered: taking in the big, tiled stove against one wall, the large brick oven in the far corner, with racks for baking many small trays of sweets at once, the big wooden table down the centre of the room with the half-completed batch of almond cakes on it, and the pots and pans and trays and sweet-making tools hanging from the walls and tidily arranged on the counters. He looked coolly impressed with it all.

It was Chereia who broke the silence. "I do have a comfortable dining-room upstairs," she said. "There is no need for us all to be standing in the kitchen."

"Oh," said Marzana. "Indeed. An excellent thought."

He had in fact noticed the stairs, with their blue painted railing, at the side of the kitchen, and guessed that they must lead up to her flat, and been wistfully certain that he would not be asked up them, since that would probably have seemed to her like something that would seem to him to be improper. Now he did not know whether he was grateful to have a pretext for going upstairs, or irritated at being prevented from remaining alone in the kitchen with Chereia.

They went up the stairs, carrying their cups of wine. Chereia brought up the lamp, and at the top lit another, double-wicked lamp on a stand, which threw a wide circle of warm light over a square, blue and white room, painted and furnished with a strangely graceful Pseuchaian simplicity. Two couches with striped cushions stood facing one another, on either side of a small, round table, in front of a pair of tall windows. Chereia walked across to open one set of shutters. Beyond the window a dark, moving gleam stretched away to the horizon.

The boy Pheres caught his breath and spoke before Marzana had seized the opportunity. "You have a view of the sea. That's wonderful."

Chereia turned back from the window, smiling—at Pheres. Marzana felt cheated. "I know," she said. "The best address in the city—everyone who visits me remarks on it. Not that I throw large parties, mind you. I haven't the space." She looked back at Bedar and Marzana. "Do sit down, both of you."

Bedar sat obediently at the end of a couch. Pheres had gone to lean in the open window, looking out at the sea.

Chereia opened the second set of shutters and stood looking out, sipping her wine.

Marzana sat down on the other couch, unable to take his eyes off her. Her hair was slightly tousled from the wind on the temple gallery, its soft strands varied in lighter and deeper shades of brown. He wondered if she knew how lovely she was. He hoped she did.

Seeing him looking in her direction, she raised her eyebrows at him slightly and looked across at Bedar, as if to say, "Don't you two have something to talk about?" Marzana remained stiffly silent, and after a moment she came over to sit on the couch next to Bedar. The boy remained by the window.

"How do you two know each other?" Chereia asked, looking from one Zashian to the other. "Is it just because you work for the same man?"

"No," said Marzana hastily, seizing on this new topic of conversation with all-too-evident relief. "We met three years ago. I was on duty at the court in Suna, in the year the last king died. Bedar's master came to court for the coronation, and Bedar was trying to find something in the palace, and asked directions of me. I suppose, since I was standing guard, I looked like I belonged to the place, and ought to know where things were."

He remembered that afternoon vividly; it had been only his second day on duty at court, and had not quite got over staring at things. The young, brisk, beautifully-dressed eunuch who came across a courtyard in his direction had seemed to him just another piece of the court's glittering furniture, and he had been very surprised when this courtly person had approached him, looking humbly at the ground, and asked for directions.

"I misdirected him—I realized it only after he was out of sight, when it was too late to run after him. I saw him a few days later, in the crowd of spectators at the coronation, and I apologized for the mistake. An official in charge of the ceremony saw that I had left my post in order to speak to Bedar, and hurried over to reprimand me. Bedar made up a story on the spot to excuse me for neglecting my duty. That cemented our friendship."

"So you both live at court?"

"No. I was living there at the time, as part of the palace division of the guard. Bedar was living in … Rataxa, was it, at that time?"

Bedar looked up from his wine cup. "Yes. But my master stayed on at court after the coronation."

"For nearly two years. This is quite ordinary, you understand, with Zashian noblemen. They attach themselves to the court in the hopes of advancement. I do not think it was very effective, though, in the case of Bedar's former master. Indeed … Well, I have never been quite sure what happened … "

"Few people are," said Bedar. "It is a long and complicated story. The gist of it is that my former master became deeply indebted to His Radiancy's cousin Zukohashkra, and a number of items changed hands, as an expression of gratitude for the favour of continued silence concerning certain issues." He smiled, and Chereia gave him an impressed look. "I was one of the items exchanged—that is how I came to be in His Excellency's service. I have only served him for one year. I was naturally delighted at the prospect of coming to Boukos, when my master was chosen to head the mission—I had long wanted to see some part of Pseuchaia. And it was a pleasant surprise to hear that my friend from the royal guard would be part of the mission as well."

"We spent most of the journey exchanging news of the previous year," said Marzana.

"Gossiping," said Chereia.

"That is what I would have said too, my lady. But *he* would say, 'That is a word from the women's quarters,' or some such thing."

"Would he?" said Chereia, looking at Bedar, only now being sure, Marzana guessed, that he really was what she had suspected he was. "And what, exactly, would be wrong with that?"

"I assure you that I do not know," said Bedar.

Chereia looked at Marzana for a moment, and Bedar looked at Chereia, and there was silence. Once again Chereia was the first to break it. She slid down from the couch and stood up, clapping her hands lightly together.

"I must go downstairs and finish the almond cakes," she said. "The dough will dry out if I leave them too much longer. Pheres—come and help me."

The boy, startled at being addressed, gave her a displeased look for a moment, and seemed to be about to say that he would rather stay upstairs with the men.

"Come," said Chereia cheerily, taking the small lamp from the table, and holding out her free hand.

Pheres pushed himself off of the windowsill against which he had been leaning and followed her downstairs, still carrying Bedar's coat.

Bedar, in the meantime, had succeeded in unbuttoning his boots with one hand, and now kicked them off onto the floor, and folded his legs under him in the way that Zashians liked to sit. He rested his injured hand in his lap, and sat for a moment looking down at it, his long hair falling around his face. Then he looked up, and met Marzana's eye.

"Tell me something, Marzana. Do you retain even the slightest interest in finding His Excellency?"

Marzana occupied himself briefly with taking off his own

boots and arranging himself cross-legged on his couch. "Do you?" he asked, looking up.

Bedar gave a sort of half-shrug. "Pheres has become quite interested in it, I believe."

"Ah. Has he? So has Chereia."

They looked at each other guardedly for a moment.

"So we find ourselves in much the same circumstances, then, I take it?" said Bedar.

"I suppose we do. Then this boy Pheres does not have anything to do with the finding of the missing ambassador?"

"Oh. No, he does, actually. He … had some information which was relevant."

Marzana felt weak with embarrassment. "So did Chereia," he replied hastily. "I happened to meet her in the street, where she was being troubled by some drunkards, and I offered to walk her home—not wishing her to come to any harm, you understand. In the course of conversation, I discovered that she knew something of interest."

"Yes. I see." Bedar was giving him a curiously surprised look. "I also happened to discover accidentally that Pheres knew something about His Excellency. I too was initially motivated more by a sense of charity than of duty to my master—it seems that we were both rewarded for our good intentions."

"Indeed."

There was a long stretch of silence. Finally Bedar looked up from his contemplation of his empty wine cup.

"I would not wish you to take this amiss, Marzana, but I feel bound to say that I hope you have considered how it may look for you to be coming into a woman's house on the night of the Psobion."

"How it would look to whom?" This was indeed not something that he had given a moment's thought; he had no reputation in Boukos to worry about, and he did not think that anyone here would have thought ill of him for coming into Chereia's house anyway.

"To her," said Bedar.

"Oh."

"She seems to be a very charming woman. It would strike me as a very great shame if she were to misconstrue you, and to think that your motivation was … other than it is."

"Oh. Indeed. But I am sure she does not misunderstand." After a moment he added, "I hope you have considered the same in relation to this boy."

"Does it seem to you that I haven't?" Bedar looked slightly worried. "I have no experience talking to teenaged boys. I feel out of my depth."

"It's not so difficult. I have had plenty of new recruits under my command who must have been about that boy's age. The main thing is not to talk down to them. They are not *quite* men, but if you treat them like children, they will often respond by behaving like maniacs. If you make them think that you think that they're men, they'll feel they need to behave accordingly."

"I see." Bedar looked doubtful.

"It's straightforward. It's not like talking to women—now that is difficult."

"No, it isn't. They're human beings, Marzana. Just circumscribed in a different way than you or I. Think about it this way. You are a soldier, so you know about weapons and battles and … oh, whatever else you know about. Siege strategies. A potter knows about clay and glazes and different shapes of pots—but you could talk to him without difficulty. A woman knows about children and clothes and keeping house—a woman like this, anyway, who has had to keep house for herself. She is just a person with a different trade than you—and sometimes it is not a trade that she wanted very much, but she has had no choice in the matter. In other cases, she is suited to it, and does it very well. I think, by the way, that you have one of the latter category here."

"Yes. I see."

It was an interesting idea, and one that he had not been aware Bedar had formulated. But then, he had never really talked to Bedar about women in the abstract. About one woman in particular, certainly, he had told him a fair bit, but for the most part Bedar had just listened to that, and said kind, sympathetic things, which was all Marzana had wished for from him. It had occurred to Marzana, of course, that in Bedar's early days as a noblewoman's attendant he must have known a good many women; he had belonged to rich men, who had large numbers of wives and concubines and daughters. But Marzana had never really wondered what sort of insights this would have given his friend into women in general.

"It is strange to be discussing women with you, Bedar," he remarked.

Bedar arched an eyebrow at him. "*Is* it?"

"No, I don't mean … Just because I never have before, I suppose."

"Have you at all, with anyone, in the last five years, Marzana?"

"I … What do you mean? Why should I have?"

"I don't know—because men do. But as far as I know, you have not even been *interested* in a woman as long as I have known you. Oh. And you're not now, either."

"No. And nor are you interested in that … " He gestured towards the stairs. "Boy."

"Pray do not be absurd. What do you take me for—some sort of Pseuchaian? He is only sixteen."

That was older than Marzana would have guessed, but of course it still made him considerably younger than Bedar. Didn't it?

"No, indeed. I said you were not interested—and you're not. Well and good."

"Precisely."

They looked challengingly at one another for a moment. Then Bedar set down his empty cup on the table, and stretched out on the couch, draping the back of his hand over his eyes. Marzana's thoughts circled unhelpfully. What if he *was* giving Chereia the impression that he was … what was Bedar's phrase? Motivated by something other than charity? *Interested*? But then, would that have been the wrong impression? He thought not. Parmatya, of course, had known from the beginning; at any rate, he thought she had known from the beginning. She had not misconstrued anything.

He could hear soft voices talking downstairs, but could not make out their words—not, he reminded himself sternly, that he was trying to, of course.

Bedar drew his hand away from his eyes. "They're gone a long time," he remarked. "I wonder what they are doing down there."

"Making almond cakes. I thought you were asleep."

Bedar sat up, rubbing his eyes, and gave Marzana a dark look. "I wish that I were. I wish that I had been asleep all day, and might wake tomorrow morning and forget I ever dreamt any of this." He looked moodily at the lamp flames for a moment. "Or do I?" he asked, in an undertone.

"I wonder if they are talking about Zashians."

"What?"

"Downstairs. The two of them. I wonder if they are talking about us." He shrugged. "We were talking about them, after all."

A short while later, the sound of sandalled feet on the stairs heralded the return of Chereia and Pheres.

"Do you think it's that?" Pheres said, as they came up into the room.

"It makes sense to me. I mean, I don't know anything about that sort of person, but it sounds likely, from what you have said."

The boy was wearing Bedar's coat now, and he carried a dish of something. Chereia was carrying a rolled-up piece of paper. There was no sign of any almond cakes.

"Hello," said Marzana, adding hopefully, "Are the cakes finished?"

"Oh," said Chereia, "the cakes. No, they are not ready yet. We had to wait for the oven to heat properly—it was quite cold, obviously, since it's practically the middle of the night."

"We brought you up some sesame sweets instead," said Pheres, setting the dish in the middle of the table. "They're very good."

"Now we must show you what we have been doing, while we were waiting for the oven to heat. I don't know if it will be useful, but we felt we ought to be doing something."

She knelt down by the low table and unrolled the paper she had in her hand, pinning it down at the ends with the dish of sweets and an empty wine-cup. Marzana recognized the lines of tidy Pseuchaian writing. They had *not* been talking about Zashians, then. He felt irrationally disappointed by the discovery.

"This is the report that they made up at the watch headquarters for Marzana," Pheres explained to Bedar. "Of all the places where people saw Ariatans. We've gone through it and numbered all the different sightings, as far as we can be sure of them, in the order they happened."

"Then we've added in the other things we know about the whereabouts of Zukohasfas—"

"–hashkra."

"Whatever." Chereia waved a hand dismissively. "The man that we're looking for."

"Wait a minute," said Marzana. "What other things?"

"And, for that matter, what Ariatans?"

Chereia looked from Marzana to Bedar and back again. "What have you two been doing up here? Were you not talking about the investigation?"

There was a moment of awkward silence.

"They're tired," Pheres offered helpfully. He reached out to take a sesame sweet from the dish. "I expect they were just taking a rest—right?"

"We are quite tired, yes," said Marzana. He took one of the sweets as well, not knowing what else to do. It was delicious: complexly sweet and sticky. At least as good as—though totally different from—the rose-water candy of Arakesh.

"Oh, of course, that's understandable," said Chereia. "Well—we've done this … " She looked uncertain.

"It's to show all the evidence we have about where Zuko and the Ariatans were, and when," said Pheres, around his mouthful of candy. "It was Chereia's idea."

"Yes, but Pheres has an idea about what might have happened."

"It's probably not true—it's just a thought."

"Please," said Bedar, "if you would be so kind—"

"We would like to hear all about it," said Marzana.

"All right. Well, here is what happened last night, as far as we can work it out." She indicated lines added in the margin of the paper in a different hand, much messier than the others. "Suko … Tsuko … hass … I am just going to call him 'the ambassador,' if that's all right. Anyway, as we all know, *the ambassador* went to this party at Minister Sosikles's house, Bedar went with him but left early, and most of the guests subsequently went out to Gorgion's, a gaming house in Fish Street. The ambassador went with them—although gambling, as we also all know, is illegal in Sasia, so one might have expected him to abstain. But never mind. The party stayed at Gorgion's for some hours, during which time we know—on the testimony of one of the employees, I think?" Marzana nodded. "That the ambassador played a couple of games, unbeknownst to his companions, with a table full of Ariatans."

"What on earth … " said Bedar.

"Puzzling, indeed," said Chereia. "But there is more. The ambassador left, with his companions, and the Ariatans left shortly after. We don't know exactly where *they* went at this point. We do know that the party from Sosikles's split up—half went to Temple Walk, and half to Old Pottery Street, depending, of course, on whether they fancied a girl or a boy."

"What?" said Marzana.

"It's girls in Temple Walk—boys in Old Pottery Street." Chereia looked apologetic.

"Do we … do we know which street His Excellency chose?"

"Yes," said Bedar, "we do."

"Old Pottery Street," said Pheres, taking two more sweets from the dish.

"Oh. I see."

Marzana looked down at the paper with its meaningless black lettering, lying on the polished surface of Chereia's table, chronicling the emerging foulness of His Excellency's adventures on the previous night. He was not going to be able to look the man in the face, if they ever found him alive. But no wonder Bedar had taken pity on this boy. Bedar had always had great compassion for such unfortunate young people.

"So this," said Chereia, indicating one of the scribbles in the margin, "is the next place we know the ambassador was—at the Horses. We don't know exactly how long he was there, but that's not important. He left in order to meet some men, probably for the consecrating of the gates. Now, we don't know what men he was meeting, except that they *may* have been recent acquaintances, and that he seemed to find them … How did you put it?"

"Quaint," said Pheres. "Odd and sort of amusing."

"Right. Odd and amusing people he had just met. Might a group of friendly Ariatans, who wanted him to play dice with them, fit that description? Possibly. And they could have invited him to meet them at one of the gates for the cere-mony—they had ample opportunity, while they were talking at Gorgion's. Now. After that—after he left the Horses—we don't know what happened to the ambassador. Except that his coat, hat, purse … anything else?"

"His dagger."

"Coat, hat, purse, and dagger were all found by Marzana, this afternoon, in a rooming-house, in an apartment that had been rented by a group of Ariatans. Along with two dead Pseuchaian men, who he estimates were killed the night before."

"The sedan-chair carriers," said Bedar.

"What?"

"At the third house that I visited this morning, seeking information about His Excellency, the master of the house was not in, but his wife told me that he had taken the sedan chair out the night before, to the party, in case His Excellency should desire a ride home. But the chair, and the two carriers, had failed to reappear that night, or the following morning. I suppose it is possible that they became … involved in whatever went on … "

"Got in the way and had to be disposed of, you mean?" said Pheres.

"That is what I mean, yes. These are exquisite sweets, by the way."

"Thank you. Have you had one, Marzana?"

"He's had three," said Pheres.

"I have. They are wonderful."

"Oh, good."

"There was a sedan chair in the alley, now that I think about it," said Marzana.

"I see. So they murdered the sedan-chair carriers," said Chereia. "But they do not seem to have murdered the ambassador. Nor do they seem to have robbed him—not in any sensible way, at least. They did take his valuables, but they left them in an unlocked room which they seem to have abandoned."

"And then," said Pheres, "they wandered around all day today doing touristy things."

"Yes. As we know from the rest of this evidence. People saw groups of Ariatan men in a couple of places the day before the Psobion." She indicated two items on the list. "But that doesn't really concern us. The rest of these entries are places where people saw Ariatans earlier today. Marzana and the public watch went about asking questions," she explained to Bedar. "The watch thinks it's all a murder investigation about the poor fellows in the rooming-house—they don't know about the ambassador. Anyway, we've numbered these in order, but I don't know what they add up to, really. It's as Pheres said—they seem to have just gone about the city, seeing the sights. They went to the barber's in the morning, near the rooming house, then they went down to the agora, and they were seen watching the procession from the Temple of Kerialos a few hours later. They *might* have bought perfume from a shop in Tanners' Row either before or after that. They were down at the East Gate around noon, buying food from a cart, and in the Vintners' District at some point later in the afternoon, going into a wine shop, and sitting on the edge of a fountain. They were seen heading down to the agora again at about the tenth hour, presumably going to see the races. They were doing all the sorts of things anyone might do during the Psobion."

"Trying to look innocent, perhaps," said Marzana.

"It would seem so. Oh, and then finally, at the twelfth hour, they were in this neighbourhood, desperate for cakes."

"Desperate for what, my lady?"

"Cakes. I was leaving my shop, which was closed, and they came up to me—one of them came up to me, in fact, while the other three stood in the street and looked worried—and said that he needed to get some cakes, did I have cakes, how much would it cost to get some cakes right away? He was *not* trying to look innocent—he was behaving rather strangely, in fact. I told him no, I didn't have any cakes—I was closed, and he should try another shop two streets down. He marched off to rejoin his companions without thanking me, without even saying good-night, Psobos give you joy. I expect they did go to the other shop, so Pheres has written down here, 'Twelfth Hour: Bought Cakes.' And that, I'm afraid, is as much as we know."

"That, I believe, is considerably more than either of us knew previously," said Bedar.

"Indeed it is," said Marzana. "It would seem that these men must have taken His Excellency somewhere else, to some secure location, and left him there while they wandered about the city."

"Yes," said Pheres, "that's what we thought too."

"Either that, or they decided for some reason to murder him elsewhere." Marzana reached for another sesame sweet.

"I don't buy that," said Pheres. "If they'd murdered an important man, I think they would skip town, not loaf about all day going into perfume shops and sitting on fountains. I think there must be some reason why they're staying."

"Well, they couldn't leave," said Chereia. "There are no ships out of Boukos on the day of the Psobion—nor the night before. The earliest they are allowed to sail is tomorrow at noon, after the Kerialos Epilogue. It's something to do with showing respect to Psobos."

Pheres raised his eyebrows. "I'll bet they didn't know about that. I mean, we don't—*they* don't have that custom in Ariata."

Marzana looked up at him, startled, but making an effort to control his expression. "That is where you are from?"

The boy nodded. Marzana felt an unexpected satisfaction. He had come to Boukos believing in the wisdom of making a reconciliation between his people and the people that his father died fighting; he had been disappointed when what he had ended up doing was chasing Ariatans after all. And here was an Ariatan who was intent on helping the Zashians, though he probably had as good a reason to hate them as Marzana had to hate Ariatans. The boy was old enough to remember the long siege of Ariata during the last war, though he would have been a child at the time.

"I am glad," said Marzana seriously, "that you realize I have not been suspicious of your countrymen simply because Zashians hate Ariatans."

Pheres gave him a rather Bedar-like smile. "No. They're murderers—I get it."

"I didn't know you were Ariatan, Pheres," said Chereia.

"You're very fair—I thought you were Kossian, actually." She made a guilty face, but she must have known that the boy was not likely to be offended by this suggestion.

Bedar, Marzana noticed, was looking at the table in silence, studying paper, which of course communicated something to him. Evidently he had heard already where Pheres was from.

"What I wonder," Bedar said, "is this: if one wanted to hold someone prisoner in a foreign city, what place would one choose, that would seem safer than a room that one had already paid for in a bad neighbourhood?"

"Some place that didn't look like a house," said Chereia. "Because it was the Psobion, and the children were going around with goats, blessing the houses. These men might have known about *that*, and thought it would not be safe to leave the ambassador in some place where the neighbourhood kids would come barging in with a goat in tow. As to what sort of a place, exactly, I'm afraid I can't guess."

"It might help if we could plot out the locations of the various sightings in relation to one another," Marzana suggested. "Something like what a general would do, you understand, to plot out where the enemy is located—only in our case we want to know where the enemy *was* located. We would need tokens of some sort to set out … "

"Very clever," said Chereia brightly. "I'll fetch the counters from my game of mercenaries." She went to a sideboard, opened a drawer, and returned with a small leather bag. She poured a small heap of bone disks, dyed black and red, onto the table. "We can do it on this table, since we don't have an actual map. Boukos is roughly circular—they have a plan of the city in mosaic on the floor of the main court, and it is basically a circle, if you include the suburbs. This dish of sweets will represent the harbour, in the west." She pushed it to the edge of the table. "And Bedar's cup—oh, it's empty. Do you want some more wine, Bedar?"

"Thank you, but I believe I have had enough."

"All right—Bedar's cup is the agora, then. That's right about here." She positioned the cup carefully. "And we'll say this inlay on the table represents the city wall, even though that's not quite accurate. Now."

"What does the lamp represent?" Pheres asked.

"The lamp?" Chereia moved it into position between the dish and the cup. "The lamp represents the house where Marzana found the ambassador's things. It's out of proportion, of course, but that's all right. Now, we start with the first item: *One. Sukohasawhatsit at dinner party.* Actually, that one doesn't really figure into our investigation."

"It might," said Marzana. "Let us be thorough."

"The party was in Old Watchtower Street," Bedar supplied.

"Very good. That's here, then." She positioned a red counter near the inlay-wall. "Next we have Gorgion's, in Fish Street, which is about here. Then Old Pottery Street … that's outside the South Gate, isn't it?" Pheres nodded. "So that's here. After that, we have the ambassador's belongings and the two poor chair-carriers here, at the lamp, this morning. Then we have … *Five Ariatans seen coming out of a barbershop.*"

"That was in the next street over from the rooming-house," Marzana offered. "We could not ask the barber for more information, because by the time we got there he had closed for the day, and gone to watch the games."

"Right. So five Ariatans exiting a barbershop near the lamp. Number six: *Ariatans seen in the agora, watching the Kerialos procession.*" She laid that counter on the base of Bedar's wine cup. "*Five men in Ariatan clothes seen going into a perfume shop in Tanners' Row. That's in the east, about here.* Then they were at the East Gate—that's not far away, just about here—buying food. *Woman selling sausages reports several Ariatan customers about noon.* But they didn't stay in that part of town, because next we have them in the Vintners' District, and that is all the way over here, on the other side of the wine cup and past the inlay. This is where they were sitting on the fountain and buying perfume—no, pardon me, buying wine—they had bought perfume in Tanners' Row." She looked back at the list. "That's an expensive place to buy perfume. There's only one perfumer's in Tanners' Row—It's where Stratos used to shop when he was still rich. Anyway. *Staff in a wine shop in Vintners' District report a group of Ariatans, one of whom became drunk and had to be escorted out by his companions.* Evidently their minds weren't all on their work. *Ten. Five men, apparently Ariatans, sitting on the edge of a fountain in Vintners' Square.* Five men? Come to think of it, weren't there supposed to be four of them?"

"There were," said Marzana. "Four came into Boukos the day before we did, according to the man at the customs house, and Stamnos at Gorgion's thought there were four Ariatans at the table where His Excellency went for a few games. But either of them could have made a mistake—Stamnos said he was not certain, and the man in the customs house was an idiot. Or it may be that there was another Ariatan who only joined the party later."

"And then left again—because I am quite sure that there were only four of them in the evening, shopping for cakes. Which is our last counter—about here, near the sesame sweets. I'm sorry, near the dish that used to have sesame sweets in it. I'm glad you liked them so well. But what does all this amount to, then?"

"I confess I cannot begin to guess," said Bedar.

Pheres stood leaning against the head of Bedar's couch, frowning down at the table with his hands tucked inside the sleeves of Bedar's coat. "He could be anywhere. They've been all over the table."

"I am sorry," said Marzana. "This does not seem to have been a helpful idea."

"No no," said Chereia. "It was a good idea—it's just that isn't any pattern to see. Or maybe there is, but we don't have enough pieces of information to see it. You know, if you try to look at something through a few tiny holes, you can't make anything out—but if you poke enough holes you'll have a screen that you can see through. Maybe it's like that."

"Or maybe we have been asking the wrong question," said Marzana. "Perhaps what we should be asking is why these men would be holding His Excellency prisoner in the first place. If their intention was to ask for a ransom, one would think they would have done so straight away."

"Oh, well—Pheres has an idea about that, actually," said Chereia.

"Yes?"

The boy shrugged. "I don't know if I'm right, it just occurred to me that they might want to trade him for Euryanos and Rhyton."

"Oh," said Marzana. "Who?"

"Euryanos and Rhyton," said Bedar. "The governors of Xia and Phiros, who defected to our side in the last Pseuchaian War. I am surprised I even remember their names—it was a minor little business."

"Not in Ariata," said Pheres. "I was only nine when it happened, but I remember the young men burning effigies of Euryanos and Rhyton outside the city gates. That's where they execute traitors, right? Their families were all exiled or put to death, after the siege was lifted. Their names went up on the list of Enemies of the State—the permanent one that they carve on the wall at the temple of Hymestos and Dion, not the one that gets painted over after you're dead."

"But," said Marzana, in stunned disgust, "did they not *save* Ariata?"

"You would think that, being a Zashian. They didn't save Ariata, they disgraced it. They surrendered. You don't *do* that, if you're Ariatan. You win, or you die. Euryanos and Rhyton surrendered on behalf of all Ariata, and they didn't even have the decency to kill themselves afterwards—I expect they'd become too Zashianized, actually. Ariatans would love to get their hands on those two—I'm sure they would, even now—and have them publicly executed, in Ariata. I'd say some of them saw a more elegant way of getting at them than busting into Xia and Phiros and trying to kidnap them personally."

There was a moment of thoughtful silence, as everyone looked at Pheres and considered what he had just said.

"I don't actually think like this, by the way," he said, looking from one face to another.

"Please do not suppose that we could imagine it," said Bedar.

For Marzana's part, he was relieved to hear it.

"Well," said Chereia, "I think it sounds likely. I mean, from the sound of it, your king wouldn't say no if he were asked to trade these Ariatan men for the ambassador—what are Euryanos and Rhyton to him?"

"Loyal administrators," said Bedar. "Replaceable, probably, though only just. But what is Zukohashkra? An idiot—God forgive me—but an idiot with royal blood, His Radiancy's first cousin. No, he will not refuse the Ariatans their demand. But after he has done that, and has Zukohashkra back safely in Zash, his advisors will convince him that he needs to attack Ariata, to avenge the insult. There will be another Pseuchaian War, and no trade alliance for Boukos.

Quite possibly, that is what the Ariatans want—to pick up where they left off when Euryanos and Rhyton defected, to have a war on their own territory again, where we can besiege them till the stars fall, and get nothing for it."

"Is that what you call them?" said Chereia after a moment. "Pseuchaian Wars?"

"Yes. What do you call them?"

"Sasian Wars."

"Of course."

There was a glum silence.

"We cannot let this happen," Chereia said finally. "I am sorry, but this has got beyond being a diplomatic embarrassment—you are going to have to tell the Boukossian authorities."

"Yes," said Marzana. "Yes, you are right."

"Indisputably," said Bedar.

"They'll be able to close the harbour, you see, or station men on the ships headed for Ariata, to catch these men when they try to get away with the ambassador. Otherwise, I don't know how they can be stopped. And they must be stopped."

"We will speak to the chief of the public watch tomorrow morning," said Marzana. "I believe you said that no ships would leave Boukos until noon?"

"That's right. Which means that at the moment we can afford to think of more pleasant things. And I believe that my cakes are about ready to come out of the oven." She got to her feet, and removed the lamp from the western region of Boukos.

"Good," said Pheres, "because all this talking about sieges is making me hungry."

"Come down and help me ice the cakes," Chereia suggested.

"I am a little tired," said Pheres.

"Oh, all right then." She turned towards the stairs.

The boy looked across at Marzana and tipped his head in Chereia's direction, with a questioning expression.

"Marzana will come help you instead," he said.

"Very good," said Chereia, pausing at the head of the stairs.

Marzana reached for his boots.

CHAPTER XIV

PHERES UNFASTENED HIS sandals, stepped out of them, and flopped onto his back on the couch that Marzana had vacated. He looked across at Bedar.

"How are you?" he asked. In the lamplight his gaze was very gentle. "Hand still hurting?"

Bedar unwound the cloth he still had wrapped around it. "It is much better."

"I'm glad. That fucker's not worth a broken hand."

Bedar stretched out on his back on the couch, tucking his good arm behind his head. "You have such a way with words."

Pheres snorted. "Where did you learn to fight? From your soldier friend downstairs?"

"No, from a, ah, another soldier friend. A former lover," he specified, thinking of the Pseuchaian frankness about such matters.

"Right. But Marzana's not … your current … "

"No! No, he is simply a friend."

"That's what I thought—you don't act like lovers—but you never know. Zashians are odd." He grinned. "Actually, if he *was* your lover, I'd say you should be worried."

Bedar laughed. "Indeed?"

"Oh, well, honestly." Pheres lowered his voice. "I've come into this shop quite often, and men are always making eyes at Chereia—everyone knows she's a widow, and anyone can see she's pretty. But she always puts them off—I've never seen her flirt with anyone. She's just not that type. And now—well, she's just met Marzana, and she's invited him into her house? On the Psobion night?"

"He claims that he defended her from some rough types in the street, and offered to walk her home because he was concerned for her safety."

"Oh, really? Do you … " Pheres frowned. "Sorry, I shouldn't be gossiping like this. It's what people say prostitutes do all the time."

"Eunuchs also."

Pheres laughed slightly, and they were silent for a moment. Then, turning on his side to look at Bedar again, he said, "Do you believe him?"

"Utterly. As far as that goes. But he also claims that she invited him back here in order to discuss something that she knew concerning the missing ambassador—no doubt this business about the Ariatans and the cakes—and he maintains that she does not misunderstand his intentions. Of this I am not wholly convinced."

"But what *are* his intentions?"

"Quite possibly he has none. He had his heart broken half a dozen years ago by some stupid noblewoman, and I don't know that he has recovered. Consider also that Zashian men have few opportunities to meet respectable women—and then, Pseuchaian women are another matter altogether."

"You think maybe he's a bit scared of her?"

"It is possible. But one would think that *she* might be scared of *him*."

"Exactly. And she's not. That's what makes me think he's … you know, he's made a really good impression. Which I can see why he would—I mean, he's very handsome. Dashing and all that. If you like beards. I'm … not sure that I do."

Bedar thought that Pheres's only experience of a man with a beard might have been His Excellency the previous night. He repressed a shudder.

"What about your other soldier?" Pheres asked after a moment. "What was he like?"

"Ah. Quite … quite like Marzana, actually."

Pheres gave him a shrewd look and appeared to be deciding whether or not to ask something else. Bedar decided to spare him the trouble.

"He is my type, as you would say, but I am not not his, and I am not thinking of pursuing him—nor wishing that I could."

"I see. What happened with the other one?"

"He ended it. He made himself believe it was for my own good. Being in love is distracting. It got in the way of my doing my work, and my master—this was my former master, before His Excellency—became upset. He made remarks about flogging which he did not really mean, but my lover was inclined to take things too literally. He said it would be better for me if we parted. I think really he looked into the future and realized that I would always have a master—that the best he could hope for was to own me himself some day, which in truth he would never have been able to afford—and he saw that was not what would make him happy. I do not blame him."

"I see."

"All this was before I came to court. There I met someone else … but we parted as well, before I left with the embassy. I am unattached."

They looked at one another in the lamplight.

"So to speak," said Bedar.

Pheres smiled.

"I could lie here and look at you all night," said Bedar in Zashian, in the formal cadence of court poetry. "You are so beautiful."

The boy's eyes widened. He had understood at least some of that.

"If I do fall asleep," Bedar added in Pseuchaian, "it will be only for the pleasure of dreaming of you dancing in that square, wearing my coat."

"Don't, though," said Pheres. "Fall asleep. I want to hear some more of this."

The almond cakes lay in crisp, golden rows on their cooling racks. Chereia looked up from the pot of honey she was stirring on the stove.

"Oh, go ahead—they're cool enough."

"Was it so obvious what was on my mind?" said Marzana, picking up one of the tiny cakes.

"It was fairly obvious, yes."

He bit into the cake, and savoured it for a moment. "Exquisite."

Chereia smiled. "I am so glad. Now. How shall we decorate them?"

She looked at him thoughtfully for a moment, but he was at a loss. He had never even seen any Pseuchaian sweets to have any idea how they were usually decorated.

"Need we decorate them?" he asked, realizing it was the wrong thing to say as soon as the words were out of his mouth. "I mean only that ... we are going to eat them immediately, so ... "

She shook her head. "Professional pride, Marzana. This is what I am known for. You can tell a cake from Chereia's by the way it's decorated." She poked the fire under the pot of honey and went on stirring.

"What about crushed pistachios?" he suggested, thinking of the rose-water sweets from Arakesh.

She laughed. "Maybe when you've negotiated that trade agreement and I can *buy* pistachios."

"Ah. I did not think."

He watched her drizzle honey over the cakes and sprinkle poppy and sesame sesame seeds, nimbly, producing a delicate and unstudied effect. It reminded him of the naturalistic decorative schemes of the potters from his home province.

He realized they were standing very close together. He thought suddenly of Pseuchaians all over the city of Boukos lying in each other's arms, lips seeking lips, hands moving over bare skin in the dark, in the warmth of lamplit rooms, breathy sounds of pleasure ... While he stood in Chereia's kitchen, watching her scatter poppy seeds.

He cleared his throat. "I see," he said seriously, "why you wished to decorate them. They look finished now, as they did not before."

She looked up at him from beneath her lashes. They were very close together. He did not know what to do.

She moved away to extinguish the fire on the stove.

"Your friend seems to have made a conquest," she said.

"I beg your pardon?"

"Bedar. Pheres is very taken with him. I would say. Is there any hope, in that direction, for the poor boy?"

"Oh. Oh, I see. Yes. That is, no. Well, what hope could there be, really?"

Chereia nodded. "I see what you mean. They are from different worlds, aren't they?"

"Different countries, at least. We are here for a month—if that."

"Well—a month is something, when you have fallen … I mean, when you have caught love at first sight. Not that—I don't know that it was like that for Pheres, exactly—obviously I didn't ask him. But here they are, having known each other for a couple of hours, and it looks to me like Pheres is in love. I just wondered if he's … well, if he's Bedar's type, as we would say."

Marzana tried to think about this, since it seemed to be a matter of genuine concern to this kind-hearted woman. He knew Bedar had had lovers, but he had met only one of them: a youngish man who worked as a junior astrologer at court and was an aggressively proselytizing Vanian. Tall and lean, and not particularly handsome, but ostentatiously romantic, and always buying Bedar things. Marzana had never really taken to him.

"No," he said doubtfully, "I don't actually think he is. He is awfully young," he offered, lamely.

Chereia tilted her head thoughtfully. "He looks young, but he's been at the Horses several years. I would think he's fifteen at least—maybe more."

"Bedar told me he is sixteen." Marzana hoped she would not go on to ask him how old Bedar was.

"There you go. That's not so young. I was married to Stratos when I was sixteen. Of course that doesn't signify, because I was a girl. But for boys too, sixteen is quite a respectable age, in Pseuchaia. You will have lots of men chasing after boys who are much younger, in fact. A sixteen-year-old is pretty close to being an adult. Nobody would say that was too young."

"Yes, I see. Only … in Zash … Well, things are different in Zash."

She looked at him for a moment with an expression that made him think she was going to laugh at him. He wouldn't have blamed her if she had.

"Yes," she said finally. "Things must be different in Zash. And men like you and Bedar are different, in Pseuchaia. I suppose that is how it seems to Pheres—that he has never met anyone quite like Bedar before … He's striking. Not my type, though, of course."

"No?" said Marzana. He had to admit he was pleased to hear it, but that was no excuse for adding, as he did now, "What is?"

"My type? Oh. Um … " She seemed startled. "Well, I like a man who looks like a man."

"He isn't," said Marzana, surprised. He thought she had understood that.

"What?"

"A man. Bedar. He's a eunuch."

"Yes, I figured that. That's a type of man, though, isn't it?"

Marzana did his best not to look astonished. "Not in Zash," he managed. "But—I see what you mean." He realized, to his surprise, that he did. In Pseuchaia they did not distinguish, since they had no eunuchs. Perhaps this was one of the reasons Bedar so admired this place. It had never occurred to him before.

"As to your question," she said after a moment, setting down the dish of sesame seeds. "I want a reliable, honest man who is not too desperate to be looked after nor too keen on taking care of me, but just a little of both. Those are the things I care about. And if I found a man like that, and he were also the sort of man I would lie awake at night thinking about when he wasn't sharing my bed—then I would know the gods had truly blessed me. I'm sorry. Were you hoping I would just say, 'I have always wanted a tall, bearded foreigner'?"

"No—no, indeed!" The time for inarticulate shame was past, he felt; now was the time for a proper apology. "I was not hoping for that at all. It was a foolish question. Forgive me. It was only that when you said Bedar was not your 'type,' I thought that meant that you had a particular style of man that you preferred, and I was curious to know what he was— and so I asked. I am afraid I may be somewhat intoxicated by the frankness with which we can speak to one another."

"Well. Welcome to Pseuchaia, I guess." She turned from the table, wiping her hands on her apron. "I am going to go up and check on the boys, to see if they need anything." Halfway up the stairs she stopped, looking down into the kitchen but not at him, and said, "Actually, I don't understand why the women of my great-grandmother's generation ever let their men give up growing their beards. *I* wouldn't have."

They left Chereia's shop at the seventh hour; they knew this because a pair of doleful watchmen were passing in the next street, calling out this information to anyone who was in- terested. Marzana said that the seventh hour was half past midnight according to Zashian timekeeping. Bedar said he was surprised it was so early.

He had fallen asleep, mortifyingly, in the middle of a story about one of Pheres's friends at the Horses, and been woken some time later to be told that he should try one of the almond cakes that everyone else had been enjoying, and then Marzana would take him home. On the doorstep of the sweet shop, while they said good-bye to Chereia, who seemed to be searching unsuccessfully for a polite way to ask when she might see them again, he had wanted to say that he was sure he could safely find his own way home. But it wouldn't have been remotely true, and he was by no means sure that Marzana would have made much of the opportunity even if he had been granted it. He seemed to have fallen into an awkward silence at the end of their sojourn in Chereia's apartment.

"Oh, I had better give you back your coat," said Pheres, after they had passed the watchmen. He stopped in the street and reached for the buttons.

"There is no need. I am not cold," Bedar lied.

Pheres looked up. "No, um … I meant because I have to go now. It's seventh hour. I have to get back. It's … um, it's been very nice."

"Where do you have to go?" Marzana asked.

"To the Horses. Where I work."

"You live there as well?" Marzana put the question with obvious distaste.

"Yes. I'm the property of the establishment."

Bedar thought of the tastefully painted little room, and the couch with the striped blanket, which must have been where Pheres slept, as well as entertained his customers. Midnight was early, for a night like this; there was no telling which of the two things he might be going back for. This was it, then, Bedar thought; the night of his interfering in Pheres's life was drawing to an end. He did not think that he would be able to afford, in more ways than one, to do it again.

"I'm supposed to be back by seventh hour," said Pheres. "So … I'm already a bit late."

Marzana yawned. "Where is this Horses, again? It was somewhere at the very edge of the table, past the city wall, I think?"

"It's outside the Eastern Gate. In the suburbs."

"Then you are not going back there tonight." He spoke decisively. "I am sorry. We are on the westernmost edge of the city now—to get to the Eastern Gate we would have to walk all the way across the city. Bedar is too tired for that, I am too tired to take him home first and then take you home, and it is altogether out of the question that you should walk there at this hour by yourself. You will have to come back with us."

Pheres looked at him for a moment, his eyes wide. "Oh," he said. "All right. That's … I'm sure that you must be right."

"Good. Let us go."

Pheres looked back at Bedar, undisguisedly pleased. "Well. I guess you're not rid of me yet."

"It seems I am not." He smiled. Pheres offered him an arm to lean on, and he took it.

The streets were quieter now, more of the revellers having retired to each other's homes for the night, and they could walk three abreast down the middle of the pavement without much hindrance. Marzana had shoved his hands deep into his sash and was looking at the buildings that they passed with a restless, thoughtful gaze. Bedar wondered what he was brooding on, and hoped that it had nothing to do with that woman from Arakesh. Simsham, or Shishi, or whatever her name was. Shamshi. Of course. How could he have forgotten? Pheres's shoulder touched his, and because he was cold, he did not draw away.

"Bedar," said Marzana by and by, "do you think that I am an honest, reliable man?"

Bedar stared at him. "Oh God, Marzana. I know of none more so."

Marzana shrugged diffidently and went back to his perusal of the house fronts. Bedar and Pheres looked at one another, eyebrows raised.

After a moment Bedar said, "Is our hostess of the sweet shop by any chance looking for an honest, reliable man?"

Marzana nodded. "Though no doubt what she really wants is an honest, reliable Pseuchaian man."

"Oh, b– stuff and nonsense! Who wants a Pseuchaian man?"

Marzana laughed.

"I'm serious," said Pheres. "They're lousy."

Marzana looked at him. "I am sure there are a few good ones, Kadesh. Or will be, at any rate."

Pheres was probably blushing, Bedar thought, but in the dark it was impossible to tell.

"What did he call me?" he asked.

"Kadesh—it is a Zashian word for the colour of a horse, that is almost the same as your hair."

"Oh, very good. I shall remember that."

"Damn!" said Marzana suddenly, tossing back his coat and clapping one hand to his sword-belt. "I have only just realized—I left my sword in Chereia's shop."

"Perhaps she hid it," said Bedar, "so that you would have to come back for it."

Pheres laughed. Marzana looked stern, and said, "I am sure that is not the sort of thing she would do."

"*Shall* we go back, though?" Pheres asked.

"Indeed no," said Marzana, looking sterner still. "We are nearly home."

CHAPTER XV

THE POST-PSOBION MORNING was cloudless but chilly, with a bright blue sky and a sharp breeze. Marzana witnessed more of it than he would have liked; he had lain awake much of the night, but was woken shortly after dawn by a commotion in the passage outside the guards' dormitory. He sat up in bed. The boy whose pallet was nearest the door had kicked off his blanket and got up to look out into the passage.

"What is it?" Marzana asked.

The boy shut the door and shrugged. "I don't know, sir. That fat eunuch carrying on about something again. He's just gone off down the hall."

One of the other sentries looked up from his pillow. "Maybe His Excellency is back, sir—do you think so?"

Marzana got out of bed and reached for his boots; he had slept in his clothes, anticipating that a scene like this might well arise in the morning.

"I have no idea," he said wearily. "No idea at all."

Smar, Chief Eunuch of His Excellency's household, was standing in his dressing-gown in the middle of the dining room by the time Marzana caught up with him, surrounded by a crowd of anxious, sleepy-looking slaves, loudly declaring that he knew nothing at all about something. Standing over him, looking as though he did not believe a word of it, had not slept at all, even in his clothes, and was in fact still drunk from the night before, was one of the youngest and least apparently useful members of the ambassadorial party, a fellow by the name of Jadresh. Between them, as Marzana observed when he shouldered his way far enough into the dining-room, lay the still and evidently lifeless body of a dog.

"What is going on here?" Marzana demanded.

Jadresh regarded him with bleary eyes. "My dog is dead!" he declared indignantly.

"I see that," said Marzana. "Is that a matter about which to rouse the entire household?"

"I am being accused of harbouring a murderer!" Smar squeaked.

"A dog-murderer?" said Marzana, fixing the Chief Eunuch with a stern look. "Is *that* a reason to rouse the household?"

"I am sorry, sir," said Smar haughtily. "But I take exception to his—his implications!"

"That brat poisoned my Fang," said Jadresh, halfway between a growl and a sob. "That shit-eating barbarian brat. Wait until I get my hands on him—just wait!"

Marzana looked down at the dog. It did indeed look like an animal that had not died of natural causes; there was froth on its mouth, and its limbs were contorted as though it had fallen in some sort of a fit. Poor creature.

"I saw the brat going about with him," Jadresh went on. "I should have wrung his heathen neck on the spot! Where is he? What have you done with him, you squinty-eyed useless capon?"

"Jadresh, control yourself, for Heaven's sake. Smar is not at fault here—I doubt very much *anyone* is at fault."

"Fang was the best hunting hound I had, and some heathen whelp poisoned him, and no one's at fault?"

"Begging your pardon, sir," said one of the younger eunuchs, at Marzana's elbow, "but I did see the Sukiyan boy giving wine to the dog, yesterday evening. I didn't think there was any harm in it, but … "

"What Pseuchaian boy?"

"That little black-haired creature that you turned over to me yesterday morning," said Smar, in an aggrieved tone.

"Oh," said Marzana, remembering the child who had come as a gift from Sosikles, with a jug of wine.

"He didn't speak a word of Zashian," Smar was saying. "I had no idea what to do with him. You would have done much better to give him to Bedar, I'm sure—*he* speaks Sukiyan so well, as everyone knows. But of course, he was *gone* all day, wasn't he, on some mysterious business with the master. Oh yes, we all know how important *he* is."

Marzana was looking down at the unfortunate dog, ignoring Smar. That child had been seen giving wine to the animal—wine that had been a gift from Sosikles, intended for the ambassador. And now the animal was dead. Only lately dead, Marzana guessed; but then, some poisons could be slow-acting. And if someone had wished to murder His Excellency surreptitiously, it would probably have seemed prudent to choose just such a poison. Did Sosikles for some reason want the ambassador dead? Had he perhaps first attempted to poison him at the dinner party, and then, fearing that this had failed, sent the wine the next morning to make sure of the job?

"Sir?" One of the sentries on duty was standing in the dining-room doorway, having come in from the atrium. "There is someone at the door, sir. He says he's come from a lawyer."

"I shall speak to him," said Smar importantly, flapping his hands at the crowd of servants, which parted obediently to let him through to the door.

"What about my Fang?" Jadresh howled after him. "You're not getting off so easily, you fat ox!"

"Jadresh!" Marzana barked. "Shut up! Nobody is going to help you with your blood feud. Collect yourself, bury your dog with dignity, and let us hear no more about it."

He pushed past the cowering servants to follow Smar out into the atrium. The person who had come from the lawyer appeared to be a young clerk, looking sour and peeved to be up so early on the morning after the Psobion.

" … wishes to press charges," he was saying, "and it was the opinion of my master that the accused would most likely be found in this house, as there are not many other Sasians in the city."

"He wants—well, somebody wants to charge somebody with something," the sentry did his best to translate for Smar, "and they think that the somebody might be one of us."

"One of *us*?" Smar squeaked. "But *I* haven't even left the house!"

"No no, I mean—a Zashian. A member of His Excellency's entourage."

"Committing a crime in Pookosh? I shouldn't *think* so! You may tell him as much."

The sentry opened his mouth miserably, but Marzana cut in. "Who are you looking for?" he asked the clerk.

The man flipped open a writing-tablet and consulted some notes inside. "My master's client gave a description of the offender." He read it out.

The sentry translated for Smar before Marzana could stop him: "He says a smallish, girlish person—he's not *quite* sure whether it's a man or a woman, but it's got long black hair, and earrings, and painted eyes, and embroidery." He looked pleased with himself for having been able to interpret so much Pseuchaian so accurately.

"Oh, *how* interesting!" said Smar, with something like glee. "I *do* think that sounds like someone I know—I *wonder* where he is!"

"I am sorry," said Marzana to the clerk, "that I have no idea what you are talking about. Smar—Smar! Come away from that door. For Pity's sake, Smar, he's asleep."

Bedar was not in fact asleep. He had, by then, been awake for some time. He had been woken by the sun on his face, coming in at the window which he had forgotten to shutter before falling into bed the night before. He rolled over in the forgetful first moments of consciousness, on the narrow bed, and realized with the shock of contact with warm flesh that he was not alone.

He opened his eyes and pushed himself back a little—wary of rolling off the bed, which was raised up in the Pseuchaian style—to look at his companion. The sunlight fell slanting across Pheres's bare shoulder and the smooth slope of his back disappearing under the blanket. It shone in individual strands of his hair. In its light, Bedar could see a trail of faint freckles over his cheekbones and the bridge of his nose.

Bedar settled back on his pillow, hands folded under his cheek, and waited for Pheres to wake.

"Sleep well?" he inquired when the pale blue eyes opened.

Pheres stretched carefully in the limited space available. "Very well, thank you." He pushed up onto his elbows, shaking his hair out of his face. "And you?"

"Marvellously." Bedar smiled.

Pheres laughed, a low chuckle. "Yeah? Waking up the morning after the Psobion with a pretty boy in your bed—how very Boukossian of you."

"I would never call you 'pretty.' I would never cheapen your beauty with such a word."

At that Pheres laughed aloud, but he also blushed, and after a moment looked away. "You can say things like that … I don't know. It's not as if I haven't heard that kind of thing before, but it's different coming from you. Maybe it's just your Zashian accent."

"I am sure that is it."

"It doesn't make me angry, coming from you."

"I am glad."

"Is that your writing?" Pheres reached for a folded paper on the clothes-stool beside Bedar's bed. He picked it up. "It's so graceful."

"Thank you. It is my writing."

Pheres read out the subscription. "*Dar and Taru, at the cottage above the mill stream, Tenhan, Narmu, Parkan Province.*" He looked up. "Not … your parents?"

"Indeed."

"You write to them."

"I do. Of course they cannot read, but there is a scribe in the next village—my mother goes down to him with my letters when they arrive, and he reads them to her, and she tells him the news from the village, and he writes it down, and they send it to me. I am informed of all sorts of fascinating details about the sheep, and who is marrying whom, how many of my sisters-in-law are expecting children, and which of my brothers is building a new barn."

"You have brothers, too?"

"I have five brothers, two sisters, and roughly a dozen each of nieces and nephews—making some allowance for the fact that more may have been born since my mother's last letter."

Pheres looked down at the folded letter with a curiously wistful smile on his pale lips.

Bedar went on: "My parents count themselves fortunate. Most parents in the Parkan who lose children to the raiders have no choice but to give them up for dead, although they know well that they may not be dead, that they are probably slaves somewhere. But instead to have a son who lives in exotic cities, and writes them letters on real Glifian paper, and sends them gifts from time to time, things no one in the village has even seen before … It is something to be proud of."

Pheres looked up. "You are lucky."

"I know."

"Have you … Have you ever seen them, since you were seven?"

"No. I hope to make the journey some day. If my master grants permission."

Pheres put the letter back down on the clothes-stool. He reached out to touch the sleeve of Bedar's pyjamas, fingering the thin cotton fabric briefly. "You wear more clothes to bed than I usually do in the street."

"Nights can be cold in Zash."

"I was just thinking, Bedar. I get a day off every other week, if I behave myself, and so I was thinking, if we find Zuko and everything is all right, maybe it would be nice if we could go out again some time?"

"Yes," said Bedar, surprised. "I should like that very much."

"Really go out, you know, not supposedly look for your master."

Bedar smiled. "I understand."

"I know of some restaurants where we probably wouldn't get kicked out. The food's not so good, but … "

"The company would be delightful."

Pheres glowed. "Yeah. It would."

That was when a heavy fist began pounding on the door, and they heard Smar's voice from the atrium, declaring, "If he's asleep, he had better wake up! I won't have him giving the embassy a bad name! I always knew he couldn't be trusted!"

The door had a latch, but it had not been fastened securely, and it burst open under Smar's blows. Bedar was out of bed by the time Smar swarmed through the door with Marzana on his heels, but he was still in his pyjamas, and Pheres was out of bed too, Bedar realized with a feeling of sick horror, but Pheres was of course naked. Smar and Marzana stopped as if they had hit a wall.

"Morning," said Pheres, propping a shoulder against the wall of the alcove and giving a little wave.

CHAPTER XVI

THEY HAD RETREATED to the cold garden behind the house because no one else was interested in it at this hour. Bedar and Marzana sat on a chilly stone bench against the wall, and Pheres leaned against the pedestal of a statue beside them. He was dressed now, but he was wearing Bedar's clothes—a leaf-green suit with black and white embroidery.

"Don't worry about it," Pheres said. "It's basically olive pits. That's an Ariatan expression—it means it's nothing, it's not a big deal. It's just a fine—even for a slave. Just maybe a few nummoi. You see? Olive pits. Boukos is a nice place that way."

"I am greatly relieved to hear it," said Marzana.

Bedar nodded weakly, looking as though he was trying hard to convince himself to be relieved too. He had dressed as well, but in an almost plain blue suit, without any kohl or jewellery or perfume, still nursing his injured left arm, he seemed scarcely like himself.

"At any rate," he said, with an attempt at a brisk and breezy tone, "it would seem that there is nothing to be done about that now. But what about Jadresh's dog?"

"I do not know," said Marzana. "It is possible that the animal ate something else that disagreed with him—I mean that killed him. Perhaps I am imagining crimes and plots now where there are none. I cannot think what Sosikles would stand to gain from poisoning His Excellency."

"It could be something that we don't even know about," said Pheres. "But maybe it wasn't Sosikles. Do you know that the wine came from him?"

"He did mention having sent a present," said Bedar.

"But," said Marzana, "was that young man who came with it necessarily his son? What was his name? Leuklios? Lyseuklis?"

"Leusiklos Sosikliades," Pheres supplied. "Tall, blond, good-looking in a boring sort of way—swaggers when he walks, and smiles a lot, to show off what good teeth he has. I could tell you more, but I'm pretty sure you don't need to hear it."

"It sounds quite like him," said Marzana, trying not to think about what else Pheres might know.

"Well. The wine came from Sosikles, then." Pheres pushed himself away from the statue's pedestal. "Is that the kitchen back there? I think I smell baking. I'll go and see if there's anything for breakfast—all right?"

"Very good," said Marzana, realizing that he was actually quite hungry.

Pheres strolled away across the garden, thumbs tucked into his white sash, the pebbled path crunching under his sandals. Halfway there he paused briefly, and executed a brisk, skipping dance step. Then he walked on.

"Is he going to be able to talk to the cook?" Marzana asked.

"Yes."

"He speaks Zashian?"

"Badly—he claims. But I think in truth quite well. He has not favoured me with a demonstration yet."

"Ah."

They sat in silence for a few moments, after Pheres had

disappeared through the kitchen doorway. His appearance in Bedar's bedroom had had an unexpected but helpful effect on Smar, who had been so wrong-footed by it that it had robbed his announcement about the lawyer of most of its force. He had retreated, afterward, regarding Bedar with something like awe.

Marzana suspected Smar had made a fairly basic misinterpretation there, but he did not mean to speak of that now. He was remembering some of the things that had been running through his mind as he lay awake that night; they had been forgotten, temporarily, in the confusion attendant on the death of Jadresh's dog and the arrival of the lawyer's clerk, but now they began to assume their proper importance once more. He looked at Bedar, who was fingering a string of prayer beads, not the flashy ones Marzana had seen him with the other night, but a plain wooden string, obviously well-used. Marzana waited until he had finished the cycle and looked up.

"Bedar," he said finally, "I am afraid I was not being quite honest with you last night."

"Oh?"

"I *did* offer to walk Chereia home because I was concerned for her safety—but then we stopped to look at a temple, and climbed up to the gallery to admire the view, and … really, when I came into her shop, I was no longer thinking about Ariatans or His Excellency or any of that."

Bedar nodded, tucking away the string of beads. "I took Pheres out to a restaurant. Then we happened to come across some dancing in the street, and we joined in—we would have stayed longer, too, except that he was worried about what would happen to me if I did not find the ambassador. I myself had long ago ceased to care about that."

They looked at one another for a moment with wry smiles.

"He seems a very nice boy," said Marzana.

"I think so. Chereia is … She's lovely, Marzana. I am very glad that you were not being quite honest last night."

"And I am glad that I insisted Pheres come back here with us. He does … seem to think highly of you."

Bedar sighed. "More's the pity, since I am undoubtedly going to be stoned to death, or flayed or at least have my hands cut off in a day or two. I am sure he cannot be right that it is only a small fine. He is merely saying that to keep me from despairing."

"Well, it isn't working, is it?"

"I take your point. I should make more of an effort."

Pheres emerged from the kitchen carrying a tray, just as the folding door to the dining-room rattled open and Jadresh strode through into the garden.

"How does he have the energy to carry on like this?" Bedar muttered. "He has obviously been up all night."

"Where is that boy?" Jadresh demanded, confronting Pheres accusingly. "Who are you, anyway? Where did that boy go?"

"I am Fereza Kadesh. I don't know where the boy is," said Pheres cooly, in Zashian. Bedar, it appeared, had been right. "Excuse me."

And Jadresh actually stepped out of the way for Pheres to pass.

"Breakfast," said Pheres brightly, setting the tray down on the bench between Marzana and Bedar. There were three saffron cakes on a dish, and a pitcher with three cups. "These are … some yellow buns, and this is … It looks like thin yogurt and smells … like beer?"

"Kilf," said Marzana and Bedar at the same time.

"That's it. Your cook was very excited because he'd found

some sheep's milk to make it with. I've never had it before—is it good stuff?"

"Yes, very," said Bedar, and, "No," said Marzana, "it's foul."

"Oh," said Pheres. He handed around the cakes and filled two of the cups with kilf. "He said he's making tea and to come back for it in a minute."

"I will go," said Bedar, getting up.

Jadresh by this time had made an angry circuit of the garden, and gone back through the dining-room door into the house.

"Who is he looking for?" Pheres asked, looking after him.

"The boy who came with the wine," said Marzana. "A small, curly-haired child."

"Yeah, I thought so. He's in the kitchen. Hiding in the wood-bin under the stove. How can you not like this stuff, Marzana? It's so good."

Bedar had gone into the kitchen by this time. Marzana looked at Pheres. He must broach the subject frankly, he thought; he would not repeat the mistakes he had made last night with Chereia. Pseuchaians were frank people.

"I must ask," he said. "When you return to your brothel—"

"Uh. It's actually not polite to call it that when it's boys."

"I do beg your pardon."

"No, I don't care—just giving you a tip. You call it a 'house' or 'establishment' or something like that. Anyway, when I go back … "

"Yes. Will you be in difficulties?"

"What, for being out all night? Nah, the doorman likes me—he'll cover for me, if the owner shows up or anything. Not that he will, the morning after the Psobion."

"That is … good, but it is not what I meant." Marzana cleared his throat. Frank. He must be frank. Although apparently even here there were limits. "I understand that in

Pseuchaian custom a boy is only considered desirable so long as he is not yet able to do a man's work in the bedroom."

The boy smiled. "Yeah, in a nutshell. A very Zashian nutshell, but yeah."

"And so?" Surely he was not to be required to exercise any more frankness than this.

But Pheres looked mystified for a moment, then he stared open-mouthed at Marzana as understanding dawned. "You think I fucked him! Smar thinks Bedar fucked *me*, somehow, and wants to know how—but *you* think I fucked Bedar. I didn't."

"I see."

"I didn't give him a blow job, either, or *get* one, or a … " He was about to start ticking off a list on his fingers, but stopped at the look on Marzana's face. "Or anything. We just slept. It was nice."

"I see." After a moment, collecting himself, Marzana added, "You seem well matched."

"Yeah." Pheres smirked. "You thought I *fucked* him." The idea obviously delighted him.

"I would never have used that word," said Marzana.

"Really? I thought you were a soldier."

"I am an *officer*."

"Ah."

Bedar returned from the kitchen with tea, to report that he had found the fugitive child but been unable to coax him out of his hiding place.

"I think he's frightened of me."

"Then he would likely be even more frightened of me," said Marzana ruefully.

Pheres drained the rest of his kilf and set down the cup. "I'll try," he said.

They all went into the kitchen with their tea and their

half-finished saffron cakes. Pheres squatted in front of the wood-bin, gathering up the tails of the green coat so they would not drag on the kitchen floor. "Hey," he said. "You're Phormion, right? Where are you from? I'm Pheres—I'm from the Horses. What about you? Where'd they buy you from?"

After a moment there was some mumbled response from behind the piled sticks of kindling.

"Oh yeah? I know that place—it's down the street from us. One of my friends used to be there. His name's Agorgios, but everyone calls him just Gorgi. Did you know him?"

The little voice inside the wood-bin said something else, and Pheres frowned.

"I didn't hear that," he said, a warning note in his voice. "You want to say that again?"

The boy under the stove repeated himself, with some elaboration. Marzana could make out the words this time, but there was a lot of idiomatic language that he did not understand.

"All right, Phormion," said Pheres, "you know what? I'm bigger than you. So you can come out of that box and tell me what happened to the dog, or I can haul you out, and we'll go look for the scary Sasian who owned the dog, together. It's your choice."

Phormion came crawling out of the box, wiping his nose and glowering at Pheres. "I don't know anything about the dog, I didn't do anything to him. All I did was give him a drink of wine because nobody *else* wanted it, and then he ate some cake out of the garbage and he died. That's all."

"Cake?" said Marzana sharply. "What cake?"

Phormion stared at him in speechless terror.

"What cake?" Pheres repeated. "You're cooperating, re-member? What cake?"

"Cake in the garbage! I don't know where it came from, it

was in the garbage. He tipped over the garbage and it fell out, but I put it back when he was done. *I* didn't eat any. We don't need to eat cake out of the garbage at Karistegion's. Maybe you eat cake out of the garbage at the Horses—"

"Yeah, yeah, all the time. Where's the bin that the dog ate out of?"

"Everyone at the Horses has the pox," said Phormion primly.

"Everyone."

"And you're overpriced. That's what Karistegion says."

"Karistegion knows what he's talking about."

"And I heard that Gorgi got sold because he bit off a customer's—"

"Do you want me to hit you? Where's the garbage that the dog ate out of?"

Phormion glanced around the kitchen and pointed to a large pail in one corner. Marzana strode over to look inside. There, amid vegetable peelings and grape stems, lay the half-eaten remains of several small cakes.

Pheres and Bedar had followed Marzana to the corner and looked in at the cakes.

"Those must be what he's talking about," said Pheres.

"Yes."

The cook, not having understood any of the preceding exchange, had come up behind Marzana and the others to look in puzzlement at what they were doing.

"Where did these come from?" Marzana demanded.

"Those cakes? They were delivered at the door yesterday evening, with a little tag saying something in Pseuchaian. I don't know who brought them." He shrugged. "Some odd Pseuchaian men, the sentry said. I threw them out, of course, because you never know what these heathens put in their pastries, do you? I mean, it might be anything—Horned Beast milk, or horse meat or … ”

“Poison.”

“Exactly. Anyway, they don't look very good, do they?”

“No,” said Marzana. The cakes were iced in thick, pasty dollops of something which might have been marzipan, with chunks of dried cherry stuck into it. “Indeed they do not.”

“Where is the tag that came with the cakes?” Bedar inquired. “Is it in the garbage as well?”

“No, no—I kept that, along with the dish they came in. I thought somebody might want them back.” The cook searched along the length of his counter and produced a rather plain metal dish with a small roll of paper inside.

Bedar took the paper and unrolled it. “*A gift for the mighty prince of spice-rich Sasia, Tsukohaskres son of Tsukosathres, ambassador to Boukos, from a humble admirer who saw him in the agora today. A messenger waits without to know whether you enjoyed the gift.*” Bedar looked up, eyebrows raised. “Interesting. I should say whoever sent this knew His Excellency pretty well.”

“What do you mean?”

“I mean this is exactly the sort of stuff that would work on him. Slavish flattery, a hint of seduction, mystery, dried cherries—he is addicted to dried cherries, and the local variety is very good. If these cakes had ever got to him, I am quite sure he would have eaten them—and then sent me for the messenger, to tell him what he thought, and by the time I came back to tell him there was no messenger waiting, he would have been as dead as Jadresh's dog.”

“So then, it wasn't Sosikles who tried to poison His Excellency—it was the ‘humble admirer.’” Marzana shook his head. “‘Spice-rich Sasia’? What is *that* about?”

“That's from *Anaxandrides and the Fearless Band*,” said

Pheres. "There's always some epithet—you know, 'fleet-footed So-and-so,' 'many-towered Ariata,' 'spice-rich Sasia.' It's the epic style. Can I see that thing?" Bedar handed him the paper. "Yeah … that's what I figured. It's Ariatan spelling."

"I am ashamed of myself for not knowing that," said Bedar. "I thought it was just poorly spelled."

Pheres gave him an arch look.

"Then the men who delivered these cakes to the door," said Marzana, "are presumably the same men I was trying to find yesterday. The ones who accosted Chereia while she was trying to close her shop, insisting on buying cakes. Which they apparently then did, from somewhere else. Which of course brings us to the question of why, if they have in fact abducted His Excellency, they are also trying to poison him."

Bedar had turned to look back in the direction of the stove. "I hesitate to point this out," he said, "as it does not really seem terribly important, but we seem to have lost Phormion."

"I hope he has not gone wandering about the house," said Marzana. "Jadresh, if he is not passed out on the floor somewhere, looked ready to eat him for breakfast. I will go see if he is in the garden."

He went out the kitchen door, but, as he had expected, the boy was nowhere in sight. So long as Jadresh had not got his hands on him, Marzana supposed this was just as well. He was about to turn back to the kitchen when the door from the dining-room opened and someone stepped out into the sunlight on the white stone steps into the garden.

She was dressed in a peach-coloured gown today, and instead of her white mantle she had a sort of gauzy lace shawl, but beyond that she was exactly as she had looked in his imagination all that night, which he accounted something of a marvel. The Pseuchaians must have some goddess, he thought, whom they envisioned in precisely this way: slender and creamy-skinned and hazel-eyed, standing on a flight of steps, looking out at you, her beautiful mouth just curving into a smile, one hand holding a basket full of fresh pastries, the other a sheathed sword.

"Hello, Marzana!" She came down into the garden. "Did you know that you left this in my shop last night? I thought I had better bring it to you, in case there is a Zasian code of honour that makes it terribly disgraceful to be without one's sword."

Marzana laughed. "It is no such matter, I am happy to say. But I am glad to have it back—I had missed it." He took the sword from her, his fingers just brushing hers.

"I brought you some apple pastries as well," she said, folding back the napkin that covered the basket's contents. A little steam rose in the cold air. "I don't know if you have already eaten."

"Not so as to notice," he said. Indeed, since he had not touched the kilf, he was still quite hungry. He took a pastry from the basket. "Thank you."

"So," she said, "how are things this morning?"

He bit into the pastry, which was sweet and warm and flaky, and considered the question. "Well," he said finally, having swallowed his mouthful, "His Excellency remains missing. There have been two delegations of anxious Boukossian ministers at the house already, wondering when they can meet with him. The house is full of useless ambassadorial aides and high-strung eunuchs who don't know what is going on. One of the aides' dogs is dead, and he wants somebody's blood, so there is a Pseuchaian boy skulking about the house in mortal fear, though it appears that the dog was in fact poisoned by some poorly-decorated cakes which were delivered to our door yesterday evening by the

Ariatans. Bedar is being charged with assault for breaking a Boukossian citizen's nose last night—and we may yet be accused of stealing an expensive prostitute."

"Oh dear," said Chereia. "I take it Pheres came home with you two, then?"

Marzana nodded. "I thought he and Bedar did not look anxious to part—I recalled what you surmised about that. Also, I was too tired to take him home, and I did not think he should be in the streets by himself."

"That was very good of you." Had this small piece of kindness cost him any trouble on earth, he could not have wished for a better reward than her smile as she said this. Since it had been no trouble at all, the smile was a gift.

"Events have proven you correct, there," he said. "They shared a bed last night. Chastely, I am told."

She laughed. "On the Psobion night! How lovely." After a moment she added, "For the two of them, I mean. It's not … what … everyone would want."

They looked at each other for a moment longer.

"No," he said finally. "It isn't, is it?"

He took a step toward her, just as she took a step toward him, and there was almost an awkward collision—almost, but not quite. Instead, there was a precise and perfect meeting. His hand touched the edge of her hair, her hand touched his shoulder, he bent and kissed her cheek, and then, very lightly, her lips. They stepped apart again. He could see from her expression that she was as pleased by what had just occurred as he was.

They went back into the kitchen. Bedar was sitting down on a crate near the door, Pheres leaning on the counter beside him, one leg crossed over the other, looking down with a little smile, apparently enjoying the experience of wearing trousers.

"Pheres!" Chereia exclaimed, as Marzana had rather expected she would. "Don't you look smart!"

"Thanks," said Pheres. "So do you. I like your shawl."

Marzana looked from the boy to Chereia, and it occurred to him that perhaps a widowed shopkeeper did not always go out in gauzy shawls, and that she might have been a little more dressed up than usual. She and Pheres were right; they did both look very good that morning. Marzana was aware that he had slept in his clothes, and not combed his hair, but somehow this did not bother him as much as he would have expected it to.

"Hello, Chereia," said Bedar. "You come as an entirely pleasant surprise."

"I found Marzana's sword in my shop this morning," she said, "and so I inquired where the Sashian embassy was—and then I thought I should bring some food, if I was coming all this way. Have a pastry? I promise these ones are not poisoned."

"You are as kind as you are beautiful," said Pheres.

Bedar looked at him. "That is just what I was going to say."

"I know."

"Marzana has been telling me what has happened so far this morning," said Chereia, when they were all provided with apple pastries. Even the cook had come over by this time, intrigued by the smell, and been convinced to try one.

"I suppose," said Bedar, "if we were Ariatans we would have fallen on our own swords by now. Well—Marzana's sword. If you were an Ariatan woman, you would be bringing it to us with that very purpose in mind."

Chereia looked stern. "I am going to take it back to my house if you continue to talk like that."

"Don't worry," said Pheres, around a mouthful of pastry. "They're Zashians. They don't approve of suicide."

"That is putting it a little mildly," said Marzana. "Oh. I forgot to mention—there was no sign of that boy in the garden. He must have got away."

There was a curious silence.

"We know," said Pheres finally. "He was still in here, as it turned out—hiding behind a barrel of pickles. We let him out the back way." He pointed to the small, latched door at the back of the kitchen. "He *is* a brat, but," glancing at Bedar and the cook, "we didn't think he deserved … "

"To be eaten by Jadresh?"

"To belong to Zukohashkra. So we let him go."

Marzana reflected that all three of them probably had good reasons to make such a judgement, and he said nothing. The cook went back to some dough that he was kneading on his work-table. Chereia's gaze followed him with interest, scanning the different types of spices that he was adding. No doubt she was wishing she could speak Zashian so that she could inquire about the recipe. Marzana found himself remembering, for the first time in years, a conversation he had had long ago with his mother, in which she had said, "For Heaven's sake, Marzana, marry a girl who can cook. I could stand anything else, but to think of you saddling yourself with a wife who couldn't feed you properly—that would break my heart." Parmatya, of course, had probably never seen the inside of a kitchen—but his mother had never found out about Parmatya.

"Oh, I almost forgot," said Chereia. "I brought this with me as well—you left it behind too, and I thought it might still prove important." She pulled the rolled-up paper from the night before out of her purse, and set it on the counter. "Though … " She looked from Marzana to Bedar and back again. "It looks as though neither of you wants very much to think about this right now. Which is quite fair."

Marzana leaned against the open kitchen door and drew out his prayer beads.

"Usually," said Chereia, "I go to the Kerialos Epilogue on the morning after the Psobion."

"What is that?" Bedar asked.

"It's when the priests restore order after the Kerialos Play. So that the gods won't be offended. Kerialos is released from his captivity, and all the leftover garlands are gathered up and offered at his temple. It's quite lovely—hardly anyone goes, because they are mostly sleeping off last night's wine. I usually make a point of it, though. There's no need to open the shop this morning—*no one* wants sweets."

"I cannot imagine why they would not want your apple pastries," said Marzana, looking wistfully at the empty basket.

Chereia looked pleased. "Oh, but I don't sell those in my shop, you know."

"No?"

"No, those were especially for you. You three. Of course, I didn't know there would be three of you, still." She smiled at Pheres. He had gone to stand behind Bedar, and was very gently but quite casually stroking Bedar's hair. He looked up at Chereia and smiled back.

Marzana was wondering whether it would be ridiculous to suggest that they should all go to this post-Psobion Epilogue together, if it was still to happen. He thought the idea of a quiet, propitiatory ceremony, attended only by a few sleepy Boukossians, sounded appealing.

Chereia looked down at the paper on the edge of the counter. She unrolled it idly, and then paused, looking at something on the list with a curious expression.

"Oh my." She looked up. "We have all been great idiots. Well—no. We have just failed to realize something which should have been obvious. It is right here: *Five Ariatans came out of a barbershop*. What do you go into a barbershop for?"

"To have my hair cut," Marzana answered promptly, anxious not to seem like more of a great idiot than necessary. "And I have my beard trimmed … "

"Yes," said Chereia. "And dyed that fascinating colour. But what does a Pseuchaian man go into a barbershop for *every single day*?"

There was a moment's pause.

"To be shaved," said Pheres, "but what … Oh!"

"You see?" said Chereia. "Five Ariatans were seen coming *out* of the barbershop. But what if someone had seen them going *in*? I don't think they would have looked like five Ariatans—I think they would have looked like four Ariatans and a Zashian. I think the fifth 'Ariatan' is your ambassador without his beard."

"Chereia," said Bedar after a moment, "you are the very wellspring of wisdom and ingenuity."

She laughed. "I don't know about that. I can't imagine why we didn't think of this before, really—except that … " She looked around at the group of them. "I guess I can see why, actually."

"So they didn't lock him up anywhere at all," said Pheres.

"No, they were parading around Boukos with him all day yesterday, clean-shaven and short-haired and dressed in Pseuchaian clothes."

"But—why?" Marzana demanded. "And *how*? What did they have to threaten him with, to get him to consent to *that*?"

"Nothing," said Pheres. "I'll bet. He did it for a lark. He thought it would be fun."

"*What*?"

"No, really—I will bet you anything he did. The night before, he was … he was really having a good time. He'd got to do all sorts of things a respectable man can't do in Zash, and he thought it was spectacular. He liked mingling with the locals—he thought everyone in Boukos was just wildly quaint and fabulous in a sort of barbarian way. I *know* this, because he talked about it—not very coherently, but I could get the gist. Then I think he went out to meet those Ariatans, after he left me, and they talked him into getting his beard shaved off the next morning, and cutting his hair, so he could pass himself off as a Pseuchaian. And he thought it would be fun."

"That would explain," said Bedar, "how they knew him well enough to write that note that came with the cakes. They spent the whole day in his company. Poor fools."

"But are you suggesting, then," said Marzana, "that he has not been abducted after all?"

Pheres shook his head. "It has to have been a real abduction—otherwise how do you explain the dead sedan-chair carriers and the poisoned cakes? I'm just saying I think he might not *know* he's been abducted."

They considered this for a moment in silence. It was preposterous; and yet it might very well be true.

"But he's become un-abducted now," said Chereia. "I mean, the Ariatans have lost him. I think they must have lost him last night. They took a risk, hauling him about through the city in the open, but it must have struck them as a better alternative to locking him up somewhere, where he'd know he was imprisoned, and where Boukossians might barge in at any moment with a goat to bless the house for the Psobion. But then they lost the gamble, because he got away from them somehow, and that was why they ended up outside my shop wanting to buy cakes to poison. They must have decided that they couldn't risk having the ambassador tell anyone about the wonderful new Ariatan friends he had made."

"But His Excellency never arrived home to eat the cakes," said Bedar. "Which means—what?"

"That he is still out there somewhere," said Marzana. "Hopefully alive."

They were all silent for a time. Marzana realized he was still holding his prayer beads and put them away again. The cook was shaping his dough into loaves now; Marzana watched him for a moment, wondering if the Zashian bread-baking technique was different from the Pseuchaian, and thinking that Chereia would be interested in this. Then he looked back at her, and realized that she had been looking at him.

"Hah!" said Pheres suddenly.

Bedar sat up to look back at him. "Hah what?"

"Chereia," said Pheres, "what time is the Kerialos Epilogue?"

"It usually starts at fifth hour."

"Have we got time to get to the agora before then, do you think?"

"We may. If we hurry."

"Then I think we should."

"What?" said Marzana, though he had been thinking about going to the thing himself a moment before. "Why?"

"Because I know where Zuko is. I know how the Ariatans lost him."

They hailed a couple of sedan chairs (possibly the only two in the city that morning, Chereia said) outside the ambassador's house, paid the bearers in advance, and asked them to hurry. The chairs were rather small for two passengers, and there was a little awkward, hasty shuffling about before they sorted themselves into the right pairs for such intimate seating.

Pheres was not telling what exactly he had guessed. Even when the two chairs came to a halt side by side at a street-crossing, and Chereia leaned across Marzana and called out, "Bedar! What's the secret? Has he told you yet?" Bedar could only shake his head apologetically.

"Tickle him!" she suggested.

"It won't work," said Pheres firmly. "I'm not ticklish."

Then the bearers picked up Marzana and Chereia's chair again, and lurched ahead suddenly, causing Chereia to fall back against Marzana, who caught her, and then found that, since she had settled back comfortably, it was easiest just to keep his arm around her for the rest of the journey.

The agora, which they arrived at all too soon, was scantily populated, as Chereia had predicted, and had rather the look of a giant dining room the morning after a party. The people who were there were wandering about, picking up trampled garlands and other bits of festival debris. In the middle of the open area the temporary stage for the Kerialos Play, a round wooden platform with steps leading up to it, still stood in place, surmounted by a sort of hut made of painted wooden cutouts of grapevines piled together and secured with cords. Around the base of the stage, a small party of priests was processing with incense, followed by acolytes playing softly on reed pipes.

Having descended from their chairs, the four of them stood still for a few moments on the edge of the agora, observing the tranquil scene before them, the spectacle of order being gradually restored after the chaos of the previous day and night. The leader of the procession began to ring a bell, in a slow, sweet chiming, and the people gathering up garlands turned their attention towards the stage.

"What is the little house made of vines?" Marzana asked Chereia.

"It's left over from the play last night. It's the vines that Psobos used to imprison Kerialos. So that he could steal his mistress, you see. That is the story that they act out in the play."

"And … Kerialos—I mean, the man who plays the role of Kerialos … "

"Has to stay in there all night, until the priests let him out. They leave him water and a basin, in case … you know … because he's always very drunk by this point."

As she said this, the priests' procession started up the steps onto the stage. The other people in the agora began to draw nearer.

"Come," said Chereia, tucking her arm through Marzana's. He followed her down into the agora, where she paused to pick up a garland of fading white flowers that the others had missed. They stood there, still some distance away from the stage, to watch what happened next.

The priests had arranged themselves in a ring around the edge of the stage, and now they knelt, facing the hut of grapevines, and three of the acolytes came forward to untie the cords that bound the structure together.

The painted wooden vines fell away in a ring, the acolytes catching them nimbly and then kneeling like the priests, and after a moment a tall figure rose up inside, rubbing his eyes and yawning. He stretched, and then, apparently noticing for the first time that there were people looking up at him, turned the stretch into a majestic pose, and stood there for a moment, arms spread wide, beaming around at the priests and the acolytes and the assembled garland-gatherers below.

"Oh!" said Chereia softly. "He *does* look the part."

He was a man just on the edge of middle age, tall and broad-shouldered, but without the muscular frame or the toughness of a soldier or an athlete: a man, indeed, who looked just as one might imagine a god of wine would. Unlike the average Boukossian he was olive-skinned, with dark curls clipped close to his temples, and his clean-shaven face was strong-featured and aquiline. He was stark naked.

For a few moments, while he thought the man was some Pseuchaian stranger, Marzana had looked at him, wincing with embarrassment but thinking that this was a custom of the land, and it would be rude to avert his gaze. It was only when recognition dawned that he looked away, as quickly as possible. He caught sight of Bedar, standing nearby, looking as though he was actually going to be sick.

"He really does look like the Polykritan Kerialos in Kos, you know," said Pheres, casting a cool, appraising eye over the man on the stage. "Without his beard."

"*That*," said Chereia, looking around at the Zashians and Pheres, "is the ambassador?"

"Oh yes," said Pheres. "That's him."

Marzana looked across at Bedar. "What are we going to do?" he muttered through clenched teeth. "Do you think he has seen us?"

"I don't know," said Bedar miserably. "I can't look again to find out."

"It makes perfect sense," Chereia was saying. "That's how the Ariatans lost him—it wasn't that he got away, it was that he was chosen to play Kerialos. There wouldn't have been anything they could do about it, without creating a terrible scene. But how clever of you, Pheres! How did you guess?"

"Oh, I just remembered that I'd heard people saying the Kerialos last night looked like the Polykritan statue—and I've been to Kos. I've seen everything they have by Polykritas. And I got a pretty good look at Zukohashkra—but then, so has most of Boukos, now." He grinned. "Not that I think he minds."

Which was evidently true. When Marzana forced himself to look up again, His Excellency the ambassador, son of Zukoshakthra son of King Zohanaza, first cousin of His Radiancy King Nahazra, was descending the steps of the stage at the head of the procession, flanked by the two senior priests, wearing a crown of vine leaves atop his newly cropped head, and smiling around at the small assembly of Boukossians as if he had never in his life gone out of doors more fully dressed than this.

"They're going to process up to the temple to burn the garlands," said Chereia. "We had better follow along. Come on."

They fell in with the garland-gatherers, who followed the procession of priests up towards the Temple of Kerialos on its green hill at the edge of the agora, singing a slow hymn to the wine god as they went. Three large braziers were set up in the porch of the temple for the burning of the garlands. Into the largest of the three, Zukohashkra flamboyantly tossed his grape-leaf crown; the rest of the procession filed up behind him to follow his example, trailing off down the temple steps in little knots of friends and hand-holding couples when they had finished. Pheres and the Zashians followed Chereia, who went up to toss her garland onto the flames. The ambassador was standing with the priests to one side of the braziers, watching the proceedings.

"Those must be your friends, there," said one of the priests, pointing to Bedar and Marzana.

"No no," said Zukohashkra, "they were not Zashians. Oh—look, that is my secretary, and my captain of my guard. Hello!" he called in Zashian. "What are you two doing here?"

"God guard you, Your Excellency," said Marzana, looking at the ground. Bedar, beside him, bowed mutely.

"Hello, sir," said Pheres brightly, in Pseuchaian.

There was a small pause. Marzana looked up; he could not help it. Zukohashkra was looking at Pheres with a benignly puzzled expression, plainly trying without success to remember who this boy was, and where he had met him before.

"Chares, yes?" he tried pleasantly.

Even Bedar had looked up by this point, though his eyes were on the boy rather than on his master.

"Pheres," said Pheres. "From the night before last. You remember. It was written above the door."

The priests behind Zukohashkra exchanged a glance, and one of them slapped a hand over his mouth, hastily stifling laughter. Clearly there was only one type of establishment in Boukos where one would expect to find a boy's name written over a door. And it was not a respectable one.

"Oh, yes," said the ambassador, apparently undaunted. "You look differently this time."

"Yes," said Pheres. "It's probably because I have clothes on."

"Yes, yes. It is very different. Very different." He smiled placidly around at all of them, and his gaze lingered on Chereia for a moment.

"We have never met," she said quickly, taking hold of Marzana's arm for good measure.

The ambassador nodded, smiling. "What are you all doing here?" he asked again, reverting to Zashian.

"We came here in search of you, Your Excellency," said Bedar. "Not having known your whereabouts all day yesterday, we had become worried."

"A most fascinating thing has happened to me," said Zukohashkra, still smiling, as if Bedar had not spoken. "These heathens are a remarkable people. They have liberated their senses. They are not ashamed of pleasure, as we Zashians are. Hah! I should rather say, as *you* Zashians are, for I have learned from these simple people—such lessons I have learned from them, in a single day! Well! Just look at me!

You can see for yourself, I am a new man. I have undergone a transformation—my life will never be the same. I met four wonderful heathens in a gaming house who have shown me the *real* Pookosh—you would not believe the things I have seen, the way they have opened my eyes. You are thinking, *a gaming house*, can he really have gone into a gaming house? Pah! I am not ashamed to admit it—why should I be? I have been all over this city, I have witnessed the charm of these people's primitive rituals, I have even stood up before a crowd of heathens in the marketplace, just as I am! *Just as I am.* It is amazing what a difference it makes, to discard these foolish excesses of hair and fabric that we hide ourselves in. One feels altogether more human." He clapped Marzana heartily on the arm. "You ought to try it some time. Of course," he added with a chuckle, "Bedar couldn't, but *you* really should."

Marzana stared straight ahead of him, and may have muttered something like, "Sir." Soldiers could adopt that sort of posture without seeming rude; he was grateful for it. He was more grateful still—indeed, he was thanking God fervently, all the while Zukohashkra talked—for the fact that Chereia did not understand Zashian. Pheres, who did, had slipped his hand into Bedar's after "Of course, Bedar couldn't," and kept it there.

But Chereia seemed to have got the measure of the Zashian ambassador pretty well, even if she had not been able to understand most of what he said.

"Has he always been like this?" she asked, as they followed Zukohashkra, who was still talking enthusiastically, down the steps of the temple.

"Like *this*?" said Marzana, trying to avoid looking at the ambassador's naked backside in front of him.

"So stunningly self-absorbed."

"Yes," said Bedar glumly.

"No no," said Pheres, facetiously. "He is a new man—he said so himself. His life has been *transformed*."

"Oh, sure," said Chereia. She looked across at her companions, standing together on one of the broad temple steps. "But does he really think that he is the only one?"

They smiled at one another. Any of them could have said it, Marzana thought. Chereia was just the one who, at that particular moment, had the necessary courage. He felt glowingly proud of her.

Below them, Zukohashkra had nearly reached the bottom of the temple stairs, and had suddenly begun waving excitedly to someone.

"Hello my old friends!" he called in Pseuchaian.

Marzana looked, and saw four men approaching, walking in a disciplined line suggestive of military training, wearing brown, hooded cloaks. One of them had thrown back his hood to display his short, dark red hair; but all held their cloaks closed in front of them.

"No! Sir!"

It was Bedar who ran down the steps first, and fastest; Bedar who threw himself against his master, ignoring his shameful nakedness, and pushed him back, away from the approaching men; Bedar, consequently, who was in the way when the Ariatans' knives flashed out from under their cloaks.

There was an unreality that took hold of one in battle, Marzana had found; one could see things without really understanding them in an ordinary way. He was not much slower down the steps than Bedar, and his sword was drawn when he arrived at the bottom. Yet he knew even as he ran down the steps that he would be too late. He did not save Bedar. It was Pheres, who tore down the steps like a green and gold comet, with a wild, ragged shout that could only have been something Ariatan boys learned to shout in such circumstances, and threw himself onto the Ariatan nearest Bedar, who did that. But Marzana saw this without understanding it, without realizing what it meant.

It was the first and the last time that he ever did what he had really been brought up to do: kill Ariatans. He felled the first one with a clean, quick cut across the throat, then brought his sword down and severed the knife-hand of the second. The man did not even scream as he fell. The third Ariatan looked into Marzana's eyes for a moment, and Marzana found himself, without surprise, feeling sorry for him. The man knew that he and his companions had failed; Marzana could see the anger of knowing it in his face. But it was not in him to acknowledge that he was beaten. He was a fanatic. *You win, or you die*, as Pheres had said. He ran at Marzana, who was not a fanatic, but who stood between the Ariatan's knife and a defenceless friend, and who swung his sword two-handed, and cut off the man's head.

The fourth Ariatan was not dead, but he was on the ground, face-down, with Pheres's knee in his back. Pheres had got a knife from somewhere, and there was blood on it. The ambassador, who had been shouting and flailing unhelpfully at first, was now crouched over on the steps, moaning. Bedar stood over him. Poor man, Marzana thought; he had believed these people to be his friends.

Pheres's captive was howling irrelevantly: "Sasian dogs! I don't want your mercy!"

"I don't give a shit what you want," Pheres retorted.

The ambassador was getting heavily to his feet, swatting Bedar out of the way with an aggrieved growl about how dare he have done something or other. He surveyed the grisly scene at the foot of the temple steps.

"They wanted to kill me!" he announced, as though it were

possible that someone there might not be aware of this. "The heathen scum wanted to kill me! How dare they?"

Marzana was looking past him at Chereia, who stood on the steps above them, not having moved from where she had been when the Ariatans appeared. How would all this be for her? he wondered. She had just watched him cut off a man's head, which could not be something she had ever seen before. Perhaps, he thought, she would find it reassuring to see him look up at her now, the same man as he had been before, not a bloodthirsty monster, just a soldier who could do what needed to be done. He thought, as he looked up at her, that he was probably right, though there was no doubt she had it in her to survive worse sights than this.

"Marzana?" he heard Pheres say behind him. "Can you give me a hand?"

He turned back to the boy, who was still holding down his struggling Ariatan. There were stunned Boukossians standing around on the hill and the temple steps whom Marzana had not noticed until now. Zukohashkra was still expatiating on ungrateful heathens, though only Bedar, who was trying unsuccessfully to quiet him, was paying him the slightest attention.

"Can you … take over?" said Pheres. "It's not that I don't want to kill him, it's just … " He paused to draw a breath. His face had gone very white, except for a gash along his right cheekbone that was bleeding badly.

"You're hurt," Marzana observed. He took hold of the Ariatan's wrists, pushing the man back down with his knee. It would be as well to keep one of them for questioning, if they could.

The boy had got to his feet, still holding the bloodied knife in one hand, but the other hand was tightly clasped to his shoulder.

"Yeah … It's not too bad, though."

He took his hand away from his shoulder for a moment to push his hair back from his face. He looked unsteady on his feet, and the palm of his hand was slick with blood, the shoulder of the green coat soaked with it. Marzana realized what he had seen in that first unreal moment as the two of them reached the bottom of the stairs. Pheres had thrown himself into the path of the Ariatan's knife. He had the weapon in his hand now because he had pulled it out of his own shoulder.

"Bedar!" Marzana called. "Look to Pheres!"

The boy would be all right, Marzana thought, if the blade had not gone into his lung. He was obviously tougher than he looked.

When he had subdued the captive Ariatan and had attention to spare again, Marzana saw Bedar had got Pheres sitting down on the pavement, but didn't seem able to do much more, as his own hands were shaking badly. Chereia appeared then, dropping to her knees beside the two of them, pulling off her gauzy shawl.

Zukohashkra chose this moment to take an interest in what was happening in front of him, and found it full of surprising pathos and charm.

"That boy was wounded in saving my life!" he declared, in awed tones.

This was unjust, Marzana thought, on multiple levels. It was Bedar who had tried to save the ambassador's life, and Bedar for whom Pheres had taken a knife in the shoulder and the face.

"Yes, Your Excellency," said Bedar quickly, looking up. "He was. His Radiancy ought to be told, don't you think?"

"His Radiancy? Yes, yes, of course. The bravery of our Sukiyan friends, and so on. He may wish to make some gesture."

It seemed to Marzana that there were more important

things to worry about just then, but he guessed Bedar knew what he was doing.

"We're going to need a surgeon here," said Chereia, from where she knelt beside Pheres, putting pressure on his shoulder. The boy was leaning against Bedar and holding a handkerchief to the cut on his cheek.

"Of course." Marzana strode out into the crowd of gaping Boukossians which had gathered by this time, and found several people willing to make themselves useful by running for a surgeon. The priests of Kerialos had by this time come down the steps, followed by a rabble of curious acolytes. Marzana put some of them to work guarding his prisoner until the watch, which had also been sent for, arrived. Then he turned his attention back to the ambassador.

"Your Excellency," Marzana said, shrugging off his coat, "there are many people here watching. You should put something on."

"I don't need to," said Zukohashkra pityingly. "I have no need of clothes." He waved a hand impatiently. "I have discovered … I have discovered *myself*."

Marzana looked him in the eye. The man was a cousin of the king of Zash. In Suna, he wielded great influence, and one would be suicidally stupid to cross him. In Suna.

"Is that all?" Marzana said. "Then I am sorry for you. If I were such a man as you are, who can achieve the highest happiness of his life in a night of gambling and drink and loveless bought sex, I would not ever want to be discovered, least of all by myself."

Zukohashkra stared at him, stunned. "You insolent—insubordinate—you—you—"

But it was not really insubordination, as Marzana answered to the captain of the king's guards and not to Zukohashkra personally.

"I have just killed three men who were coming for you with knives, Your Excellency. It is soon going to be necessary for you to explain to the Boukossian authorities—as well as to these priests on whose temple steps this has taken place—why I was obliged to do this. I would strongly advise you, before that time, to put on some clothes."

He held out the coat again, and Zukohashkra, looking as haughty as he possibly could, took it, and shoved his arm into the wrong sleeve.

The watch were not long in arriving, and Marzana turned the fourth Ariatan over to them. Two surgeons arrived at roughly the same time, and Chereia took charge of sending away the one who looked most hung-over. Some of the acolytes helped Pheres up and inside the temple. There followed a long period of loud questions and confused explanations. Zukohashkra was shouting at the top of his lungs about heathens, and Bedar, who got to his feet when Pheres was taken inside, was managing, although shaky and bloodstained, to be as elaborately polite as usual. News of what had happened had apparently reached the ambassador's house, because several useless members of the embassy burst worriedly upon the scene and began asking everyone all the same questions they had already answered.

Marzana turned to see that Chereia had come down from the temple and was waiting uncertainly for a chance to speak to him. He realized that a moment of decision had snuck up on them. He was about to be swept away in the tide of his duties and the aftermath of the attack. She would wisely and discreetly absent herself. But if she did, could she be sure that he would come to her shop seeking her out when he was free? Could *he* be sure she would want him to? The blood of the men he had killed in front of her was still wet on the pavement.

"The surgeon's finished with Pheres," she said.

"Ah, yes. Good."

"He said it's not serious, but of course Pheres will need to rest the shoulder for a while to let it heal. I've offered to let him stay with me, at least for a couple of days. We've sent a message to the house where he works, and I'm on my way to look for a sedan chair. Also to see if I can pry Bedar away from all this, to come see that Pheres is all right. I think he will be worrying."

"Indeed." He looked across to where Bedar was talking to the ambassador. "I will take care of it. Is it … Is it permissible for Bedar to enter the temple?"

She looked surprised by the question. "Oh, of course. It's the temple of Kerialos. Everyone is allowed in. And Kerialos was a foreigner himself, you know."

He didn't quite understand that, but he nodded. And it struck him that he would like to ask her about it some time. There were many things he would like to ask her about.

"When can I see you again?" he said abruptly.

"Oh. Any—Whenever—Tomorrow? Can you come around in the evening?"

"I can," he said. "I will."

She went to fetch a sedan chair, and he strode over to the ambassador and announced that Bedar was needed inside, then escorted him into the temple for good measure. Inside, he satisfied himself that the surgeon had done a tidy job bandaging Pheres's shoulder, and pronounced his approval. The cut on the boy's cheek had needed a couple of stitches, and would probably scar. Marzana wondered what they would think of that at the "establishment" to which he belonged. It could be a good thing.

He stood at a distance in the temple's cool, marble-columned central hall while Bedar talked with the boy as they waited for Chereia to return. He watched the two of them together, wondering again what the difference in their ages was. He would never ask Bedar about it, but it suddenly struck him that it might not be all that much.

When Chereia returned to take Pheres back to her house, Marzana and Bedar stood at the top of the temple steps for a moment before going back down into the crowd. Bedar, Marzana noticed, was wiping his eyes. Marzana offered him his handkerchief.

"Thank you. You know, that is a marvellous woman that you found in the street, Marzana."

"Indeed. And a very brave young man that you found."

Bedar nodded. "I am glad that we found them. I am glad, because if all that we had found after all were that … object standing down there in your coat—which, I note with revulsion, he has not buttoned up—I am afraid I would feel that it had not been remotely worth the trouble."

CHAPTER XVII

THE LETTER WAS written not in Bedar's elegant secretarial hand but in the brisk, businesslike script that was taught at the schools for gentlemen's sons in Zeleush. It came straight to the point—as much as any Zashian letter ever did.

To Aza son of Varazda son of Aresh, Captain of the Guard of His Radiancy King Nahazra, whose house may God prosper forever, Marzana son of Sorgana, Captain of the Guard of His Excellency Zukohashkra, ambassador to Boukos, sends his humble blessing.

I write to convey to you the very good news that, thanks be to God's mercy, His Excellency and all the members of his household in Boukos are safe and well. I wish also to inform you of some recent events in this city.

On the third day of the month of Swallows, the ninth day after our arrival in Boukos, an attempt was made on His Excellency's life. Four Pseuchaian men were responsible. All but one were killed in the attempt, the remaining assailant being kept for questioning by the Boukossians.

The man was an Ariatan and harboured strong prejudices against Zashians, which seem to have provided the principal motive for the attack. He denied that he and his fellows had acted with the knowledge or instruction of any state or government. They seem to have been hired assassins in the employ of some individual who wished to destroy the trade alliance. The four men were known to His Excellency, with whom they had struck up a slight acquaintance on the previous day, in the course of a local festival. Choosing to ignore advice given to him by the captain of the guard appointed for him by His Radiancy, and failing to inform any member of his staff of his intentions, His Excellency had spent the day taking part in this festival. Evidently, the assassins whom he thus encountered spent the day seeking an opportunity for their planned outrage, but were unable to find it until the following morning. All of His Radiancy's subjects should praise God for their failure.

One further matter remains to be brought to your attention, and, I hope, through you to the attention of His Radiancy. His Excellency's secretary, the eunuch Bedar, deserves praise for his diligent, and ultimately successful, efforts in tracking down his missing master, for employing great diplomacy in placating the Boukossian ministers who were anxious about His Excellency's whereabouts, and finally for courageously endangering his own life to protect his master when the assassins made their attack. It is a matter of grave doubt whether His Excellency would have survived this incident if it had not been for Bedar's intervention.

"If you would be so good as to turn the prisoner over to us for interrogation," Bedar said, "we feel that it may not be necessary to torture him."

The official gave a little start, then answered earnestly, "Oh, of course! We wouldn't want to offend against your customs. You know it is something we only resort to in very rare cases. I would not wish you to think it was common practice in Boukos—of course it is not something that the customs in Sasia permit, I understand."

Bedar was looking at the man as though he wondered whether he was thinking of a different "Sasia" altogether.

"It is not so much that," said Marzana hastily, "as that we don't feel it would accomplish much in this case. The man being an Ariatan."

In fact, what Bedar had said, when they talked it over privately, was, "I daresay they could make him talk in Suna—but these people are amateurs. *And* they have peculiar ideas. They'll leave a dagger lying around for him to stab himself with, on principle, or something. And then we'll never know if Pheres was right or not."

"But," said Marzana to the official, "we have an idea that we might be able to get some information out of him in another way."

As they followed the official down the passage to the cells—clean, white-washed, well-lit, the whole place—Bedar whispered in Zashian, "Don't laugh, Marzana."

"I haven't so far."

"Yes, well. Just don't."

The remaining Ariatan sat on the narrow stone bench in his cell, staring gravely out the barred window. When the Zashians came in he cast them a brief, haughty look, and spat on the floor to signify his contempt.

Bedar came and sat on the bench beside the man, leaning indolently against the wall, thumbs tucked into his sash. He sat there, looking coolly at the Ariatan, until the man turned and glared haughtily back at him. Bedar smiled.

"Now look here, Karestes—that is your name, is it not?" The man gave no response, but Bedar went on, pleasantly, his Zashian accent exaggerated. "Let me speak candidly. We know—you and I know—what this was all about, all this … unpleasantness at the temple the other day. My associate here"—he gestured at Marzana, who stood by the door, arms folded, looking very stern—"my associate has some idea of there being a political motive of some sort—and, you know, for all that you and I know, Karestes, there might have been, mightn't there? But I have *told* him that it is perfectly absurd for him to imagine that *you* would know anything about that. Isn't it? I mean, you were hired. You and your—regrettably departed—colleagues were hired by someone to … well, I don't know what the term is that you would use, but where I come from we say, 'to send someone on'—'to send him on', you see? Of course we don't usually fall upon people with knives—those such as myself, you understand—our method would usually be to have something put in his food, or his wine. It *is* a surer way, in general. But never mind. The main thing is, I understand that you did this for money, and of course we would very much like to know who hired you—so any little hint that you can give me, always understanding that of course you can have no idea what the man's motives were, will go a long way to securing your own freedom. Is this reasonable, do you think? I am concerned to seem reasonable. After all, we are a civilized people, you know. Just as you are."

The man had listened to all this with widening eyes; now he had heard more than he could bear quietly.

"Don't you even think to compare your people to mine, you spayed barbarian dog!" he shouted, starting up from the bench. "You soft, painted, ass-licking piece of heathen horseshit! Hired? Hired? Hah! We did it for glory! All Ariata knows what we had planned! If your pig-fucking ambassador could hold his drink any better than a Kossian *girl* it would have succeeded, too! We *had* him—we would have had your goat-buggering heathen king by the balls—if *he* has any—he would have shipped Euryanos and Rhyton back to us with nooses around their goat-buggering necks, and we would have pitched your ambassador off Katagion Rock to thank him, if the horse-fucker hadn't got himself picked for Kerialos—how were *we* supposed to know about these shit-eating Boukossians' customs? Oh yes, Orgion was all for sending poisoned cakes to the house in revenge, to keep the ambassador quiet, but I *told* him that was a Sasian dog's trick—hah! I spit on his grave! I was right! We did it for glory, and we'll have glory! They know our names in Ariata! They will remember us!"

He stood shaking with defiance in the middle of the whitewashed cell, evidently expecting to be fallen upon and slain on the spot. There was a cool silence, and the man looked almost reproachfully at Marzana, who was no longer bothering to look stern.

"They will not have any need to merely remember *you*," said Bedar, getting up from the bench, "since you are going to be flogged and then escorted back to Ariata. We have no desire to start a war. But *thank you* for telling us all this. It is most interesting."

They were leaving the cell when Bedar paused and turned back to the Ariatan.

"I forgot to mention something," he said. His tone was still cool, but no longer entirely pleasant. "I think you may know the name of Hesteus Stesiphanis? I gather it is a prominent one. Should you have the opportunity, on your return to Ariata, of speaking to the man himself, you may tell him that you owe your life to his son."

The Ariatan looked scornfully puzzled for a moment; then understanding dawned. "That—that boy?" And then, before the elaborate mechanisms of Ariatan honour could begin working, before Karestes remembered that the boy had been wearing trousers and consorting with Zashians, there was a moment in which he reacted just as any man anywhere might who realized that he had stabbed the son of one of his nation's famous men. He looked at Bedar with horror, and stammered out: "He's not—I didn't—did I … ?"

Bedar held his gaze for a moment or two before replying. "You cannot, I think, be altogether unaware whom Pheres Stesiphanis was defending when he put himself in the way of your knife. *Do you think* that if he had died from your pitiful assault, I would walk out of this room and leave you breathing?"

Pheres, when he heard about it, said that he heartily wished he had been there to see the man's face. Marzana said that rarely, off of the field of battle, had he seen anyone look so frightened.

CHAPTER XVIII

EVEN IN THE shadowed colonnade of the house it was hot: moistly, foully hot, with flies buzzing languidly in the soupy air. Out in the courtyard the sun blazed on the white pavement, and it seemed hard to believe that the painted statues were not sweating. Bedar sat leaning against a column, which felt pleasantly cold against his back through the thin fabric of his shirt. He was fingering a bracelet on his left wrist, a string of small red glass beads. He owned a pair of trousers which matched the colour of the beads exactly, and he was wearing them this morning. The red coat, which he did not even like to look at in this heat, had been packed already.

It was high summer in Boukos. *The hottest summer in ten years*, everyone kept saying. Shopkeepers and bureaucrats and perfect strangers in the street would apologize to the Zashians about the temperature, as though they felt they were letting these foreigners down, somehow, by allowing such weather to occur.

The house door opened and Jadresh slouched into the colonnade. Bedar had half-risen, to bow respectfully to him, before Jadresh noticed and waved a hand to obviate the gesture, as Bedar had hoped he would. It was wise to be polite in this weather, as many people's tempers were short; but it was also better not to move more than one needed to.

"Good morning, sir."

"Good morning, Bedar. Did you sleep?"

Bedar smiled. "Not very much, I confess."

There had been a terrific thunderstorm the night before, which everyone had hoped would break the humidity, though it hadn't. But Bedar doubted he would have slept much anyway; he and Marzana had been up most of the night talking.

"Haven't had a wink myself," said Jadresh, yawning ferally. "Only three more days, though, Bedar. It will be good to get home, won't it? My mother has been sending me letters by every available ship, you know, wanting to know how much longer we're going to be here. Nine weeks—can you believe it? It was only supposed to have been a month."

Bedar gave him a sympathetic half-smile, shading his eyes with one hand against the sun to look up at him. This morning Jadresh was wearing a sleeveless waistcoat with no shirt under it, and lilac cotton trousers which looked strikingly like they belonged to a pair of pyjamas. It was the sort of thing that did not even raise an eyebrow, these days. Everyone had been obliged to take some measures, within the bounds of decency, to cope with the heat. No one had actually resorted to wearing Pseuchaian clothes yet, but servants had learned to knock very loudly before entering anyone's bedroom, because it was hot even at night, and there were rumours that some of the younger aides had taken to sleeping naked. A whole delegation of the guard, their captain included, had gone together to a bath-house, and returned declaring that it was *not nearly as weird as you would think.*

Bedar, for his part, had bought a pair of sandals at the market and taken to wearing his hair twisted into a knot to keep it off his neck. But he had had some expert help in picking out the sandals, which were made of tooled dark leather and were really rather smart, and he took as much care in putting up his hair these mornings as he did in painting his eyes.

"So, Bedar, I hear that you had your trial finally, for that assault business."

"Yes. Last week."

"I hear it was quite the thing. You pleaded guilty?"

"My dear Jadresh, I *am* guilty. I *did* break the young man's nose. No one has ever tried to deny it—though I believe that the victim himself, when faced with me in the courtroom, where everyone was able to judge our relative sizes, would dearly have liked to."

Jadresh let out a bark of laughter. His opinion of Bedar had improved considerably since the nose-breaking incident had become general knowledge at the embassy.

"And what did they fine you?"

"Forty nummoi. A bargain, for the amount of entertainment it has afforded my friends."

Not to mention that it was His Excellency who had actually provided the funds, since Boukossian law made the master responsible for any fines incurred by his slaves. Of course the master possessed the power of life and death over his slaves and could extract that debt in any way he saw fit. That was the theory, but in this case the ambassador had simply handed over the money and said no more about it.

"So you got away with breaking a free man's nose, eh?" Jadresh shook his head wonderingly. "They could hang you for that in Zash, couldn't they?"

"They could, yes." Bedar looked at Jadresh for a moment, with a faint smile. Jadresh shifted his weight and looked a little less merry. "Well. They are barbarians, these people, after all."

"Oh! Yes. Well, I had better get back inside and make sure

those lazy slobs are packing my things properly." Jadresh stretched, showing off an expanse of hairy stomach, and shambled back inside.

Nine weeks, Bedar thought. The time had seemed short enough to him, but he had been grateful for its lengthening, and had not let it run by him unheeded. Each new postponement of their departure, greeted by most of the household with howls and moans of impatience, had been a blessing for which he had been hard pressed to conceal his gratitude. Marzana had agreed that he felt the same.

The trade mission had suffered a predictable setback from the near-assassination of its leader on the day after the Psobion. The Boukossians had been anxious to conciliate after that embarrassing incident, but the ambassador himself had simply wanted to leave. In the end, a combination of flattery from the Boukossian ministers and firm orders from his royal cousin had kept him in Boukos, and he had contented himself with not leaving the house except under heavy guard, and making dark pronouncements about heathens at every opportunity, which two policies had done their own work to help make the trade negotiations more difficult. As for shaving, gambling, frequenting brothels, or appearing in public in any condition other than fully dressed, with coat, hat, boots, and earrings, one did not dare mention such subjects in His Excellency's hearing. His love affair with the Boukossians and their simple ways had been a short one.

Bedar had almost made up his mind to give up waiting for Marzana and leave when Marzana finally did appear in the doorway.

Of all the Zashians in the household, Marzana seemed the least bothered by the heat. It actually seemed to suit him; his skin had gone brown with the sun, and with his hair tidily pulled back, his sleeves rolled up, and his shirt unbuttoned, he looked, Bedar thought, more dashing than ever. Bedar did not think he was the only one to hold this opinion.

"God guard your coming and your going, Marzana."

"And yours."

"Well?"

Marzana stood at the edge of the colonnade, fists on his belt, looking out at the sunlit courtyard. "Well what?"

"Well, have you made your decision?"

"Yes. Have you?"

"Yes. And … is it what we talked of last night—that which you have decided?"

"Yes."

"I am glad."

Marzana smiled out at the courtyard for a moment, then looked back at Bedar. "And yours?"

"Of course." He shrugged. "Mine was easy."

"Mine was not difficult, either. Though there will be some regret … "

"For both of us, my friend. But one can always write."

"One can. Yes. You are right—thank you for that."

"Shall we, then?"

"Go, you mean?"

"Yes."

"Yes, I suppose we had better."

Bedar laughed lightly. "It will be well, Marzana. I cannot think but that it will be well."

They parted ways at the end of the street, since their paths these days lay in opposite directions. Each offered the other his blessing on the enterprise at hand, in gravely formal terms.

Old Pottery Street was silent as a street of tombs, which was ordinary at this time of day; at this hour, most of the brothels' inmates would still be asleep. Bedar paused in the shade under the eaves with the plaster horses. He stroked the tail of the nearest one, wondering whether he would remember these ghastly things with nostalgia, at home in Zash. They did not deserve to be remembered, these third-rate plaster statues of lumpish stallions with flared nostrils. Or rather … Well. He was pretty sure they *had* been stallions, before.

The doors between the horses were closed, but not, as Bedar knew from having come here on many previous mornings, actually locked. He opened one and walked through the front hall, across the familiar mosaic of Psobos, to look in at the inner archway.

"Bedar! Hello." A black-haired boy sitting on the edge of the large central bath was the first to notice him.

"Hello, Gorgi. What happened to the bath-tub?" It was empty of water.

"It started to leak yesterday. Flooded the basement and everything. Skyphos says it's going to cost a fortune to repair it."

The doorkeeper himself appeared at that moment, climbing up the steps out of the bath and pausing at the top to mop the sweat from his forehead. There were large, expensively glazed windows above the main bath, and the space beneath them was oven-hot.

"Good morning, Skyphos. I see you are having troubles. I am sorry."

"Bedar! Good morning—this is early even for you. Well, yes, you might say we are having troubles." He nodded towards the empty bath, rubbing his broad, stubbly chin. "Cheap, inferior workmanship—I could've told you it wouldn't last. The owner won't be happy, but there it is—we may as well close our doors until it's fixed. But business was falling off anyway, with the heat. Nobody thinks of sex when it's this hot, you know—it's just not natural."

Bedar smiled.

"Mind you," said Skyphos hastily, "it doesn't *get* this hot, most summers. I wouldn't want you to think it's always this hot here."

"Indeed I would not. I have heard it said that this is the hottest summer you have had in ten years."

"Oh, I think so. I think so."

"Hey, Bedar!" called another boy, who had just hopped up onto the side of the bath near Gorgi.

"Hello, Lekki!" Bedar waved.

"Bedar, did you see what the goat-fuckers from Karistegion's did to our horses?"

"Lekistheus!" said Skyphos reprovingly. "Don't use that kind of language in front of Bedar."

"Why not?" Lekki retorted. "He's not a customer."

"That has nothing to do with it, Lekistheus. Bedar has manners. You could learn a great deal from him."

Lekki snorted. "Sure, sure. Anyway, *did* you see what they did to our horses, Bedar?"

"Yes," Bedar admitted. "Are you certain that it was someone from Karistegion's who did it?"

"Who else could it have been?"

"It's disgraceful, really," said Gorgi. "Oh … sorry, Bedar."

Bedar laughed. "I assure you I am not in the least insulted."

"Come now, you two," said Skyphos. "Bedar didn't come here to listen to your nonsense. Pheres was out in the yard, the last I saw."

"Thank you, sir," said Bedar, with a slight bow.

Skyphos looked, as he always did, slightly disoriented at being called "sir" by Bedar; but he was a freedman, and he had been kind to Pheres, and really it seemed only fitting.

Pheres was sitting in the shade of the colonnade in the small yard at the back of the Horses. He did not immediately hear Bedar come out, so Bedar had a moment just to look at him. His bright hair was tied back, untidily, in a little tuft at the nape of his neck. He wore a plain tunic and sandals, and he sat with his long legs stretched out, leaning back on his hands, a broom propped in the corner beside him, where he had finished his morning's work. This was the sort of thing he had been doing at the Horses since his shoulder healed. By the time he had been fit to return to work, he had been judged unfit for the work he had been doing. His beard, when it had begun to show, was a shade or two redder than his hair. He was clean-shaven now.

"Bedar!" Pheres looked up with a start. "How long have you been standing there?"

"Not long. God guard your coming and your going."

"And yours." He got to his feet and pulled Bedar into a tight, almost fierce embrace. He kept it brief, in consideration of the heat, releasing Bedar and brushing a light, glancing kiss across his cheek.

For two months it had been like this: clinging to each other as if they might be torn apart at any moment, pouring their souls into every conversation as if it might be their last. Soft, respectful kisses that marked a careful and definite limit.

They had talked about it. (Of course they had talked about it; they talked about everything.) At first they had decided that on their last night together they would do something. They had discussed what exactly "something" should be; they agreed it shouldn't be left to chance. But they had not been able to settle on one thing that they were sure they could do and also enjoy. It was Bedar who had finally suggested that the whole thing was turning into a dark cloud on the horizon, and that perhaps their last night together should be the same as their first, and in between they should go on together as they were doing. Pheres had seemed relieved to agree.

So they had not shared Bedar's bed again, nor Pheres's, which was now in the basement of the Horses and too narrow for two anyway. But they had been all over Boukos together, they had watched the sun rise from the top of the sea wall and eaten fried cheese at an inn on the edge of town and climbed to the gallery of the temple of Hesperion. They had danced together at a party hosted by some of the girls of Pigeon Street, shopped for earrings and sandals, and talked late into the night about poetry and religion, music and food.

They sat side by side on the cool paving stones now, shoulders just touching.

"I didn't know whether to expect you today," Pheres said. "Have you got the whole morning free?"

"The whole day. I packed Zuko's papers last night and my own things this morning. Zuko told me yesterday that he had no more work for me, and should he change his mind today, he will not be able to find me." Bedar had stopped calling the ambassador "His Excellency" in conversations with Pheres some time ago. They both referred to him as "Zuko."

"He doesn't know that you come here?" Pheres asked curiously.

"He has no idea."

"Well!" Pheres stretched, beautifully. "*I've* nothing to do, as we're closed. We have a whole day ahead of us, jewel of my heart's desire, thanks to that stupid bath."

"God bless it and its inferior marble."

"Yes, so what shall we do?"

"Sit here in the shade—at least for a little longer. I have had some news I want to tell you about."

"Good news?"

"Very good."

"They're not delaying again? They've decided to stay for

good? No, I can't see Zuko ever agreeing to that—he'd throw himself into the harbour first."

"Very likely. No, we leave in three days—that is definite. But ... I have two pieces of news. I'll tell you the one I wasn't expecting first."

Bedar drew a breath. The moment when he would have to hear Pheres's answer would soon be upon him. He did not really know why he feared it, since he was pretty sure he knew what it was going to be. It was as he had said to Marzana; he could not think but that it would be well.

"Last night," he said, "the ship that will be taking us back to Zash arrived in the harbour. It came from Zeleush, by way of Pyria, where it was delayed by a storm, which is what we have to thank for this last, extra week in Boukos. It is a ship of the king's fleet, and His Radiancy sent messages for his cousin with the captain, along with presents for the Boukossian ministers, and a few other items significant to our last days in this city. You know of course that His Radiancy has not been pleased with how Zuko has behaved in Boukos." Pheres raised an eyebrow at the understatement, and Bedar laughed. "He has reprimanded him, in this latest dispatch ... Zuko likes to have his correspondence read aloud to him—he *can* read, but he finds it beneath him to do so ordinarily. Thus I was privy to the content of His Radiancy's message—indeed, slightly before my master was. It is quite usual in Zash for a superior to demand a present, by way of reparation, from a dependant who has failed him or angered him in some way. This His Radiancy has done, in a way which took my master by surprise—and did not, I must add, please him very well at all."

"Wh ... what's he asked for?"

"You cannot guess? I said that this was good news, recall. Good news, at any rate, for me."

"I don't know. What does he want?"

"Me."

"You mean … " Pheres was a moment taking this in. "You mean the king wants Zuko to give you to him? To serve him, you mean? You'll be going back to join the royal household?"

"I will."

"Bedar!" His eyes lit with unforced joy. "How wonderful! How *perfect*! It must be because of what Marzana … " He bit his lip.

"What?"

"I forgot you didn't know about that. It, er, was supposed to be a secret. But I guess it doesn't matter now. Marzana put a line about you in his letter to the captain of the royal guard, that's all. Commending you for everything you did to save the mission and protect the ambassador."

"Did he? Well. I wondered what gave His Radiancy the idea to ask for me."

"It's just what you wanted, isn't it? To be in the king's service?"

Bedar nodded. "It is very good. Anyone with any ambition would say that it was an excellent thing to have achieved— and you know that I am not altogether without ambition." He smiled wryly.

"Yes, sure, but you also like the king. I'm so happy for you—I'm so glad this news came now. It's good to think of you going back to join the royal household, and not belonging to Zuko any more." He slipped his hand into Bedar's. "That was the news you weren't expecting. What was the news you *were* expecting?"

"Ah. Well, while Marzana was campaigning on my behalf, I was making sure Zuko's letters—"

"Which you write."

"—which, as you say, I write—I was making sure they

mentioned the contribution made by a brave Pseuchaian youth to saving the ambassador's life and forwarding our cause in Boukos. What I said—what Zuko said—was no more than the truth. I did make sure to indicate in the letter that you were an enslaved aristocrat—I hope you will forgive me, but I felt it was the sort of detail that would strike His Radiancy as … ah, romantic. He did indeed respond as I hoped. He has sent a sum of money and instructions for its use."

"The king of Zash sent me a reward?" Pheres looked amused.

"Not exactly. He does wish to reward you, but the money was sent for me to use. His Radiancy wishes to add you to his household as well."

At this, Pheres's smile faded to a look of blank shock, as if he had never considered this possibility. Bedar was not surprised, though to him it had seemed fairly obvious.

"He sent you money to buy me."

"If you wish it."

Pheres let go of Bedar's hand. "I … would we be … I suppose you don't know whether we would get to see each other. Since the king of Zash has so many palaces, and he must have armies of slaves all over the place."

"I can tell you what would happen. You would come to Suna with me, to be presented to His Radiancy. He would take one look at you—or, at least, hear one word out of your mouth—and free you with his own hand. You see, he thinks … " It was all very well to know that Pheres would not be insulted, but still it was impossible for Bedar to forget that it *was* an insult.

Pheres finished the sentence for him. "He thinks I'm a eunuch. Of course! Because I suppose any nobleman's son made a slave in Zash would get gelded—he sent you money to buy me and bring me to his court because he thinks I can't just be freed. He won't be disappointed when he finds I'm, you know … "

"A man?" Bedar shrugged. "It was a gamble, but I think he will not be offended. I think His Radiancy is a man of good humour. If he *is* annoyed, it will be only with me, for misleading him. I know he will free you, in any case. Then … you can go wherever you like."

"Or stay in Suna with you?"

"Or stay in Suna with me."

Pheres turned toward him. "Can I kiss you?"

"Of course."

"I mean really kiss you—like a lover."

"I've had those, you know. I am accustomed to how it goes."

Pheres was frowning slightly now. "Yes, but you haven't done—haven't been what I've been, and if you don't like the thought of … I'd understand, I'd still … "

"Oh, Pheres, no. No, no, no. How have I ever let you think that."

In fact, in everything he had been very careful, scrupulously careful, to let Pheres take the lead, set the pace, choose what happened and when. And if nothing much *had* happened, nothing but those careful kisses, clasping hands, and chaste hugs now and then, he had thought that was because those were all that Pheres wanted. It simply hadn't occurred to him that Pheres might put another interpretation on it.

He drew Pheres's face toward him and pulled him down to bring their lips together. It was not the most artful kiss he had ever given, but it was the most emphatic. And it did what was needful for Pheres. He kindled like a fire of dry twigs, taking control of the kiss as Bedar yielded happily to him. They went over together onto the newly swept stones of the porch, Bedar beneath, Pheres on top, strong and young and eager, loosing Bedar's hair so he could tangle his fingers in it, kissing Bedar's throat and flicking open the buttons at the neck of his shirt.

It really was too hot for much of this, and the place was only very tenuously private. Either of these things might have made Bedar protest in another moment, but Pheres pushed himself up on his hands before that. He was obviously reluctant, but from the way he smiled, Bedar thought Pheres knew what he had been thinking.

He allowed himself a moment to lie there, sweaty and dishevelled, looking up at Pheres.

"You haven't … I think I know what it is, but … you haven't actually given me your answer."

"Yes. My love. Of course. Of course I'll come to Suna with you."

They went in to meet Skyphos, tidied up and acting as nonchalant as they could manage. But the doorman took one look at the two of them holding hands and guessed the situation.

"This is the day I've been expecting since you took him out that first night, isn't it?" he said to Bedar.

"Is it?" Bedar replied blandly.

"You're going to take him off my hands at last."

Pheres made an indignant noise.

"I am," said Bedar, squeezing Pheres's hand. "We're leaving in a few days, and I want to take Pheres with me—since he wants to come." No need to go into the whole story about the king; he wanted to let Pheres leave here with as much dignity as he could. Pheres squeezed his hand back.

"I wish you both happy," Skyphos was saying, actually looking a little teary. "I'll miss you, that's the truth. Well, let's see—what can I let you have him for? He's a good worker, been a lot of help around here, but it's not as if we don't have a steady supply of able-bodied lads needing something to do. And between you and me, the owner has been after me to sell off a few of our hangers-on. Let me see … ”

He quoted a sum, and Pheres made another, even more indignant noise.

"Look, it's not what I think you're worth, you know that—I'm just trying to do Bedar a favour."

Outside in the street, having finally escaped the excited questions of Pheres's friends, they stood for a moment between the plaster horses.

"What should we do with the rest of our day?" Pheres asked.

"We should go shopping," said Bedar. He hefted the purse he had brought with him. "I have … *a lot* of money left over."

Pheres swatted him. "Because you haggled like a heartless—"

"Because His Radiancy thought you were a eunuch."

"What does that even … ?"

"We're very expensive."

CHAPTER XIX

MARZANA STOOD ON the familiar corner, looking at the painted facade with its jaunty dishes of cakes and candy. They clustered around the inscription which was so far, fittingly, the only piece of Pseuchaian he knew how to read: CHEREIA'S. That, he thought, like the sweet shop, was what he was. He had long known it.

Up here on the edge of the city, where the wind arrived fresh from the sea, it was not nearly so hot as in the streets below. Even inside the sweet shop, which had wide open windows shaded with a deep awning, the temperature was bearable. The warm air was laden with the scent of honey. Counters with cool marble tops held dishes piled with crisp, deep-fried fruit pastries, pyramids of sticky candied figs, candied oranges, bowls of candied fennel, small, fluted tarts, iced almond cakes, and a big, round dish, sitting in the front window, of the shop's latest specialty: Zashian-style rose-water candy, better than any you could get in Arakesh.

The shop was full of customers when Marzana entered. A group of small boys stood just inside the door, blocking everyone's way while they pored over their handfuls of copper coins and conferred earnestly about what to buy. A short queue had formed in front of the counter where Chereia, in her light blue apron, with her hair tied back in a white kerchief, was busily packing orders, taking money, and at the same time giving every appearance of listening with interest to the gossip which a couple of languid young men leaning against the counter to her right were relating. One of the latter looked up and saw Marzana enter, and began to nudge his friend urgently and remark on the probability that it was later than he thought, and that they needed to be somewhere, for some reason, quite soon. Chereia paused in handing an elderly woman her change, looked at the two young men, then looked up and saw Marzana, and smiled.

When the young men had left the shop, the queue of customers had been dealt with, and only the group of boys remained, still deliberating about the best way to spend their coins, Marzana leaned across the counter and kissed the proprietress.

She rested her elbows on the marble countertop and smiled up at him. "Will that be all today, sir?"

"No, indeed." Marzana turned back to the sweet-laden shelves of the shop. "I should like a few sesame sweets as well." He located the dish and picked out a handful.

Chereia untied her kerchief and shook it out, and lifted up the hinged section at the end of the counter so that Marzana could join her behind it. He gave her another kiss before popping one of the sesame sweets into his mouth. It was so easy to kiss her—she was so eminently *kissable*—that he rather wondered how all the young men who came into her shop to make eyes at her could stand not being permitted to do it. He rather wondered how he had managed himself, during the first evening of their acquaintance.

"Do you have the day off?" she asked.

He chewed honey-crusted sesame for a moment and re-plied, when he was able: "More or less."

"Lovely. If you'd like to stay to dinner, I've some more of

that excellent cheese from my brother-in-law, and some fresh mushrooms, and I thought of making omelettes."

"I should very much like to stay for dinner."

"Good."

The little boys had made their choices at last and came to the counter to pay for their sweets. As they were leaving, two young women carrying baskets came in, followed by several more children, in the company of a white-haired nurse.

"It's been like this all morning," said Chereia. "I don't think the shop has been empty for a moment since I opened. For such hot weather, it's remarkably good custom."

"It may be partly because some of the competition has shut down. Someone told me Phileidion's in Old Embankment Street had to close—a fire in their kitchen, apparently."

"Oh, dear! Who told you that?"

"Some woman, in the street. She was no one I knew, but I think that many people have seen me here and remember me as that foreigner who is always in Chereia's."

"Yes, my dear, I know they do. You've become quite famous." She stacked up some coins on the counter and swept them away into her cash box. "She wasn't a *young* woman, was she?"

"I don't know … " He shrugged, then looked at her. "Yes. She was young, and very beautiful." He gazed off reminiscently out the window.

"Really?"

"No. She was middle-aged. She had beady little eyes and a face like a pudding."

"Good, good. Excellent." The two young women with baskets came up to the counter, and Chereia smiled and greeted them cheerfully.

"I have had some news," she said, turning back to Marzana when they were gone.

"Oh?"

"Good news. It's about the lawsuit. Tyreus thinks it may be wrapped up pretty soon, and that the court is going to decide in my favour after all."

"Really?"

"Yes, and it promises to be rather good. Listen to this. There's some evidence—he thinks he has some witnesses who will be willing to speak about it—that Speutokrates, you know, one of the worst of the creditors—"

"I remember. The one who exports olive oil to the colonies."

"At extortionate rates—he is already in another lawsuit about that. Anyway, it *looks* like Speutokrates used some very underhanded dealing with Stratos, gave him some very unfavourable rates of interest and promised some favours which he never delivered on, which might mean—if the jury accepts it—that Speutokrates actually owes *me* damages, rather than my owing him anything."

Marzana whistled. "That would be satisfying."

"Oh, it would."

The two girls whom Chereia employed as shop assistants came out of the kitchen at this point, to say that they had finished cleaning up and would be on their way home, if there was no further work to be done. They smiled shyly at Marzana. Chereia gave them leave to go.

The shop was briefly empty after that. Chereia retied her kerchief and went about tidying the dishes on the shelves. Marzana sat on the tall stool behind the counter which was Chereia's usual seat. When she sat on it, her feet dangled, or she tucked them under one of the stool's rails, but Marzana could easily sit on it with both heels on the floor.

"Oh, by the way, Marzana—I was tidying the flat yesterday, and I gathered together some things that you've left upstairs, and put them on the shelf by the clothes-cupboard. You should go up and get them before you forget them again."

A cool breath of wind came in at the window in front of the counter where Marzana was sitting.

"Mm," said Marzana. "Mm-hm. Things upstairs." He ate the last of his handful of sesame sweets and did not move.

He considered asking Chereia if she would fetch him some more candy, since she was up, but then he remembered how she had said once that it was probably a good thing he was not staying long in Boukos, as too much eating of her products would eventually make him fat, and *that*, she had added, cocking one eyebrow at him in an irresistible way of hers, would be a *terrible shame.* He had gone to the local exercise facility to swim laps in the pool that same afternoon, and had a long conversation with one of the trainers there about what other exercise he might take without aggravating by his bad hip. But he had not told Chereia about that.

She came back around the counter, he took her waist between his hands, and she hopped up to sit on his lap.

"Ah, that is a nice breeze," she said, leaning her head back, eyes shut.

He kissed her throat and felt a little tremor of laughter run through her. *This would be a good moment*, Marzana thought. But the mention of the lawyer had made him stop to think. Tyreus was a new lawyer; the old one, Phoronemos, had not, in fact, killed himself in the bath, but someone had recommended this other man to Chereia shortly after Phoronemos's disgrace, and she had found him to be much more useful. But Marzana was pretty sure—and indeed, he thought Chereia knew perfectly well herself, from some hints she had let fall—what Tyreus had in mind in helping out a pretty young widow for a very reasonable fee. Tyreus was about Marzana's age, and he was unmarried. He had never seemed very much worried about Marzana, who was evidently not thought to represent a permanent threat.

An elderly man came through the door of the shop at that moment, and Chereia slid down hastily from Marzana's lap, turning rapidly pink. The man pursed his lips and looked reproving; but he did not leave without making a large purchase. On the whole, Marzana had not, as he had at first feared, been bad for business.

Several more customers followed the old man.

"Why don't you go upstairs and get the things I told you about, dear?" Chereia suggested. "Put them somewhere where you won't forget them."

"Oh, all right."

He got up from his seat and went back through the kitchen and up to the flat. The front room, with its tall windows open to admit the air, was bright and cool. The bedroom had no window, and was as usual somewhat stuffy. Chereia had a plan eventually to buy the adjoining flat, which was rented out and had two bedrooms on the front, and to have a door knocked through to connect the two. It would have to wait, she said, until the business of her late husband's debts was finally settled. Anyway, she said, though it would be nice to have a bedroom on the front of the house, she didn't really need the extra space, for herself.

Marzana sat down on the bed. It was certainly true that she had tidied, he thought. All her clothes had been put away in the cupboard, there were no gowns or scarves draped over the chair at the foot of the bed, and her few small items of jewellery had been put back in the little inlaid box on the shelf by the cupboard. Even the spiderweb-thin white shawl which she had worn almost incessantly since he gave it to her two weeks ago had been put away.

Did she, in some way, want him gone? he wondered. Was

that what all this insistence on taking his things was about? He knew very well that she loved him; he hoped he would not have allowed himself to become so familiar with the inside of her bedroom if he had not known *that*. But she had known what she was getting into from the beginning. *A month is something, when you have caught love at first sight.* In the event, it had been two months, and he would not have been surprised if she were beginning to wish, by now, that she could get on with her life without him, since she knew—or thought she knew—that she would have to do it some time. He should have made his proposal sooner. That was all it amounted to. But he hadn't, and so here he was, looking at a heap of things that she had gathered up in preparation for putting her life back in order after he was gone.

He got up from the bed and looked over the things on the shelf. There was his dark blue coat, neatly folded, which he had worn here one evening and left behind when the following morning had proved brutally hot. There was his other pair of earrings, which he had been looking for yesterday, and been puzzled at not being able to find. He remembered now the occasion on which he had taken them out, and smiled to himself, wondering how he could have forgotten it. There was also his copy of *The Thirty-Six Parrots*, which he had been reading to Chereia—slow going, since he had to translate as he went—and a horrible wine cup with a picture of an awkwardly entwined couple on the inside, which he had bought, reluctantly, upon specific instructions in a letter from his brother-in-law, who had heard that such things were to be had in Boukos and wanted one to scandalize his friends at parties. And there was a maroon leather Pseuchaian-style sword belt, stiff and new, with gleaming bronze rivets and that ingeniously practical design of sword-hanger which would perfectly accommodate even a curved Zashian blade.

That cunning woman! he thought, picking up the belt. He remembered the amused tolerance with which she had, as he had imagined, only half-listened to him extol the virtues of this style of sword belt, after he had seen some Boukossian guardsmen wearing them. That had been weeks ago; he had not even imagined that she would have remembered. But she must have had the thing made for him. He tried it around his waist and found it was a perfect fit; it had certainly been made to measure. That cunning, cunning woman.

This was why she had been so anxious for him to come upstairs and collect his belongings, then. It was just her devious way of giving him his present.

He came back downstairs with the sword belt in his hands. Chereia was busy commiserating with a stout woman whose son had taken up with an actor.

"Yes, I'm sure it does seem a shame, for a boy of his promise," she was saying, "but you know, I have known some actors who were really very good men, and I do think your neighbour is right—you *should* have him to dinner and see what sort of a person he is, before you begin forbidding Antilokos to see him altogether."

"Chereia," said Marzana gravely, when Antilokos's mother was finally gone, "this is not mine. I have never had a sword belt like this."

Chereia looked at it and widened her eyes. "Oh, dear! Where can it have come from?" He laughed, and she smiled. "I hope I did get the right style?"

"Yes," he said. "Thank you. It is perfect."

"I'm glad." She sorted some more coins and stowed them in the cash box. "Did you put the other things somewhere?" she asked, still busy with the coins. "I really *don't* want you to forget them and go back to Zash without them—I mean, the earrings I wouldn't mind keeping for myself, but that awful piece of smut that you bought for your brother, I don't want that."

"Chereia … "

There was no help for it. There were half a dozen people in the shop, she was counting money behind the counter, not even looking at him, and he had not had time to think about what he was going to say. But it could not wait, not even a moment longer.

"Chereia, if our hearts agree, it is my desire—no, it is my intention—not to go back to Zash."

She dropped her handful of coins, which bounced and scattered into the wrong compartments in the cash box and onto the floor.

"Oh!" She glanced at the people in the shop, who were staring because of the noise. "It's all right, it's nothing," she said, waving a hand breezily at them. She reached for Marzana's hand. "My darling," she said, lowering her voice as best she could, "if you *would* stay, if you would, of course you can live here—the shop really does bring in enough money, especially with business so good these days, that I can afford to feed you—I … I mean I can afford to feed both of us, and—"

"Chereia," said Marzana hastily, alarmed, "I have been to see the chief of the public watch and told him I might stay in Boukos, and he said he would be willing to hire me, as he suggested a long time ago, to run the new investigative squad that they have planned—I made it *very clear* that I would only do it on condition that they paid me a salary, I had not the slightest intention of asking you to keep me! Though … though the thought that you would … " He smiled. He had to admit that it was surprisingly pleasing.

"You really mean it, don't you?"

"Of course I do." He took her other hand. "I have known all along that I could never ask you to come to Zash—you have so much more to hold you here, and rightly, than I have to draw me back to my homeland. If I have not spoken to you of this before, it is only because I did not wish to give you false hope, until I knew that I could stay here—that your countrymen would tolerate me, and that … well, that I could tolerate them."

A woman had come to the counter, neither of them knew how long before, and chose this moment to say, "Excuse me!" and rap the edge of her coins repeatedly on the countertop to get their attention.

Chereia looked at her vaguely for a moment and then smiled. "Thank you," she said. "Please take them with my compliments today. Good afternoon!"

"Look here!" said the woman, tremendously affronted. "I have the money, I have it right here! Do you think I'm a beggar? Is *that* what you think?"

"No," said Chereia, "I don't think that, but I am a little busy just now."

"Too busy to take my money? Is my money not good enough for you, that you can't be troubled to take it?"

"If you'll just leave it on the counter … "

"I would *like* some change, I am not *such* a spendthrift that I am pleased to spend *ten* obioi on candy that is only worth *seven*!"

Chereia let go of Marzana's hands and turned to count out the woman's change very methodically from the cash box and set it down, with a precise click, in a little pile upon the counter.

"Thank you," she said very sweetly. "Please have a *lovely* afternoon."

She turned back to Marzana and stood looking at him for a few moments in silence. Finally she drew a long breath and let it out slowly.

"My parents will expect us to get properly married," she said.

"Yes," said Marzana. "That is what I had in mind."

"Oh! Of course. Good. And … my brothers will make threatening jokes at the wedding about what they will do to you if you get it into your head to have any more wives."

"I should be disappointed if they missed that opportunity."

A man had come to the counter now, with an elaborate question about what sort of honey was used in the sesame sweets. Chereia dealt with him politely and waited for him to leave before she looked back at Marzana.

"We may well have children … "

"I hope that we do."

"You do? Oh, I am so glad. You seemed so alarmed that time when I thought I might be pregnant that I was a little afraid … oh, I don't know—that's silly, isn't it? Of course you were just worried about what might happen to me with a child and no husband."

"Yes."

"Well, our children would be Boukossian citizens. I … out of curiosity, I asked Tyreus about that the other day, and he said that they would be. And … you know they will want to believe in something or other."

"When they are old enough to understand it, I shall tell them what I believe, which is that Boukossians are good people who worship God in many forms because that is how He chose to reveal Himself to them. You may tell them what you think of *that*, and they will be in a good position to make up their own minds, I suppose."

"Very good. Yes. I was pretty sure that is what you would say."

"Wait a minute—you asked Tyreus what would happen if you had *my* children?"

"I said, hypothetically, if a Boukossian woman married a Zashian man, what would be the legal status of their children—but he knew what I was talking about. I mean, half of Boukos knows about us, Marzana." She glanced back at the shop full of customers.

"No, no—I understand that. I don't mind that. I meant—I thought Tyreus wanted to marry you himself."

"Oh, yes, he did. Does, I suppose. He proposed to me almost the moment I came to him with my suit."

"He *did*?"

"Yes. I didn't tell you, because it seemed like the sort of thing a woman would say if she wanted to … you know, to drop a hint, or something, and of course I didn't intend that. I told Tyreus no, of course. I didn't think it would be at all fair to tell him, 'Wait a month or two, until I find out whether my Zashian lover can be persuaded to stay in Boukos, and then I'll let you know.' You weren't thinking I *wanted* to marry him, were you?"

"No."

Three girls came giggling up to the counter, withered slightly under Chereia's cool gaze, and handed their money over meekly, scurrying out afterwards with backward glances at Marzana.

"I will of course have to go back to Zash," he said, "from time to time, to see my mother and my family."

"Oh, of course you will. Good. I would worry about them if you didn't. Perhaps, if we do well at the shop, we can afford to close it for a few months so that I can come with you. I would love to meet your people."

"They live on the coast, so the journey is not an especially long one. I should like to bring you."

She looked around the shop, where several customers were still poring indecisively over the dishes of candy. Then, rather suddenly, she leaned on the counter and called out cheerily, "The shop will be closing in a minute—please make your choices! Thank you!"

When the lingering customers had at last been cleared out, and Chereia had flipped the sign in the window to CLOSED and locked the door behind the last of them, when she and Marzana had run up the stairs to the cool, inviting front room of the flat, and Chereia was negotiating, as she always insisted on doing, the intricacies of Marzana's buttons and other fastenings, she remarked, "I do hope you're not intending to give up wearing trousers, darling, because I'm just getting good at this."

Much later, when the sky out over the sea beyond the windows was beginning to turn a deeper blue, and they were finishing their omelette and discussing how they would arrange the furniture when they had expanded into the flat next door, they became aware of some young voices which had begun shouting up from the street below.

"Disappointed customers, I expect," said Marzana. They laughed.

"Wait a minute," said Chereia. "What are they saying?"

They listened a moment.

"Hello!" the voices were shouting. "Open up! It's terribly important! We need sweets! We're spending the king of Zash's money, and we need sweets!"

ABOUT THE AUTHOR

A.J. Demas writes about love and imaginary politics in a fictional world based on the ancient Mediterranean. She has been making up stories since she was a little girl but only recently discovered the romance genre. She lives in Toronto, Canada, with her husband and cute daughter.

Find out about upcoming books and more here:
www.ajdemas.com

A.J. also publishes fantasy and historical fiction with a metaphysical twist under a different name (her real one). You can find those here: www.alicedegan.com

They met on a battlefield and saved each other's lives. It's not the way enemies-to-lovers usually works.

Adares comes from a civilization of democracy and indoor plumbing. Rus belongs to a tribe of tattooed, semi-nomadic horse-breeders. They meet in the aftermath of battle, when Rus saves Adares's life, and Adares returns the favour. As they shelter in an abandoned temple, a friendship neither of them could have imagined grows into a mutual attraction.

But Rus, whose people abhor love between men, is bound by an oath of celibacy, and Adares has a secret of his own that he cannot share. With their people poised for a long and bitter conflict, it seems too much to hope that these two men could turn their fleeting happiness into something lasting.

Unless, of course, the relationship between them changes the course of their people's history altogether.

Something Human is a standalone m/m romance set in an imaginary ancient world, about two people bridging a cultural divide with the help of great sex, pedantic discussions about the gods, and bad jokes about standing stones.

9 781988 086101